The Fall Girl

Kaye C Hill

CREME DE LA CRIME

There is something in omens.

– Ovid

First published in 2009
by Crème de la Crime
P O Box 523, Chesterfield, S40 9AT

*All the characters in this book are fictitious and any resemblance
to actual persons, living or dead, is purely coincidental.
Except Old Shuck, of course. Everybody knows he's real.*

Typesetting by Yvette Warren
Cover design by Yvette Warren
Front cover image by Peter Roman

ISBN 978-0-9557078-9-6
A CIP catalogue reference for this book is available
from the British Library

Printed and bound in Great Britain by CPI Cox & Wyman,
Reading, Berkshire

www.cremedelacrime.com

About the author:

Kaye C Hill lives in Guildford. A career involving steel-capped boots, chainsaws and railway embankments somehow inspired her to start writing crime fiction.

www.kayechill.com

Thanks to Lynne, Jeff and all at Creme de la Crime for unstinting support and shared pasta; thanks to my family for always being there; thanks to Jane, Gail, Roy, Rosemary, Cathy and Mary for laughing in the right places and thanks to all my other friends for putting up with me.

For Nick

1

This was a tricky one.

Lexy Lomax studied the teenage girl sitting opposite her. Heart-shaped face, earnest eyes, black glossy hair that swept across her face like a swallow's wing. Polite. Well-spoken. The type of kid a parent would be proud of.

But if Lexy had understood her right, this clean-cut paragon of virtue had just confessed to a murder.

Rowana Paterson had phoned earlier that afternoon. She'd seen Lexy's advert in the local paper and wanted to make an urgent appointment. She couldn't say what it was about over the phone. It wasn't until she had turned up, an hour later, at the front door of the elevated fisherman's cabin that served as Lexy's office and home in the prim Suffolk village of Clopwolde-on-Sea, that Lexy realised she was little more than a schoolgirl.

She was wearing the typical teenage uniform of black jeans, black trainers and a black pullover, which in her case was slipping off one slim shoulder.

Lexy tried to back-pedal straightaway.

"You're a bit younger than my usual clients. Are you sure it's a private detective you're after?" She didn't want to play mother confessor to some insecure adolescent with boyfriend problems.

"Yes."

"So you actually want something discreetly investigated?"

"Yes." The girl nodded as she replied this time, as if Lexy were slightly dense.

"OK. You'd better come up." Well, what else could she say?

They tramped up the wooden stairs to the octagonal living room that looked out over the bank and quay of the river Younge and the silver line of the North Sea beyond.

A scarred, caramel-coloured chihuahua was sitting on the

arm of a sofa by a window. A silver disc hanging from his collar was inscribed with the name Kinky.

Despite her obvious distraction, Rowana Paterson managed to smile at the sight of the dog. Most people did, except the ones who screamed, 'Rat!' and ran for the hills.

"So, how do you think can I help you?" Lexy asked when they were seated.

The girl drew a deep breath. "Six weeks ago a woman died – here in Suffolk. Elizabeth Cassall, her name was."

"Someone you knew?"

Rowana hesitated. "Not exactly."

"OK." Good. Lexy didn't want the kid blubbing over her desk. "So… how did she die?"

"There was an accident. She… fell from an upstairs window. Over a balcony. Backwards."

Bummer. "How awful!"

"Yes, it was, actually. I feel terrible about it." Rowana's dark lashes were lowered. "The thing is, I didn't know her. I mean, I didn't even know she existed at that point. I was living with my family in London – we'd never even been to Suffolk." Her voice had risen.

"OK. So, what you're saying is, although you didn't know this Elizabeth Cassall, you were very upset when you got the news she'd died?" Lexy attempted to clarify.

"Yes. Exactly."

"Why?"

"I… don't think her death was accidental."

"How do you mean, not accidental? You think she committed suicide?" Backwards?

"No. I think she was killed."

"What, murdered? Who by?"

Rowana regarded her gravely. "Me, actually."

Lexy quelled an impulse to laugh. "Steady on. Didn't you say you were in London when Elizabeth Cassall died?"

"Yes. I was."

2

"So… how did you do it? By magic?"

The girl blanched, her hand going to her mouth. "How… how did you know?"

Lexy shoved her chair back. "Are you taking the mick? Because if you are, I've got better things to do."

"No. I really mean it." Tears were sparkling on those dark lashes now. "I found this book on the occult and I carried out a magic ceremony. A proper one."

Oh boy. She'd been gathering herbs by the light of a waxing moon and dancing around circles waving incense – and now she'd convinced herself she'd magically offed this Cassall woman. Lexy clenched her teeth. Perhaps she had. When were people going to learn that they shouldn't mess with this stuff?

She ran a hand through her spiky black crop. "OK, Rowana – so how do you think a private detective can help you with this?"

"Well, I want you to find out for certain."

"Find out what?"

"Whether it was an accident, or whether I did it."

Lexy tipped her chair back, eyeing the enticing silver sway of the Younge through the window beyond Rowana's shoulder. She'd take the mutt for a nice, relaxing walk as soon as she'd broken the news to this aspiring acolyte that she didn't deal with the esoteric. As she worked out a polite way of putting it, something hove into view. The tip of a large white marquee. It was being erected on the other side of the river, bang opposite her cabin. Why?

She brought the chair back down with a sharp clack, and screwed her face into a look of apology. "Rowana – it's not that I don't want to help you, but…"

"I've got money," the girl said. "How much do you charge?"

It was an interesting question. Lexy was keen – no, frantic–for a healthy dose of cash. Private eye work, as she was discovering, didn't exactly bring in a regular income, and the debts were mounting. Unfortunately, her only significant payment so far

3

had been in the form of a cat, albeit a very rare and pregnant one called Princess. Princess Noo-Noo, to be precise. The intention had been that Lexy should benefit from the sale of her very rare and valuable kittens. Lexy chewed her lip, glancing involuntarily at her desk calendar. Kittens that would be appearing any time now. Although she'd have to wait another couple of months after the birth before any money could actually change hands. A person could get very hungry in two months. And it wasn't as if she could ask her landlord to hang on for the rent. She had some pride. Edward de Glenville had already done Lexy more than her fair share of favours, and on top of everything else he had agreed to put up Princess at his ancestral home until the kittens were grown enough to sell. Repaying him was going to be tough.

Lexy hauled her mind with difficulty from this problem and back to the whey-faced girl sitting in front of her. However hard up she was, she couldn't justify taking candy from this deluded baby.

"I charge two hundred a day, plus expenses," she said. "Seventy-five up front." That should settle it. There was no way the girl would...

Rowana didn't flinch. She reached for her bag, a camouflage back-pack with badges on it, and brought out a blue fluffy pencil case. It was stuffed full of notes. She counted out seven tens and a fiver and held them out to Lexy. "OK. When can you start?"

Lexy's mouth twitched. "How old are you, Rowana?"

"Sixteen. Nearly seventeen." Lexy was surprised – she would have put her a year younger.

"Where'd you get that money, if you don't mind me asking?"

"From my savings account." Rowana gave Lexy a sideways glance. "But it's not like I can't pay it back, because I've just had an inheritance, haven't I?"

"How do you mean?"

"Well – from Elizabeth Cassall."

"She left you money?"

"Yes – thirty thousand. And the cottage, of course."

"Thirty… ?" Lexy felt her eyes glazing. "And the… ?"

"See my problem?"

"Yeah. I think I'm starting to."

"I mean, can you imagine how I feel? Two months ago we lose the family business and everything we own, and we're, like, desperate for a miracle. So I turned to magic. Then a woman I've never heard of dies and leaves everything to me."

She flipped compulsively through the bundle of notes in her hand. "And, to make things worse, my dad's acting really weird about it."

Lexy folded her arms on the desk in front of her and stared intently at Rowana Paterson.

Things were beginning to assume a very different complexion.

"Was there a coroner's report on Elizabeth's death?"

"They're waiting for the official one to come out – it takes weeks – but everything is pointing to a verdict of accidental death." Rowana eyed Lexy. "Not that that makes me feel any better. Because I know what I did."

"Well, let's not jump to any conclusions." Especially not mad ones involving the forces of darkness. "Let's try to look at this logically. Where did Elizabeth live?"

"In a cottage called Four Winds, about two miles from here, out on Freshing Hill."

"Sounds bracing."

That bought a pale smile to the girl's lips. "You'd better believe it."

"So, apart from the wind, what's it like, this cottage?"

Rowana pulled a face. "Completely isolated. Halfway up a hill, surrounded by trees."

Sounded good to Lexy.

"We just looked in a couple of windows when we went up there. We couldn't go inside, because the solicitors haven't drawn up the paperwork yet to sign the place over to us. Well, to me. We've been staying in a B&B in Clopwolde for the past few days.

You know, it was pretty difficult being up at the cottage – I couldn't help thinking about what had happened. I mean, the balcony Elizabeth fell over is right at the front. And Dad was having problems being there, too. If I could, I would have just got the solicitors to sell the place without us even looking at it."

Rowana flipped the notes again. The rustle made Kinky sit up straight. He knew about how money converted to dinner.

"But my sister Gabrielle made us all go there. She's very… assertive."

So she had a pushy sister. "Why do you reckon your dad felt so reluctant about going up to the cottage?"

Rowana shrugged, looking uncomfortable. "I don't know, really. But, when we got the news from the solicitor about the will, he seemed – well, almost as freaked out about it as I was.

It was only Gabrielle who was acting like we'd won the lottery. That is, once she'd got over her jealousy that I was the one who inherited it all."

"So, did you find out from the solicitor who Elizabeth Cassall was, exactly? And why she left you all of this?"

"Kind of. It turned out that Elizabeth originally left her cottage and estate to my mother."

Aha. Now we're finally getting somewhere. Why did teenagers have to be so obtuse? "You haven't mentioned your mum yet. Is she… not around?"

"She's dead," said Rowana. "Years ago."

"I'm sorry. But clearly Elizabeth knew her if she made her a beneficiary in her will?"

"Yes – apparently they were friends. This was before I was born. And my mum died not long after I was born, so…"

Lexy gave the girl a sympathetic look.

"Elizabeth wrote in her will that in the event of my mother dying, the cottage and estate would come to her daughter."

So Elizabeth knew there was a daughter.

"And your dad never knew any of this?"

"He says not…" Rowana's eyes became guarded.

6

"But if your mum and Elizabeth were friends, surely he would have known her?"

"He says not."

Lexy wasn't liking the sound of this. Nevertheless she changed the subject. She'd do some subtle probing about Paterson senior later.

"What about your sister?" she said. "Wasn't she mentioned in the will?"

"Oh – I forgot to say. Gabrielle's my half-sister. From my dad's first marriage. She died too. Gabrielle's mother, I mean."

"Bl... blimey." Both Paterson senior's wives dead, now Elizabeth Cassall.

"It was pretty awful for my dad," Rowana went on. "But I think he always felt worse about my mother. His one true love. You know, like Henry the Eighth and Jane Seymour. Except that Dad was only married twice. And no one was beheaded."

Lexy nearly choked. This kid was priceless. "Er... how old is Gabrielle, by the way?"

"Nineteen."

"How did she take all this?"

"Well, like I said, she was fairly gutted that I was the one who inherited it all. But when I said I was going to sell the cottage and put the whole lot back into starting a new business, she was OK about it. I mean, I have to do that, don't I? I can't keep the money to myself."

She looked down at the notes in her hand. "Except this, because I really do need to find out what happened to Elizabeth."

Poor kid. Not only did she think she'd dispatched this unfortunate woman by some clandestine magic ritual, she was also having to cope with an uppity half-sister, and a father who, by the sound of it, might have a guilty secret or two of his own.

"So, will you help me?" Rowana held out the money again.

Lexy took it. She knew she should have dropped this one like a hot cauldron but something about the girl tugged at her heartstrings. And intrigued her. And she had that rent to pay.

"Before I do anything, I'll need to know every detail about this. Right from the start." She flipped open a notebook on her desk, uncapped a biro, then arranged her features more sensitively. "You say you lost the family business?"

The girl nodded. "We're confectioners. Paterson's Fine Cakes, we're called. Were called. My great granddad started the business in 1899."

Lexy raised her eyebrows in respectful interest.

"Our shop was in Bloomsbury, in London – near the British Museum. You know it?"

"I know the British Museum." It was one of the places Lexy used to go to get away from her husband, Gerard. For an antiques dealer he was surprisingly averse to culture.

"We lived in a flat over the shop," Rowana continued. "I was brought up there. It was a bit…" She searched for the word. "Unorthodox."

Lexy looked at her with new sympathy. She knew all about unorthodox upbringings.

"Thing is, Paterson's never changed with the times. My grand-dad took it over in the nineteen fifties, and he kept things just like they always had been. He died when he was eighty-four, still running what was left of the business. Then my dad took over."

"So… did he try to turn it around?" asked Lexy.

"You're joking. He's as obsessed with the past as granddad was. More. In fact, up to this year we were still using the same copper saucepans, dipping forks and caramel cutters that great granddad used. The same ones!"

"Sounds good to me," said Lexy. "People are really into retro stuff these days, aren't they?"

"Maybe. But when customers came into the shop and saw the old 1920s till and everything, they thought we were doing it as a gimmick. They didn't actually realise it was for real. That we were living it. I suppose it wouldn't have mattered to us if it was only the shop, but you should have seen the flat above." She gave a helpless grin. "In a funny way, I really liked it. I mean, it was inconvenient and cold, no central heating, and having to take our washing to the launderette and stuff like that. Gabrielle couldn't stand it – she wanted all the home comforts. But somehow it felt to me like we were really alive. You know, not wrapped in cotton wool."

Lexy found herself nodding. Her own upbringing in a series of caravans bore that out.

"But everyone Gabby and I knew – well, from school and that – thought we were barking. Our dad actually is barking. I mean, he was restoring a Squirrel in the living room."

"A squirrel?"

"Scott Squirrel. It's a motorbike from the 1930s."

"Ah." That kind of barking.

"So, you get the picture," Rowana went on. "Until the day I found the letters I thought that Paterson's Fine Cakes would just go on and on forever."

"The letters?"

"It was the day I discovered how bad things really were – two months ago. I found a bundle of letters tucked behind the range. It turned out to be a load of correspondence from a firm of solicitors to Dad, threatening to take legal action against him over non-payment of rent."

"So you didn't own the place?"

"No. It's always been owned by a property company who've had it ever since great granddad set up in business. I think he must have done them some sort of favour, because we only paid what's called a peppercorn rent – practically nothing, really – and there was a very long lease agreement. Which is why I'd always just assumed that things would go on as they had been."

"But," prompted Lexy, "something had obviously gone wrong."

Rowana nodded. "I found out that last year the company had been bought out by this big corporation of developers. They used an old covenant in the lease agreement to raise the rent to what they described as a 'realistic reflection of the commercial potential of the property'. Totally out of our league."

"Did your dad try to fight it?"

She nodded. "Apparently he refused to pay it, and he went to a fair rent tribunal last year. I mean, Gabrielle and I had no idea about any of this. All we knew was that he'd turned from being someone fairly happy with life into a miserable… well, git. We thought he was having the male menopause."

"What happened at the tribunal?"

"It ruled in the property developers' favour, of course. They gave us four months to vacate the premises, unless we came up with the money."

Lexy gave her a look of commiseration.

"But by the time I found the letters, we only had eight weeks left. God knows when Dad was going to mention it to us. Although I think he probably meant for one of us to find the letters." She said this with a kind of fond resignation.

What a strange mix she was, thought Lexy. An intelligent, charmingly naïve kid who had lost her mother but not her sense of humour. Stuck with an eccentric father, and an angry half-sister, and weighed down by a floury family legacy. Can't have been an easy life.

"Anyway, Gabrielle and I spent every waking hour from then on trying to decide what to do. Blimey, Gabby even offered to marry her rich boyfriend, because he could have bailed us out, but Dad totally put his foot down there. Can't blame him. I mean, not only is Russell nearly thirty, he's also going bald and his main topic of conversation is carburettors. I think Gabrielle was only going out with him because he had a Ferrari, although…" She tailed off, then shook herself. "Anyway, it caused a massive row, and didn't get us any further. It wasn't like Dad had any useful ideas – in fact, he seemed to have given up completely. So I realised in the end it was down to me." She fumbled in her bag. "I found this in a jumble sale."

Rowana handed a book to Lexy.

It was a slim hardback in matt black, the title picked out in ornate silver text.

Thirteen Moons – The Magical Cult of Helandra.

Lexy nodded to herself. She'd seen this kind of thing before. She turned to the first page and read aloud.

"*Welcome, Fellow Seeker, to the ancient art of Ceremonial Magic. Transform your existence through Helandra, Supreme Goddess of the Moon, Arch-Mistress of Change.*"

She skimmed the pages. Helandra was associated with an ancient and powerful form of natural magic. The book explained how to summon the goddess in order to bring about change.

The transformation, it said, *may be constructive, for example, the gift of love, or the increase of material wealth, or destructive, perhaps the elimination of something unwanted.*

This last made Lexy look at Rowana sharply. She was following the words too.

"It was the idea of the increase of material wealth. Got me hooked."

Lexy could see that. She read on. Apparently Helandra could be summoned by anyone game enough to try. *However,* the book admonished, *magic is a dangerous tool when exploited by the unprepared. The purpose of this Handbook, therefore, is to guide the initiate safely through the basic Arts. This may be accomplished in the time that it takes for the moon to circle the Earth thirteen times.*

"I'm guessing that you taught yourself the magical arts in a rather shorter timescale than a year?" Lexy said.

"Yup. Basically, I had about a fortnight to get the Supreme Goddess to intervene before we had to leave."

Lexy shook her head wearily.

"But look at the inscription on the fly-leaf," Rowana implored.

It was written in tiny, spidery script:

To R. Hesitate Not.

2

"So what exactly did you do?"

"Took it home, learned as much as I could, and went out and bought all the stuff I'd need – you know, incense, candles, herbs. Then, one night, six weeks ago, when Dad was away and Gabrielle was out for the night with Russell, I went to the greenhouse… "

"The greenhouse?"

"Well, I wasn't going to set up a pagan altar on the back lawn," Rowana reasoned. "For a start, the ritual I was doing needed me to be, um, naked."

Lexy held back a grin. "Right."

"So I set up my circle, with the altar in the middle, facing east, of course, and I got out my wand…"

"You have a wand?"

"Yeah. It was a nightmare getting it, too. I was meant to cut it from a branch of hazel at midnight under a waxing moon, but the only tree I could find that was anywhere close was an elder, in the park opposite the shop."

Despite her private amusement, Lexy felt a sudden chill. Elder. The witch's tree. Bad luck if you cut it. She could hear her dad saying that.

"And the moon was waning."

Waning? Not a good time to mess with the spirit world.

"And I got chased by a tramp."

Lexy shook herself. She wasn't sure how folklore interpreted that one. But it was unlikely to be lucky.

"Anyway," continued Rowana. "I lit this little charcoal burner and sprinkled on some incense, and some dried parsley and snail shell…"

Lexy interrupted her before she got to eye of newt. "Sounds like you did a thorough job."

"I thought so, too," said Rowana. "I lit four candles, rang my silver bell – well, actually it was the shop counter bell – then I stepped into the circle, er… dropped my robe, took up my knife and invoked the goddess."

"Your knife?"

"Bread knife." Rowana's expression changed. "Invoking Helandra made me feel…" She searched for the right word. "Empowered. It was like I suddenly knew that the magic was going to work."

Lexy felt herself nodding.

Rowana took a deep breath. "I started dancing and chanting. I had this picture in my mind, this vision of the shop doing well and us paying the new rent, and everything continuing as it always had."

She looked directly at Lexy, her pupils wide. "Then suddenly this weird little thought popped into my mind."

"What?" Lexy could feel the hairs on the back of her neck springing up.

"Well – I was summoning a goddess. You know, actually summoning a real goddess! I wanted to make it worth my while."

"In what way?"

"A bad way. I tried to shake it off. But by then I was down on one knee, with my wand aloft, and this bolt of energy shooting through me. The wand didn't exactly glow, but it was a bit of a Darth Vader moment. I felt this… this… presence… expanding and floating above me."

"You mean you saw it… her?" Lexy's hands were clenched.

"No. I stared down at the ground. I was too scared to raise my eyes in case the spell was broken. But she was there, all right." Rowana swallowed. "Thing is, when it came to it, instead of asking Helandra to help us with the shop and the rent and all that worthwhile stuff, I… well,… I found myself blurting out something else."

"What?" For the love of…

"I said 'Make me rich, Helandra. Whatever it takes.'"

"Ah."

"It was, like, a moment of madness. I knew you should never do magic for personal gain. But, before I had a chance to take it back, I heard a noise – a door banging. It was Gabrielle and Russell, back from the cinema."

"What did you do?"

Rowana gave a short laugh. "Dived out of the circle, grabbed up my robe, blew out the candles, shoved everything into a bag and legged it up the fire escape to my room. Not the best way to end an invocation, but I knew I'd blown it, anyway. Even so, part of me still thought Helandra would sort it all out. You know – lead me to some kind of lost inheritance, or something." She laughed again, harshly this time. "Trouble is, she did."

Lexy leaned forward, palms up. "Rowana – Helandra doesn't exist."

"So it was just a coincidence that this woman fell from an upstairs window straight over the balcony, the very next morning after I'd done the magic, and died, leaving me a small fortune?"

The very next morning? Lexy tried not to hesitate. "Yes."

Rowana looked almost truculent. "So you don't want to take this job?"

"I didn't say that," Lexy replied. "And I agree that it's a bit odd that Elizabeth fell backwards to her death." To put it mildly. "I'd like to go up to the cottage and take a look around."

"I've got the key here," said Rowana, digging once again in her bag.

"How come? I thought you said…"

"When we went up there yesterday I found it under a pot by the front door. I didn't tell the other two because I didn't want to go in. Too creepy."

She handed the key to Lexy. "Please just go there. See if you can find out anything. It was the front bedroom window she went out of. On to the rockery."

14

Lexy grimaced.

"That's why I didn't want to go there." Rowana looked down at her watch.

"One more question," said Lexy.

"Oh, no – I'm going to be late. Dad's waiting at the pier. He doesn't know anything about this. He'd go loony tunes if he did. Got to go."

"But… " said Lexy.

"I'll call you," the girl said. "We can meet somewhere, when I can get away, that is."

"But…"

Lexy's protest hung in the air. Rowana had slipped out of the door, and was clattering down the wooden stairs that led to ground level.

Lexy stood at the window, clutching the key, and watched the girl run across the scrubby garden, her long hair flying out behind her, over the river bridge, and up the road towards the distant pier.

Kinky, disturbed by the drama of the moment, jumped awkwardly from his perch and made his way through the still open living room door and down the steps. Moments later Lexy heard the scrabbling sounds that told her he was clambering through the cat flap that a previous occupant had thoughtfully put in the main door to the cabin.

Lexy paced around her octagonal living room. How had she managed to get talked into this? More importantly, should she try to get out of it before it was too late? But how was she going to contact Rowana? She pulled up short by one of the windows, glanced out, then stared hard through the fading, slanting rays of sun.

"What the… ?"

Cursing freely, Lexy clattered down to the front door herself, and yanked it open.

"Kinky!" Her voice was unnaturally sharp.

The chihuahua, despite his residual limp, appeared with alacrity around the side of the cabin.

"You didn't see it, then?" Lexy grabbed his collar, relieved. "That big black dog… thing? Running down the edge of the dyke?"

He couldn't have seen it, otherwise he would have done his usual party trick. But she'd probably got there just in time.

Lexy hustled him back into the cabin and locked the cat flap. Although he was a choice example of the smallest dog breed in the world, Kinky was blissfully unaware of this fact. He would cheerfully square up to rottweilers, rampaging horses, harbour seals, ruddy great herring gulls… and anyone who took a pop at Lexy. In fact he had a past history of it, which explained the scars, and the limp. Whatever it was out there, soon as he saw it, he'd have it. No doubt about that.

Lexy shook herself. There wasn't anything out there. Not of the sort she thought she'd seen, anyway. That loopy kid had got right under her skin. She was starting to imagine things herself.

3

She was in pitch darkness, her heart slamming against her ribs. She had been running – no, bolting – from some faceless pursuer. But now her legs had turned to lead. She could only stagger, unable even to turn, while the thing behind her gained ground, until she could feel its hot breath on her neck.

A claw raked her cheek.

Lexy yelled out, her hand grabbing at the flowery curtain beside her.

Flowery curtain?

Pale dawn light filtered into the room.

"Kinky! You little shite!" Lexy shoved the chihuahua away, glancing at her watch. Six-thirty. She groaned. He usually had the decency to wait until at least ten past seven before waking her up.

Her heart was still racing. She lay back, trying to control her breathing. Perhaps the dream was a warning from her own subconscious, telling her not to get mixed up with that Paterson girl and her peculiar paranormal problems. And somehow, that black... thing she'd seen the day before, that was all tangled up with it. That's what had been chasing her.

Lexy gave a snort. She was going soft. There was no black creature! It had just been a trick of the light. There was nothing supernatural going on, either in Clopwolde or in the world according to Rowana Paterson. The kid hadn't killed Elizabeth Cassall by magic, and the bad dream was just...well, a bad dream.

Lexy would nip over to Four Winds Cottage today, have a quick look around, just for the sake of form, then come back and convince Rowana that Elizabeth Cassall had toppled over her balcony accidentally. Just as the coroner would soon confirm. Charge her for a half day, seeing as the kid was flush. But she wasn't going to take advantage. And she wasn't going to have any more peculiar visions or bizarre dreams. That would be an end to it.

She sat up, rubbing her eyes. Kinky dashed eagerly to the stairs.

"No way! It's too early for breakfast."

He sloped back, tail down, jumped on the bed, and sat with his back to Lexy. She rolled over with a sigh. Might as well get up and feed the little git. She wasn't going to be able to get back to sleep again, not now.

Nevertheless she lay back for a moment and surveyed her surroundings with quiet pleasure.

Her bedroom used to be a fishing-net loft, and was accessed by a set of steep wooden steps from the main living area. Not quite what she'd been accustomed to in her previous life as a trophy wife in South Kensington, but it suited her just fine. And it provided a perfect refuge from Gerard Warwick-Holmes, the husband from whom she had fled three months earlier. Each passing day at Clopwolde, Lexy had relaxed a little more. He hadn't tracked her down yet. Perhaps he never would. A genteel Suffolk coastal village had to be one of the last places he'd look.

Lexy smiled up at the protective rafters over her head. The sturdy wooden cabin used to be a base for offshore fishermen in the early nineteenth century. They took boats out into Clopwolde Bay, in the North Sea, a rich herring ground. At least it was until they'd caught them all.

There were about a dozen cabins originally, but with the demise of the herring population, half got neglected and fell down. Then the remaining ones were rediscovered by artists, and after that the river fishermen and holidaymakers moved in. Suddenly the humble dwellings were commanding as much as a semi-detached house in Reigate.

Lexy's friend Edward owned the cabin she was now in. He wasn't really a beach hut kind of man, and she had been desperate for a base, as her previous home had met with an unfortunate end three months previously. So an arrangement had been made.

Lexy sat up and glanced out of the window. She hadn't been wrong about that marquee yesterday – some kind of tent village was springing up on the opposite bank, a sea mist rising rapidly behind it. Obviously a local show of some sort, probably involving home-made jam and peculiarly-shaped vegetables.

She continued to watch the activities, until the rising swirls of mist began to obscure the bank and blot out the sunlight.

"Right, I'm gonna have a quick shower, then I'll get your grub," she informed the chihuahua's stiff, caramel-coloured back. She took the three strides into the small bathroom and picked up her toothbrush. A minute later she heard Kinky barking savagely in the room below.

Muttering darkly, Lexy descended backwards down the steep steps to the living area, and joined him at the window that looked west, over the water meadows. Kinky's hackles were raised, not that anyone would notice, they were so tiny, and he was scrabbling at the window.

She stared out. Nothing, of course.

"Knock it off, Kinky. You've got me down here now, which was what you wanted."

Lexy tore open a packet of dog biscuits and poured them into the chihuahua's bowl. Uncharacteristically, he ignored the sound, remaining with his nose pushed against the window.

She turned to go back to her shower. Perhaps he'd gone deaf?

"Oi, dummy – your breakfast's here."

He gave a sharp bark.

Lexy stopped short, then moved to the window, staring into the eerie vapours outside.

What the hell was that, making its way along the raised meadow dyke to the side of the cabin? She pressed her face against the cold glass.

It was the thing she'd glimpsed the day before! Big, black and shaggy, with a large head, and gleaming yellow eyes. If it was a dog, it was a huge one. No wonder Kinky was so incensed. At least he'd seen it this time, which meant it was real. She blinked rapidly. Damn – it had disappeared into the mist.

She ran for the door. Kinky leapt after her. If Lexy wanted to chase the black interloper along the river front wearing just her t-shirt and undies, he wasn't going to argue.

They sped down the wooden stairs together, Lexy just managing to grab the chihuahua before he launched himself through the cat flap, locked or not. She fumbled to unlatch the front door, one hand on the dog's collar. They peered out. The cold sea mist was now furling around the cabin, making it difficult to see anything further than ten yards away, although Lexy could just make out the ghostly outlines of the marquees on the bank opposite. Metallic clanks and clashes echoed from the site. Kinky struggled to be free.

"No way," Lexy muttered. She reached up with one hand to grab a small chain from a hook by the door, and clipped it to his collar. Until she'd cleared up this mystery, Kinky would have to be supervised at all times. She couldn't afford any more vet bills. And she wasn't talking about vet bills for the chihuahua.

"Morning, moi luvver!"

Lexy jumped violently as one of her neighbours, a hale and hearty type called Lonny, loomed out of the mist, carrying a fishing line.

"Blimey, girl, aren't you cold in that little outfit? Oh, yeah – I can see you are. Want warming up?"

"No – you're all right, " Lexy assured him, folding her arms in front of her chest, wishing that Kinky would hurry up with the activity in which he was now engaged. "Er... Lonny – let me know if you see anything unusual today."

The fisherman stopped with a grin. "Like what? A bird in scanty underwear?"

"No," said Lexy, patiently. "A... well, a big, black, shaggy dog-thing, actually."

"You mean Old Shuck?" The fisherman gave an explosive laugh.

"What – you know it? Is it someone's dog?" Lexy felt a pulse of relief. She'd have to keep Kinky under close surveillance until she had a chance to introduce him to this particular canine neighbour. Must be a wolfhound or something. But at least it wasn't…

"No, luvver. Old Shuck's one of them local legends. A 'uge black hound of the Devil. Oh, dear, oh, dear – you ain't seen him, 'ave you?"

"Course not," Lexy snapped. "Come on, Kinky." She dragged the indignant chihuahua back into the hallway, listening to Lonny's laughter echoing through the mist.

A mythical hell hound. Great. Lexy might kid herself she wasn't superstitious, but even she knew it was supposed to be bad luck to see one of those things on the loose.

She began to trudge back up the stairs, her expression dubious. No: that thing she and Kinky had seen had been flesh and blood – she would stake her life on that.

Two hours later, dressed in her usual combats, t-shirt and faded denim jacket, Lexy left the cabin with the chihuahua, both peering apprehensively out first. The mist was clearing as quickly as it had arrived, blown away by a brisk sea breeze that Lexy was by now accustomed to, after three months of living on the east coast. She unlocked a rusting lime green Fiat Panda parked in a lean-to next to the cabin.

"Four Winds Cottage, Freshing Hill," Lexy muttered, checking she had the key that Rowana had thrust at her the day before. Freshing Hill was only a couple of miles down the coast – she'd checked it on the map. Probably take at least twenty minutes to drive there though, as she'd need to negotiate the network of little lanes through the farms and salt marshes south of Clopwolde.

Lexy checked her watch. There were a couple of things she needed to do first. She turned the ignition key a few times, waiting anxiously for the engine to fire. Depressingly aware that the car was on its last legs, she drove into Clopwolde village centre, stopping off for a local newspaper. As usual, visitors cluttered the picturesque high street, and as usual, Lexy had to park on a double-yellow.

She rushed across to the newsagent's, then, halfway in, she glimpsed something that chilled her to the marrow.

It was a tastefully designed poster displayed in the shop window.

CLOPWOLDE-ON-SEA ANTIQUES EXTRAVAGANZA!

A WEEK OF ANTIQUES FOR EVERYONE!

It explained the marquees.

But it wasn't the prospect of a week-long antiques fair that had filled Lexy with so much horror.

No – it was the name of the resident host.

GERARD WARWICK-HOLMES.

Her estranged husband.

Not good. And there was her thinking earlier that a genteel Suffolk coastal village would be one of the last places he'd look for her. Well, she obviously hadn't reckoned on Clopwolde having an annual Antiques Extravaganza, and inviting Gerard, of all C-list celebrities, to host it.

And the worst of it was, whether he was working or not, Lexy's husband would always be on the lookout for her. Went without saying. Not that he'd want her back or anything. Oh, no. He'd just be missing the half-million quid she'd stolen from his safe three months ago.

It was actually the second time that the cash had been stolen, as Gerard himself hadn't exactly earned it by the legal sweat of his brow. However, it had been the last straw in a long line of last straws as far as Lexy was concerned. She had made it her personal mission to ensure that every penny was used as its rightful owner intended, even though she and Kinky had nearly been wiped out in the process.

Lexy's plan to hide out in Clopwolde and keep a low profile had been somewhat hampered when she became a suspect in a murder case on her second day in the area. But at least she'd managed to avoid having her name splashed all over the newspapers.

However, trying to escape notice by her abandoned husband when he was spending a week in a marquee bang opposite her rather eye-catching, elevated home might be a little more problematic.

Ignoring an elderly woman who was trying to get out of the shop, Lexy checked the dates of the antiques jamboree. It was starting the following day. Christ, Gerard would probably be in Clopwolde already.

She shot a glance up and down the high street.

"Looking for someone?"

Lexy jumped violently and twisted around. A tall, grave-faced man in a dark suit stood behind her. Not for the first time she wondered why Detective Inspector Bernard Milo hadn't pursued a career in undertaking.

"You have to do that?"

"Do what?"

"Creep up behind me."

"I've been standing here patiently for ages, waiting to get into the shop, listening to you swearing. I was starting to think you were suffering from Tourette's Syndrome."

"Yeah, well, I've got an excuse. Look who's coming to town." Lexy jabbed a finger at the poster.

"Gerard Warwick-Holmes," he read aloud. His ice-grey eyes flicked blankly back to Lexy.

"Warwick-Holmes?" she said significantly.

Recognition dawned. "Ah."

"Yes. Ah. I think that just about sums it up. If he sees me, I'm dead meat. Especially if I tell him where the money went."

"What money?"

DI Milo had always refused to acknowledge his part in helping Lexy off-load the stolen money. He was utterly dedicated to his career, and to the general upholding of the law. General, that is, rather than specific.

"Let the people out of the shop," he said, guiding Lexy away from the poster.

"I need a drink," she told him.

Milo consulted his watch. "It's ten-forty five in the morning."

"And?"

"How about a coffee?" He turned firmly towards a gingham-themed café two doors down.

"Can't go in there," said Lexy. "I'm banned."

"You're banned from Kitty's Kitchen?"

"Long story." Lexy jerked her head at Kinky. "Involves him and… a cream horn."

"Say no more. Please."

Lexy trod warily along the high street, Milo and Kinky in tow, making for the Jolly Herring, one of Clopwolde's main watering holes. But as soon as they were in, Lexy glimpsed the back of a head that looked horribly familiar. Blond, bristly, might have been fashionable in the late eighties. She turned on her heel, almost cannoning into Milo. "Not here," she muttered.

"What… ?"

A moment later Milo joined Lexy on the street. She was crouching low to avoid being seen through the pub window, with Kinky thrust under one arm.

"I think he's in there," she said. "Let's get out of here."

"Actually, I'm meant to be on duty and…"

Ignoring him, Lexy scuttled down an alley that led to a narrow, dark lane lined with terraced Victorian houses. She knew Milo would follow her. He had a habit of it, on duty or not.

"Let's try here." She dived into a pub that was barely advertised as such, having only the name The Dutchman painted in black letters over the door.

"I'd rather not…" Lexy heard Milo cursing under his breath as he followed her in.

"Who's got Tourette's now?" She was already ordering a vodka and tonic. The place was empty, apart from an unsavoury-looking character nursing a pint in the corner. He scrambled half up at the sight of the policeman.

"Relax, Sidney," said Milo. "I'm not here for you."

The man sat down again, but he glared at Lexy.

"What's his problem?" she snapped.

"One of my snouts," Milo explained quietly when they were out of earshot. "I expect he thinks you're muscling in on his territory."

"Terrific. Just what I need. A jealous police informant waiting for me in a dark alleyway."

"Don't be ludicrous."

"Just when I might need to spend a week lurking in a dark alleyway myself, hiding from a husband who's after my blood."

They took a seat in a dingy booth by the window. Kinky busied himself with the previous night's dropped crisps.

"You're being very melodramatic about this." Milo took a sip of his orange juice. "All you have to do is stay out of Clopwolde for the next few days. Take a holiday or something."

"And how, exactly, do I pay for a holiday?"

"I was only suggesting."

Was it then that Lexy felt herself fingering the key to Four Winds Cottage, tucked in her jeans pocket?

She examined Milo in the light filtering through from the greasy window. "Are you on a case at the moment?"

He nodded.

"Thought you looked distracted. Is it a juicy one?"

"Usual rape and pillage. Not so good for the victim."

"Oh."

"Are you on a case?" Milo asked, looking as if he sincerely hoped she wasn't.

"Yeah, as it happens. Bit of a weird one, too."

He shut his eyes. "Please don't tell me there's a suspicious death involved." He clearly hadn't recovered from the last murder case Lexy had accidentally stumbled into.

"Well, actually…"

"I'm not joking here."

She gave a forced laugh. "Relax. It's just that this dippy kid has got it into her head that she killed someone by the force of magic."

Milo narrowed his eyes.

"She wants me to check it out. I mean, y' know, make sure this person definitely died by accident."

"When you say 'kid'?"

"Well, young girl. Young woman." Lexy wasn't sure she was allowed to be hired by a sixteen-year-old.

"When did the victim die?"

"Six weeks ago. I haven't got the full story yet. Actually I'm meant to be going over to her cottage today. The dead woman's, I mean. On Freshing Hill." Sod it. Why had she blabbed that?

"Freshing Hill?" Milo gave her a sharp look. Bugger.

"Yeah – a place called Four Winds." Resignedly, Lexy watched his face change.

"Happened in mid-July," he said. "Woman lived up there alone. Went backwards out of an upstairs window, straight over one of those little Juliet balconies on to a rockery. Died of head injuries sustained on impact."

They exchanged a glance.

"That'll be my one, then." Lexy took a nervous sip of her drink. "Were you...er... involved in the case?"

"Not personally. One of my lot was investigating officer. I looked over the case notes."

"And... ?"

Milo hesitated.

"Go on – I won't tell. Sounds like it was all cut and dried, anyway."

"There were no suspicious circumstances. No sign of a struggle. No reason to think she'd topped herself. No letter, certainly. Conclusion was she either tripped, or went off balance. When the coroner's report comes out it will most likely return a verdict of accidental death." With these last two words he gave her the benefit of his best steely look. Like an approaching aircraft carrier.

"Fine. No problem." Lexy twiddled a beer mat. "I just have to convince witch-girl and we can all go home happy. Or at least I can go home happy in a week's time."

"Lexy," said Milo. "Please don't do anything that attracts the interest of Lowestoft CID again."

"Goes without saying. Anyway, I'm more concerned at the moment about not doing anything that attracts the interest of my husband."

Lexy noticed the snout called Sidney prick up his ears at that and look with lascivious interest between Milo and herself.

As if.

Some ten minutes later, Lexy turned into a rhododendron-lined gravel driveway, and pulled up beside a maroon Jaguar parked outside a substantial manor house.

She was greeted at the studded door by a well-groomed man with a devastatingly neat pencil moustache.

"Lexy, darling!" exclaimed Edward de Glenville. "You've been a positive stranger. How's life in Captain Birdseye's cabin?"

"Great. I love it, Edward," she smiled. "How's Princess?"

"Almost ready to pop. She's in the west wing, lurking in a wardrobe. Come through. Peter and I are about to have lunch. We had rather a late one last night."

"Drinking and fighting again?"

"No, sweetie, although, *entre nous*, I feel like killing him. He's trying to get ready for this ruddy antiques fest tomorrow…"

Lexy felt a nervous spasm.

"… talked about nothing else for days. He's got a stand in the main marquee, and he's doing a little chat on Art Deco. Anyone would think he was doing the Queen's Speech." He grinned. "Hey – if you open your front window at the cabin you'll be able to hear him – the marquee's right opposite…"

"Yes. I know," Lexy said tightly.

27

"In fact, I'll join you – we can get drunk and heckle him from across the river."

"Yeah – that would be really funny, Edward."

"What's the matter, sweetie? You're not your normal ebullient self."

Lexy teetered on the verge of telling him about Gerard. Edward knew she had left her husband, but she'd never explained the circumstances, or indeed the identity of the obnoxious ex-celebrity spouse. Generous and delightful friend though Edward was, he wasn't exactly the soul of discretion. The only person in Clopwolde who knew her secret was Milo, and Lexy decided she'd better keep it that way.

"New case. Sorry – it's been making me distracted."

"Ooh, I say – are we going to be relentlessly pursuing cold-blooded murderers again?" Edward had somehow become entangled in Lexy's first job, and had been immediately addicted to the thrill of the chase. "Do let me know if you need my assistance for car chases or stake-outs."

"I think this is going to be a quiet one. More a case of proving that someone didn't do it."

"How disappointing. But you will let me know if it hots up?"

"Naturally."

Grinning, Lexy followed Edward up a large flight of stairs, through a grand living room and out on to a sunny balcony that overlooked miles of flat countryside. A hostess trolley bearing a large coffee pot and some covered plates stood in one corner. In the other, a slightly-built, serious-looking man with a 1930s hairstyle and clothes to match was striking a pose. "… and this inspired him… " he declaimed.

"Inspired who?" Lexy asked.

"Bum. I've forgotten. Oh, yes – William Moorcroft, of course. God, I'm know I'm going to screw this up."

"Peter – give it a rest," Edward sighed. "Have a break. Let's talk about something else. Say hello to our guests."

"Yes, sorry. Hi, Lexy Lomax." He leaned over and kissed Lexy on both cheeks, then bent and plucked Kinky from the ground to give him a smothering hug which made the chihuahua's eyes bulge.

Edward, having distributed sparkling wine and hors d'oeuvres, was scanning the countryside with binoculars.

"All he needs now is a pair of net curtains," said Peter.

"What's he looking at, then?" Lexy bit into a warm tartlet.

"Well, it's not the lesser-horned swamp tit, dear."

"Aha!" Edward exclaimed. "I see that Pilgrim's Farm is let at last!"

Squinting, Lexy followed Edward's gaze down the coast. A distinctive wooded promontory rose, wedge-shaped, from the flat meadows. It had cliffs to its seaward side and she could just make out a spread of buildings nestled at its neck.

"To a single man of good fortune, by any chance?" she asked.

"Yes," said Peter. "Only trouble is, he happens to be Bruce Gallimore, a crusty old farmer with an eye for a good scam. Rare breeds, to wit. Punters will pay silly money to see odd-shaped mutton. Anyway, Gallimore's been there for a while now, Eddie. That's old news."

"But what you don't know is that he's been joined by his two lusty sons," said Edward.

"What? Let me see." Peter grabbed the binoculars from Edward, half strangling him in the process.

"Look who needs net curtains now."

"And a telescope. I can't make out anything with these."

"It is over a mile away, lovie."

"That's not Freshing Hill, is it?" Lexy asked.

"Correct. Do you know it?" Edward gave Lexy a searching glance.

She shook her head.

"It's to do with your new case is, isn't it?" he said, mischievously. "What's old Gallimore been up to? Or is it one of his sons?"

"What's this?" demanded Peter.

Lexy rolled her eyes. "It's nothing to do with the farm. It's just some people who've been left a cottage over there. One of them wants something looked into."

"Ah – the old Mickey Spillane stuff again, is it? Well, if you're involving Edward, try to give him back in one piece, will you? It took weeks of valium and aromatherapy massage to calm him down after last time."

"Didn't know there was a cottage," Edward frowned, still staring across the countryside.

Peter and Lexy sat down and sipped their wine.

"Er… either of you guys heard of Old Shuck?" Lexy asked casually.

"Old who?" Peter dabbed with a napkin at a small drip on the table.

"What, the legendary Black Dog of Suffolk?" Edward made a grisly face. "If you see it, it means you're about to die? That Old Shuck?"

"Yeah. That Old Shuck."

"Why?"

"I've seen it."

"Oh, god. What did it look like?"

"It looked like a big black dog, Edward."

"With red eyes?"

"Well… no. It had yellow eyes."

"Wasn't Old Shuck then. He's got red eyes. What you saw was probably the Clopwolde Hound of Death."

"The what?"

Peter threw a sausage roll at Edward. "Shut up with your nonsense. He's extracting the Michael, Lexy."

"Well – you don't seriously believe in any of that supernatural hoo-hah, do you, sweetie?" Edward passed the sausage roll to Kinky.

"No. I just saw a… big black dog-thing."

"Well, never mind, dear. Finish lunch then come and see a small cream cat-thing."

Leaving Kinky stretched out on a sun lounger on the balcony, they went into the cool interior.

Edward and Peter led the way, like proud parents, to a lavishly decorated bedroom. But as soon as they were in, they heard the sound of a cat in distress.

The din was coming from a large walnut wardrobe. The door was half closed. Edward rushed over, pulled it wide, and dropped to his knees in front of it, Lexy and Peter peering over his shoulder. An odd-looking feline, thin and angular despite her condition, with a cream coat as short and curly as a newborn lamb's, was walking around in circles on a soft, now damp blanket, yowling vociferously.

"Quick – call the vet," gasped Edward. "Emergency number's by the bedside phone."

Peter hurled himself, commando-style, across the immaculate silk quilt and grabbed up the phone.

"It's OK." Lexy squashed in beside Edward. "I think it's just that her waters have broken. The kittens are on their way – aren't they, Princess?" And each one was going to be worth several thousand pounds. She mentally rubbed her hands.

The cat flopped on her side, displaying a neat set of teats, and with her audience in place, she heaved.

A watery pink parcel appeared. She regarded it in surprise for a few seconds, then leant round and began to clean it.

"Ooh, bless," said Edward. "It's like a little mouse."

"Looks like she knows what she's doing. Let's leave her to it." Lexy straightened up.

Peter touched Edward's arm. "What are you blubbing for, you big Jessie?"

"And you're not? It is our first-born."

The following half hour brought two kittens, further tears, and an efficient-looking female vet.

"Three. That's the lot," she proclaimed. "Still – she is very young, isn't she?"

"Yes. There was an unfortunate incident with a farm cat," Peter explained.

And that was only the half of it, thought Lexy, exchanging a glance with Edward as they recalled the events of three months earlier.

"I'm going to have to go." Lexy glanced at her watch. "But I'll be back later with twelve knitted bootees, or whatever it is the well-dressed kitten wears nowadays."

She collected Kinky, who had slept through the drama, and left Edward and Peter gazing through misty eyes at the single-parent family.

Lexy sighed. They obviously hadn't noticed yet.

4

Lexy glanced at her watch. Half past three. She was bowling along a narrow country lane towards Freshing Hill, which was visible in the distance across acres of farmland.

When she'd left Edward's place, Lexy had briefly returned home, where she'd crept in like a thief, one eye on the big marquee across the river.

She was now trying to ignore the packed rucksack on the back seat. It was there just in case, although she wasn't seriously thinking about spending the next few days at Four Winds Cottage. Of course not.

At the verge a kestrel hovered, then swooped. Bad moment to be a vole.

Lexy slowed, map propped on the steering wheel, and turned awkwardly into an even narrower lane. A road sign informed her that a place called Nodmore lay one mile ahead.

Overhead, the sky had swelled to a threatening black, and fat drops of rain began hurling themselves against the windscreen. Lexy turned the wipers on, frowning as they set up their customary screech.

"Nearly there now," she said through gritted teeth.

Not for the first time, Lexy wondered exactly what Rowana expected her to find at Four Winds Cottage. Perhaps the Goddess Helandra had dropped an amulet when she was shoving Elizabeth over the balcony. Or left a set of sandaled footprints on the stripped pine floorboards.

She shook her head at the madness of it all. Still, the money was going to come in handy. Especially now the kitten dosh had fallen through.

Because Lexy couldn't but notice, even in their newborn state, that each of those little dark-haired bundles was going to be the spitting image of its father. Which meant they would all grow into dirty great black farm moggies that Lexy would have trouble giving away, let alone selling for thousands. Princess Noo Noo had kept her very rare Suffolk Rex, curly-haired gene to herself. How typical was that?

The rain was falling so hard that Lexy nearly missed the small winding lane, set deep between unkempt hedges, that led towards Freshing Hill. Halfway along she slowed, crashing through the gears, squinting at the map again as the Panda came to a ragged halt in front of a single track tarmac road protected by a cattle grid and a five-barred gate. It bore a sign:

PILGRIM'S FARM (RARE BREEDS)

Silhouettes of various misshapen farm animals laboured this point.

Lexy rolled down the window. The smell of cow pats and wet countryside filled the car. Must be close – Pilgrim's Farm was right at the bottom of Freshing Hill. But should she follow this track? There was no indication that...

Then she saw it, half hidden among the bedraggled hogweed in the hedge. A weathered sign with three words roughly daubed on it in black paint:

FOUR WINDS COTTAGE

An arrow pointed up the tarmac track.

Lexy's heart began to hammer gently.

Annoyed with herself, she jumped out of the car, unfastened and pushed open the gate, getting drenched in the process, then got back in and juddered over the cattle grid. The farm owners weren't making it easy for visitors. By the time she'd shut the gate again she was shivering with cold.

She drove slowly along the road. On one side was a wooden post-and-rail fence painted white. The enclosed field was divided into paddocks with small stables. A handful of odd-looking sheep nonchalantly grazed the soft grass near the fence, looking like they'd been born in a downpour. One had sharp twisted horns, another elaborate cream dreadlocks, and a third was thickly banded in black and white like a giant humbug. They looked up, still chewing, their bland, insolent eyes following Lexy as she drove past.

Next to her, Kinky stood precariously with his paws against the dashboard. He gave a blood-curdling growl.

"You wish," muttered Lexy.

Through the vertical rain she could just make out a farm-house and a huddle of out-buildings, and beyond them, the grey smudge of the North Sea.

On the other side of the track, a tangled meadow merged into woodland.

They drew to a halt at another five-barred gate, bearing the Pilgrim's Farm sign.

To the left, a dark, rutted track led up a tree-covered hillside.

"That'll be us, then," Lexy guessed.

Kinky's eyes tightened.

Lexy turned the wheel and the Panda jolted up the track, spraying mud as it lurched through deep puddles. The dripping tree canopy overhead conspired with the rain to make it unnaturally dark.

Halfway up, it petered out to a levelled area. Lexy pulled up in front of a building that sat in the very centre of the clearing.

Four Winds Cottage. Rowana Paterson's inheritance.

It was a square grey pile with white gables, set in a walled garden. Lexy could see why the original builder of the place took the trouble to lug all the materials up there. On a clear day the views across the countryside would be spectacular. But this was not a clear day.

The front elevation of the cottage had four blank-looking windows. Two on the ground floor, either side of the front door. Two on the first floor, directly above the ground floor ones. The latter were both full length, with a little balcony in front. More of a window guard, really. Except that in Elizabeth's case, it hadn't worked.

Lexy's eyes were drawn to the rockery below the left-hand

window. Not exactly a soft landing. If she'd been expecting dark stains on the decorative stones, she was – well, disappointed wasn't exactly the word. More relieved. Anyway, if there'd been any in the first place, they'd have been washed away by the rain long before now.

Lexy switched the engine off, and unclipped her seat belt. "Ready?" With a glance at the chihuahua, she grabbed her shoulder bag and popped the car door, and they dashed through the downpour, arriving, dripping, on the doorstep.

Lexy fumbled for the key. The lock turned with unexpected ease.

She pushed open the door and they entered a musty-smelling hallway. A worn striped rug lay on the wooden floorboards, and a series of prints lined the wall. Kinky sniffed the air suspiciously, then tucked himself next to her leg, hindquarters shivering like a namby-pamby poodle's. Lexy frowned. Wasn't like him. Did he know something she didn't?

Trying to quell her rising trepidation, Lexy slowly pushed open a door to her left. It led into a kitchen, with a blind pulled three-quarters down at the window, making it almost dark in there. She groped for a switch and a fluorescent strip light flickered into life.

The kitchen was a fitted one, inexpensive but serviceable. A row of cooking implements hung from a stainless steel bar, with a set of saucepans above. The fridge had been unplugged and emptied out, and the beech effect worktops wiped down – Lexy surmised that someone must have come in and set things straight.

Kinky usually liked kitchens – he had a nose for dropped scraps – but he didn't like this one. He made straight for the back door and whined.

"You want to go out in the rain?" Lexy unlocked the back door, bemused by his behaviour. Outside was a storm porch, with a worn stone step leading down to the garden. The dog stood in the shelter of the porch, quivering.

"You wait there, then," Lexy told him. "I'll be back in a sec." It was odd to see him like this. He certainly hadn't been such a wuss when he'd caught scent of the thing that Lonny had called Old Shuck. Lexy gave a mirthless smile. At least that particular beast wouldn't be bothering her here.

She went back through the kitchen into the hall, and glanced up the stairs. The stairs that would lead to the room where Elizabeth had made her final descent. Lexy turned away quickly.

Next to the kitchen was what must originally have been a dining room. It had been converted into an art studio. An easel stood on a paint-spattered sheet, and brushes and pots lay on a table covered in newspaper. The smell of linseed oil lingered in the air. A few completed oils were stacked against a wall, all local landscapes. Not bad either.

Still reluctant to climb the stairs, Lexy pushed open the door opposite the studio and found herself in a large living room, furnished with a squashy dark blue sofa and two easy chairs arranged in front of an open fireplace. A tall wooden bookcase against one wall was full of neatly arranged volumes, mainly classics, together with art and gardening books.

On the mantelpiece a clock ticked hypnotically.

Lexy's eyes were drawn to a curtained alcove, to one side of which stood a small piano. A flowered silk wrap lay across the piano stool, looking eerily as if someone had only just left it there.

Beyond this, a set of double doors led to a patio.

She peered through the glass into the grey gloom. Terracotta tiles, a few large plant pots containing sprawling geraniums, overblown petunias and some late tumbler tomatoes. No one to tend them since mid July. A big rhododendron bush intruded across the side of the patio from the garden beyond, its shiny, rain-washed leaves pressed up against the window.

Lexy moved around the room, methodically opening cupboards and drawers, looking for clues as to why Elizabeth took the quick way down to the rockery six weeks ago. There were a few utility bills in a desk drawer, all seemingly paid. A neat pile of bank statements in another confirmed the healthy state of her savings account – the money that had now passed to Rowana.

No obvious indication that Elizabeth had been in any kind of financial trouble – the sort to make a person want to end it all – or any other trouble, for that matter.

She might have been, it was just that there was nothing, no papers or letters, to give any hint of something amiss. There weren't even any personal letters, cards, or photographs anywhere. It was almost as if someone had come through and cleared the lot out.

A plaintive whine came from beyond the kitchen.

She'd forgotten Kinky. She retraced her steps. He was still hovering in the storm porch.

"You might as well come in," Lexy told him. "We're going to be here for a while."

Kinky didn't look pleased at this news. He slunk back in and adhered himself to her leg again.

Shrugging, Lexy turned back to the living room, then checked herself. She hadn't been upstairs yet. To the front bedroom.

She peered up the hall. What had made that creak? Hell, why was she so jumpy?

"You've put the wind right up me," she scolded Kinky. "It's just an ordinary cottage. A nice cottage. The fact that its owner has recently died is neither here nor there. We're doing a job, right? Need to stay professional."

The chihuahua didn't look convinced.

They trod slowly up the stairs.

An oil painting hung on the landing wall, a portrait of a man. A rugged, distinctive-looking bloke, with silver hair, and decidedly decadent eyes. It was signed EC.

Elizabeth could do people, too.

Lexy stared at the painting for a few moments, then pushed open doors up and down the landing. A bathroom straight ahead; three bedrooms, two at the front and one at the back together with a boxroom.

Steeling herself, Lexy went into the bedroom that looked over the rockery, ignoring the whine Kinky had set up at her heel. It must have been Elizabeth's main boudoir. It was furnished with a double bed, dark wooden wardrobe, tallboy and dressing table.

A photo of a stern-looking young man in army desert combats stood on the tallboy.

Lexy glanced at the dressing table. Among the usual toiletries was a pair of black binoculars.

"Odd," she muttered.

Tail down, Kinky started a detailed sniffing of the carpeted floor.

Lexy moved towards the set of double windows opposite the bed. They were framed by white curtains, and offered a ceiling to floor vista, opening inwards. The keys were hanging on a hook behind the curtain.

Lexy unlocked the windows and pulled them open. The sound of drumming rain filled the room. Braving it, she stepped out on to the balcony. It was standing room only out there, but on a better day it might be pleasant to lean on the white rail and watch the sun go down. Lexy turned and stood with her back to it. Wouldn't be too difficult to take a tumble either, if you tilted back far enough.

Perhaps Elizabeth had been cleaning the outside of the windows and stepped back to admire her handiwork. She might have overbalanced. But if that had been the case, surely a cloth or duster would have been found too? Anyway, the fact that the windows opened inside the room meant that she didn't have to stand on the balcony to clean them.

Perhaps she had simply missed her step in the room while both windows were wide open. Trod back quickly, tripped on the floor-bar between room and balcony, then kept going, arse over tip straight over the railing. But Lexy had to concede that was unlikely – she'd have to have been as clumsy as a carthorse.

Maybe it was just that Elizabeth had let herself go out backwards in a suicide bid. Lexy looked down at the rockery with a shiver. It would be an unconventional way to do it, to say the least. Anyway, the police report, according to Milo, indicated she had no obvious reason to want to kick the bucket.

Lexy surveyed the dismal sky. Unless it always rained like this on Freshing Hill.

There was another option of course.

Perhaps someone pushed her.

Not an impartial goddess acting on a whimsical enchantment, but a real flesh and blood person who knew what was in her will.

Lexy stepped back inside with alacrity, shaking rain from her hair, pushing the unwelcome thought from her mind.

She wondered what to do next. This wasn't going to be as easy as she thought. How could she prove to Rowana that Elizabeth had suffered a genuine accident? It was the most logical explanation, given the alternatives, but Lexy needed to find something to back it up. Kinky was still sniffing the carpet.

"Found anything, pal?"

He looked up, large dark eyes distracted. Nothing he was going to tell her.

The rain seemed to have brought dusk early. Lexy was aware that she needed to make a decision about where she was going to stay that night.

She walked back through the bedroom and took a quick look in the other rooms. The adjacent front bedroom had an identical balcony arrangement. It seemed to be the official guest room. There was a clean quilt and pillows on the double bed. Tempting. A stack of white towels, together with a cake of fancy soap, had been placed on a blanket chest at the foot of the bed.

The only other furniture was a wooden chest of drawers, on top of which were three small candles shaped like penguins.

At the back of the house was a single bedroom with a sofa bed, and adjacent to that was the boxroom, which Elizabeth apparently used as a dressing room. A long rail of clothes stood along one side, with a full-length mirror opposite.

Kinky was sniffing along the hallway carpet now. Thoughtfully, Lexy made her way back downstairs to the kitchen. She pulled up a chair and sat at the table, chin in hand. She had come to Four Winds Cottage half-intending to stay for a few days, and there didn't seem any logical reason why she shouldn't. The Patersons weren't likely to return until the paperwork concerning the cottage was sorted out and that wasn't going to be immediate. It was isolated enough for her to be safe from Gerard. So why did the thought of staying here overnight scare the wits out of her? Lexy shuddered. Kinky seemed to feel the same way. There was definitely something creepy about the place. The thought of returning to her friendly fisherman's cabin on Clopwolde quay was almost irresistible.

However, the idea of running into Gerard wasn't, although he probably wouldn't even recognise her if she did. The last time Gerard had seen her, Lexy had waist-length blonde hair and killer heels. He wouldn't be expecting a tough-looking woman sporting a black, spiky crop and a Celtic armband tattoo. Why, the only thing Lexy Lomax had in common with Alexandra Warwick-Holmes these days was a caramel-coloured chihuahua.

Nevertheless, she wasn't prepared to take the risk.

So, did she have any other options? She could always beg a bed for the night from Edward – he wasn't short of a bedroom or twelve. Trouble with that idea was how to explain to him why she didn't want to stay in her own place, just down the road. He would find it highly odd, and anything that Edward found highly odd he would worry at like a dog with a bone, until he got the marrow out.

Lexy cursed aloud. Sodding Gerard. Why had he taken the job of hosting the Clopwolde antiques fair? It was exactly the kind of provincial thing he'd always sneered at in the past.

Perhaps he was having to take whatever he could get these days, since his last series of *Heirlooms in the Attic*, destined to be shown on BBC Two, had been cancelled.

Lexy glanced down at Kinky, who had just joined her. "OK. You win. We're won't stay here tonight, we'll go to Edward's. Tell him the cabin's sprung a leak, or something."

She pushed her chair out. Kinky darted down the hall ahead of her. Lexy locked the kitchen door, and the two of them left by the front entrance.

Just being back in the worn fabric seat was a relief.

"Right – take me to Clopwolde, car," Lexy commanded, turning the key. The Panda made a noise like a startled pheasant. The next time she tried there was no reaction at all.

"Not quite the glorious exit I'd planned. However, let's not panic."

But Lexy's heart was in her mouth. The car had just picked the worst possible place to die. And time.

Kinky shifted uneasily.

Lexy took her mobile phone out. She'd ask Milo for a lift. But he'd probably be tied up on his case, which meant, even worse, that she'd have to call Edward to come and get her, like she was some ditsy teenager, rather than a thirty-year-old woman. Only just thirty, mind.

She flipped open her phone and waited for it to fire up. The battery icons built themselves up obediently. Just needed a signal. It took Lexy a couple of minutes to realise there wasn't going to be one.

A ripe Anglo-Saxon expression rent the evening air.

Lexy bundled out of the car and walked around in the rain, holding the phone up high as if the elusive satellite might spot it from the sky. It was useless.

She couldn't even call a cab.

She tried the car once more, leaning in to turn the key. Nothing. They weren't going anywhere.

Lexy grabbed the rucksack from the back seat.

"Come on," she snapped at Kinky. He slunk out after her. Back into the house they went.

Lexy stopped short in the hall as she hung her damp jacket

up. There was one other option. She could walk down to the farmhouse. She chewed her lip. It was at least a mile away, down that winding track in the sheeting rain and gathering darkness. And how could she explain herself when she got there? On top of that, hadn't there been something just slightly odd about the place when she went past earlier? She remembered the insolent eyes of the sheep, following her along the tarmac road.

"OK, Lomax, quit with the Hills Have Eyes stuff," she said loudly. But she didn't put her jacket back on.

She went into the kitchen, making sure the blind was pulled right down before she put on the light. She wasn't scared of the Gallimores of Pilgrim's Farm. She just didn't want them knowing she was up here.

5

Lexy hadn't thought to pack any food. She checked out the cans in the larder. Rowana wasn't going to mind if she nicked a tin of baked beans – there were enough of the things in there. Nothing else, mind, except an ancient-looking bottle of home-made elderberry wine.

Lexy felt Kinky's eyes burning into her.

"Haricots?" she queried, scraping some out into a bowl for him.

Legumes in tomato sauce weren't quite to the chihuahua's taste.

Lexy shrugged. He might feel differently about them in the morning.

She washed down her own beans with black tea, wondering where to lay her head. She certainly wasn't going to use any of the rooms upstairs. No – she'd kip in the living room.

She went in, chucked her sleeping bag on the sofa, and prowled restlessly around, fighting the rising creepiness that clawed at her at the thought of the coming night. Checked through the drawers and cupboards she'd already looked in. Went over to the piano. The keyboard was covered in a light film of dust. Lexy played a few notes, then shut the lid before Kinky started howling. She picked up the flowered silk wrap, and lifted the lid of the piano stool. Inside, under a Chopin score, was a brown envelope, unsealed. She opened it.

It contained two photographs.

The first was of a face that Lexy instinctively knew to be Elizabeth's. Wasn't difficult. She'd been photographed in the studio across the hall, wearing an artist's smock, with a palette in one hand. She had turned to look at the photographer, her expression one of great tenderness. Made Lexy wonder who'd taken it. It was a black and white print, taken with old-fashioned film, perhaps ten or fifteen years ago?

Lexy flipped it over. To her surprise it had Elizabeth's name and the previous year's date on the back. She gazed at it again.

Her vague preconceptions of Elizabeth had been of a spinsterish woman in her sixties. But the Elizabeth in the photo wasn't sixty and spinsterish at all. Far from it. She only looked to be in her late forties. Lexy hadn't even thought to ask Rowana.

It almost gave a new dimension to the fall. Could there have been a love angle? Had she been spurned by someone? Or perhaps angered someone? Again, Lexy wondered who had taken the photo.

She turned her attention to the other print, which was in colour.

There were three people in it. Lexy found herself doing a double take. One of them was Rowana Paterson.

With her was a slim, rather tired-looking man with dark auburn hair, whom Lexy assumed to be her father, and a taller girl with pretty but hard features. Rowana's sister, Gabrielle. It wasn't a posed photo. They were walking along a street together, a crowded street at that – seemingly unaware that the photo was being taken. Gabrielle was glancing sideways at a shop window, Rowana was talking to her father, her mouth slightly open, her hair sweeping across one side of her face. He was smiling down at her.

Lexy turned it over. There was a date hand-printed in one corner. It had been taken just over a year ago. Nothing else was written on the back.

The Patersons might not have known Elizabeth, but Elizabeth knew them.

Lexy ran a hand through her hair. What was going on? She needed to speak to Rowana again. Lexy wondered what the girl's reaction would be if she saw the photo. She wasn't sure it was something she wanted to put to the test yet.

Feeling thoroughly disquieted by this discovery, Lexy turned on the TV, needing noise and distraction. The reception was bad, but she managed to tune into a cop show.

But she couldn't get Rowana out of her mind, and what the girl had said about her strange upbringing, and her anachronistic father, who had been acting 'really weird' since he'd heard the news about Rowana's inheritance. And who, like Rowana, hadn't wanted to come here. Why? Anyone in their right mind would be intrigued to look at a country property their daughter had just been left in a will. Especially if they were strapped for cash.

Lexy silently berated herself. The whole point of coming here had been to have a quick look around the cottage, assure Rowana that she wasn't a teenage murderess, collect the dosh, and go on her merry way. So what had changed?

It was that photo. Why would Elizabeth have a secretly-taken snap of the Patersons?

OK, fair enough, she'd left everything she owned to Rowana's mother. That was her choice. But had she known that she'd died? That the daughter was already the beneficiary?

Even if she had, Elizabeth wouldn't have anticipated Rowana inheriting her legacy for another thirty, maybe forty years. So, perhaps the really big question was – who else knew about the will?

Lexy chewed her lip. The police had already carried out an investigation of sorts. Wouldn't it be easier if she just kept her head down?

Of course it would be easier. But would it be right?

Kinky sat opposite on an armchair, fixing Lexy with an aggrieved stare. It had obviously sunk in that she wasn't intending to take him home that night. Or even give him any Doggy Chomps.

It made thinking very difficult.

With one last look at the photo, Lexy tucked herself into her sleeping bag. It was still raining, not in great grey rods now, but heavily enough to keep the gutters gurgling and splashing.

She turned out the tasselled lamp on the table next to her and lay in darkness, unable to sleep.

Was that clock getting louder? She stared blindly around. Where was the cold draught coming from? Surely not the patio door? She'd shut it, hadn't she? And locked it. Perhaps it was Elizabeth's spirit haunting the cottage. Writhing and moaning…

Come off it! This wasn't like her. Lexy pulled the sleeping bag up to her chin and firmly closed her eyes.

She awoke, disorientated, at dawn. Sunlight was extending slim, bright fingers around the sides of the roughly pulled curtains. She'd made it through the night. Grinning sheepishly at her earlier fears, Lexy pulled on her t-shirt and combats and padded across to open the curtains and unlock the patio doors. A rush of morning cool and birdsong assailed her. Kinky pushed past her to get out.

She'd have a spot of breakfast – beans, again, unfortunately – then she'd get on to Milo and…

Lexy's mouth fell open. The garden looked almost magically transformed from the grey gloom of the previous day. The early autumn sun sleeked over the flint wall and shimmered in the dew-soaked lawn, enticing her out like the Pied Piper of Hamelin.

She pulled on her trainers and went into the garden, breathing in the fresh, clear air.

The cottage lay in a low-walled garden bordered with native trees and shrubs – holly, elder, spindle and hawthorn. A sunny raised bed had been planted out with herbs, each carefully marked up with its name on a wooden stick. Borage, ginger mint, chives, rosemary, golden sage, thyme – there must have been over twenty different varieties, some tumbling and rampant now, needing to be tended and harvested.

In the centre of the garden, a picturesque mountain ash tree was laden with a mass of orange berries. Birds flitted and chirped in the foliage.

It felt like a little slice of Eden. Certainly a world apart from the rain-lashed scenario of the night before. But then, any amount of rain would be worth it for just one morning like this.

In the corner of the garden was an old lean-to shed. Lexy peered through the cobwebby window. It housed what she supposed to be Elizabeth's car, a small red model with a serious rust problem. Obviously hadn't been driven for a while. Did she walk everywhere? Then Lexy spotted the bicycle, an old-fashioned sit-up-and-beg type with the word Pegasus printed along the frame. It looked well-maintained, with a sizeable basket on the front, and seemed to fit the image of the woman very well. Lexy imagined the Elizabeth from the photo spinning along the country lanes on this metal steed, her long, dark hair flying behind her.

She turned back to the garden. Across the grass was a wicker gate. Lexy headed for this, her footprints clear in the dew. It let out on to a path that ran further up the wooded hill. She opened it, took a step out, and stopped, arrested by a shrill bark behind her. Kinky was standing in the centre of the lawn, looking wary.

"Don't you want a little walkies?" Lexy coaxed.

In a series of grumbling whines, the chihuahua explained where to shove her little walkies.

"Please yourself." Lexy set off.

Below her lay Pilgrim's Farm and through the still, clear air she could see a tiny figure moving about in the yard.

The path led upwards through woodland that thinned as she climbed, eventually revealing an open area of grass, gorse and scrub which extended as far as the cliff edge. The view across Clopwolde Bay was spectacular.

Kinky caught her up, panting and glaring. Lexy smiled to herself. He was so predictable.

They continued to the edge, the chihuahua again sticking close to Lexy's heel, a model of canine probity. Lexy couldn't figure it out. It was as if the cottage and Freshing Hill were exerting some strange, restraining force on him.

Although it was early, the sun already felt warm on Lexy's face. She stood looking out over the restless grey-green North Sea, dimpled with sunlight, and felt a stab of envy for Rowana.

What a shame she had to sell the place, and what a shame Lexy didn't have a spare few hundred thousand in the bank to buy it. She couldn't imagine why she had found it so sinister the previous night.

A low mist hugged the shingle shore, some thirty feet below. The beach extended in a wide crescent all the way to Clopwolde, formed over centuries by the sea taking bite after patient bite from the land's edge.

She followed the path along the edge of the cliff. It wasn't long before she came to a set of rough stone steps leading down. A wonky tubular metal rail ran beside the steps.

"Come on, fella." Lexy began to descend.

Kinky dithered at the top.

"Stay there, then."

Lexy was getting a mite fed up with the little caramel-coloured sod and his inexplicable moods. As she clambered down, a large, loose stone slipped from under her and tumbled heavily down to the beach. Lexy clutched at the railing, falling on her backside. There was a rustle in the undergrowth, and a couple of rabbits shot away.

Kinky began barking. That was more like him.

Lexy pushed herself up. "Don't even think about chasing them."

Then she noticed it. Moving away from them through the mist.

"Not again," she whispered.

But it was happening again. Old Shuck was at large, making along the beach for Clopwolde.

It was exactly the same creature she had glimpsed coming along the dyke towards her cabin yesterday morning. Head down, big powerful shoulders, drumming feet. As she gazed, the black, shadow-like form disappeared into the mist. Drumming feet? The creature had to be mortal. Lexy clambered awkwardly to the beach, Kinky slithering down in her wake.

They found themselves on cool shingle glazed with silver wash from the sea. Pretty to look at but not great for running along in pursuit of mysterious black beasts. After five minutes Lexy was exhausted, and Kinky had given up completely. There was no sight of the creature, or any trail of animal prints – no hope of that on the uneven ridges of pebbles. Thoroughly disconcerted, Lexy trailed back to the steps, meeting up with the panting chihuahua on the way back.

They climbed back up the steps to the cliff top, and Lexy stared down at the beach until the mist lifted in shreds, revealing – nothing. Nothing other than a couple of early fishermen, arriving and setting up on the shore. She debated whether or not to go down and ask them if they, too, had seen it. Then it occurred to her that Lonny had doubtless already regaled the entire fishing community of Clopwolde with tales of a lush bird in underwear, gabbling about a sinister black apparition. She didn't want to fan the flames of that one. She had a feeling she wouldn't be taken seriously, even fully dressed.

6

Half an hour later Lexy was sitting in the sun on Elizabeth Cassall's back doorstep, drinking black tea, and eating cold baked beans straight from the tin.

She'd just tried the car and it had started first time. Seemed like her luck was beginning to change.

"Points must have been wet," she told Kinky, without really knowing what this meant, other than that she could now drive to the village and get him some food before their relationship deteriorated beyond repair.

"Remind me in future," Lexy told him, "to keep some emergency packets of Doggy Chomps in the car, for the next time we illegally enter a remote cottage and spend the night there."

Kinky raked her knee, pleadingly.

Neither of them heard the stranger coming down the path at the side of Four Winds.

"Hey – who are you?" He rounded the wall, pushed the front gate open and advanced on her across the lawn.

Kinky gave a belated bark.

Lexy shaded her eyes and looked up in alarm, her mind swiftly formulating explanations as to why she should be sitting on Elizabeth Cassall's back doorstep, eating cold baked beans and drinking tea.

She assessed her interrogator. Mid-twenties, straight nose, high arched brow, light brown eyes. A Norman countenance, bit like one of those knights from the Bayeux Tapestry. His brown hair was cut short, and a little ruffled, as if he had just removed a chain mail helmet.

He took a brief, almost furtive glance back up the footpath from where he had just come, then fixed his autocratic gaze back on her.

"I could ask you the same question." Might as well meet fire with fire.

"I'm Tyman Gallimore, Pilgrim's Farm." As if she should have known.

Gallimore. Must be one of the lusty sons Edward and Peter were discussing the day before.

"Lexy Lomax. I'm a friend of the Patersons."

"Oh. Right." She could see him struggling to think who the hell the Patersons were.

"Perhaps you haven't met yet?"

"No… I don't think…"

"The new owners." Lexy jerked her head back at the cottage.

She really had him on the back foot now. In fact, he looked like she'd just slung a sandbag in his gut.

"W… what? You… you mean it's been sold already?"

"Not sold. Elizabeth Cassall bequeathed it."

"What?"

"You know. Left it to someone in her will."

Uninvited, Tyman Gallimore sank down on to the path opposite the step. He eyed her, heaving a sigh. "Yes. I know what bequeathed means."

"Problem?" Lexy enquired.

"You could say that." He shot another quick glance up the path. "We just assumed it would go straight on the market."

"We?"

"My dad, my brother and me."

"You want to buy it?"

"We were planning to, yes. Do you know what these… Patersons… intend to do with it?"

Lexy shook her head. "Bit early to say."

"Who are they, anyway? Not relatives of Elizabeth?" He was crushing one fisted hand tightly into the palm of the other, nails digging hard into the flesh. What was his problem?

"There's some kind of family link." She chose her words with care. "It's a father and two daughters. Elizabeth left the place to the younger daughter."

He looked perplexed, as well he might. "And you say they're friends of yours?"

"Yes. I kind of… help them out. That's what I'm doing here now, actually. Checking over a couple of things while they sort out the paperwork in Clopwolde." Although they don't know it.

"That your dog?"

Lexy considered Kinky, who had been sitting at her side throughout the whole exchange. "What, him? Nah. He was just hanging around the place."

Tyman rolled his eyes. "It's only that I would have had you down as more of, I dunno, a lurcher owner. You know, something with a bit of street cred."

Was that a compliment? "So a chihuahua isn't cool?"

"Well… no. Has he been in an accident?"

"Fight."

"He fights?"

"Let's just say he has a tendency towards risky situations." At least he used to have.

The light brown eyes looked politely sceptical. "We've got a German Shepherd." As though theirs was a proper dog.

"Better not bring it up here when Kinky's around. Mincemeat."

Tyman laughed then, a little too long and loudly. He was very nervous about something.

"Glad the weather's picked up," Lexy said, to fill the sudden lull.

He nodded. "You should have seen it over here last night. It was crazy."

"I know. I was here."

He sat bolt upright. "You mean you were here last night? Actually here in the cottage?"

"Uh… yeah. Is that bad?"

He rubbed his forehead, eyes distracted. "Course not. I was just a bit surprised. I mean, it's so isolated up here, you know. For a girl on her…" He clocked Lexy's expression and moved on. "So, are you off back home today? Have you done what you need

53

to here?"

"Why?"

"Surely you don't want to spend another night up here on your own?"

Why didn't Tyman Gallimore want her staying at the cottage?

"It doesn't bother me." Much. Lexy remembered the loudly ticking clock and imagined cold draught.

There was another silence. Again, Lexy was the one who broke it. "Did you know Elizabeth?"

"Yes." His voice was guarded. "Didn't you?"

She shook her head.

"But you live locally?"

"Clopwolde. Although I've only been there three months." She pressed on with her original line. "I guess it must have been quite a shock for you when Elizabeth died the way she did?"

"Of course it bloody was."

Lexy raised her eyebrows.

"Sorry. It's just that it was actually me who found her. You know… just after the accident."

"Oh." For a brief, crazy moment Lexy wanted to ask him if he had spotted an ancient robed deity fleeing the scene. "Guess that must have been pretty awful."

"Just a bit." His expression made Lexy wonder what sort of state Elizabeth must have been in. "It's something that's happened to me twice, now. I saw… someone else… fall like that, too."

"I'm sorry."

"It was a while ago. But Elizabeth…" Tyman launched into the story as if he had been desperate to tell someone ever since it happened.

"I was coming down the hill for breakfast after I'd been checking on the sheep. I go up there every morning." He broke off, his eyes roving up the path again.

"It was just on nine o'clock. It all seemed pretty quiet when I came to the cottage, which was a bit unusual. Elizabeth was normally up and about well before that time in the morning. I went to the kitchen door and knocked, then I went round the corner of the house to the front door." His eyes became unfocused.

"Found her on the rockery. She was lying at an odd angle. I knew immediately she was dead. Guessed she'd fallen from the balcony."

Lexy gave him an enquiring look.

"You don't get injuries like that from just tripping over."

She winced.

"Must have just happened, she was barely cold. But there was nothing I could do. Like the kiss of life, or anything."

Lexy digested this. "I wonder if she died straight away, when she fell?"

"Oh, yes. It was immediate. At least, that was what the doctor said."

"Right. So she didn't…"

He caught her drift. "Suffer. No."

Lexy nodded. At least she could put Rowana's mind to rest on that count.

"Thing is, I feel really guilty about it." There was a terrible sadness in his voice.

"Guilty? Why?"

He stammered slightly. "W… what I mean to say is that I could probably have prevented it."

Lexy's tawny eyes narrowed. "Do you know how it happened, then?"

"What?"

"I mean, what caused her to fall?"

"No." He shook his head, face pale. "But perhaps if I'd been there earlier…"

Lexy let up. After all, she herself knew what it was like to stumble on a recently dead body. Something you don't forget in a hurry.

Tyman glanced at his watch.

"Can you tell me a bit about Elizabeth?" Lexy said quickly. "I mean, what she was like as a person? I didn't know her, and… well… I guess I'm just curious."

He seemed to consider this, squinting down the hill towards Pilgrim's Farm.

"Elizabeth was quite intense," he began. "Mad about our four-footed friends…" He gave a nod at Kinky. "And well into her causes. Animal charities and the like." A humourless laugh escaped him.

"Well, that's good, isn't it?"

"Generally, yes." Tyman shaded his eyes against the sun. "Trouble is, she was a little on the over-zealous side. Especially where we were concerned."

"Why?"

"Oh, there was this… misunderstanding about six months ago. Elizabeth was under the impression that we were mistreating the animals on the farm."

"Which you weren't?"

"God, no – they live like royalty. Much better than we do, in fact. Unfortunately, Elizabeth happened to come down to the farm the day we were shifting one of our Tamworth sows, a particularly bad-tempered one, from her nursery pen into a paddock. She'd taken it into her head to make a run for it, and my dad was sort of…" He searched for the right word. "Sort of grappling with her in the yard. So, there she was, screaming the place down, and all her eleven piglets running mad. Blood everywhere where she'd bitten Dad's hand open. Looked like a battle scene. Anyway, Elizabeth took a photo, and it got in the paper. You know. *Suffolk farmer brutalises pig.* That sort of thing. Took a hell of a lot of sorting out."

Lexy suddenly found herself trying not to laugh. She saw that Tyman was trying not to, as well.

"When we finally managed to persuade the farms inspector that the old man wasn't a direct descendant of Caligula, Elizabeth had to come down and apologise to us. Damned nearly killed her."

His hand flew to his mouth. "Sorry. Didn't mean to say that. But it meant that we never really saw eye to eye after that." He smoothed out the loose threads around a tear in the knee of his jeans.

"Then one day," he continued, "a few weeks ago now, I ran into her on the path. There was a barn owl perched in an oak tree nearby – she pointed it out to me. Beautiful thing. We got talking, and, well, after that I saw her most days. Dad had put a flock of sheep out on the hill to graze, and I came up past her house every morning to check on them." She watched a muscle twitching in his cheek. "So we put our differences behind us."

It was as Lexy was contemplating this that the second stranger suddenly appeared.

She jumped in alarm, but Tyman actually leapt to his feet, striking an almost defensive pose. Explained why he'd kept glancing up the path.

The newcomer stared at the two of them from the gateway. He was about Lexy's age, a large, dark, brooding presence, with narrow, watchful eyes. At his side was a large, dark, brooding dog.

Lexy grabbed Kinky's collar, just as the chihuahua broke into a storm of snarling barks.

The stranger regarded him with contempt.

"What's going on?"

"Ward – this is Lexy," said Tyman, speaking loudly and quickly over Kinky's continuing racket. "She's a friend of the new owners of Four Winds."

"What are you talking about?"

"Four Winds Cottage is in new hands."

Lexy caught the disbelief that flashed momentarily across the other man's face.

"Apparently, Elizabeth left the place to a distant relative in her will," Tyman gabbled. "Bit of a surprise, eh? Lexy's been staying here. Lexy, this is my brother, Ward."

So this was big brother. Lexy could see the family resemblance now, in the arched brow and straight nose. Just seemed that Tyman had inherited all the charm.

"Hi." She stood up, still holding the enraged chihuahua. Ward barely glanced at her, his attention fixed on his brother like a stoat with a rabbit. Lexy felt a rattle of resentment.

"We need to talk. Now."

"Yeah – I know." Tyman stepped back, upending the mug and sending tea splashing around their feet.

He threw a helpless look at Lexy. "God. Sorry. Do you want me to… ?"

"Just leave it, Tyman. Django, heel." Ward turned abruptly and began striding back up the path in the direction he had come from, the dog keeping pace beside him as if its nose was velcroed to his trousers.

"Something I said?" Lexy enquired.

"No – it's just that we've got… stuff to do." Tyman grimaced at his brother's disappearing back. "Sorry about him. He's under a lot of pressure. Er...incidentally, it's all private land round here, except the cottage and its access road. That is, Pilgrim's Farm owns the peninsula, and, you know, with the sheep and everything…"

"Don't worry, I'll stick to the cottage," Lexy lied. "Guess that's why you want to buy it. So you'll have it all?"

Tyman gave her an apologetic smile, turned and hurried after his brother.

She watched them go, feeling the tension crackling in the air.

What a look of shocked disbelief there'd been on each of their faces when they learned that the cottage had been left to the Patersons. They had obviously been banking on getting it themselves – Tyman had said as much.

Was that why they didn't like the idea of her being in the cottage? Well, tough. If Lexy had any lingering doubts about remaining at Four Winds Cottage they were gone now. She wanted to find out all she could about this Gallimore family.

An impatient bark reminded her that she had more immediate things to attend to.

"Come on then." Lexy grabbed her bag, locked the back door and headed for the car.

She flipped her wallet open. She'd go and get a few supplies from the village store and check her phone messages while she was there. There might be one from Rowana.

"I hope you don't think you're going home," she warned Kinky as they set off. "Because you're going to be sadly disappointed, mate. I've got the bit between my teeth now."

He threw her a long-suffering look.

They bounced along the track under the thick canopy of oak and sycamore. Rain water from the evening before lay in deep ruts, dappled by sun shining through the branches.

At the bottom of the hill, they turned on to the tarmac lane, and went past the farm. The trio of weird sheep had been joined by some white geese, tearing at the grass with gusto. In a further field, a big flock of more ordinary brown and white sheep were moving restlessly around.

At the gate Lexy turned into the lane, sunk deeply between hedges thick with late summer flowers, and after just half a mile the village of Nodmore came into view.

It was clustered around a green. There was an old-fashioned pub called the Unicorn; a small church with a walled graveyard shaded by yew trees; a garage with one petrol pump; a general store – hallelujah – with a garish sign; a rash of unimaginative grey bungalows; a couple of original Suffolk long houses, the type built by Dutch settlers and settled by rich Londoners, and a mellow-stoned thatched cottage.

Lexy and Kinky got out of the car and headed for the shop.

"Bet I'll be served by a plump middle-aged woman with a face like a currant bun, who'll call me 'moi luvver', and ask all sorts of awkward questions," Lexy predicted, as she tied Kinky up outside. She'd been to these rural outposts before.

A bell jangled as she opened the door. Standing behind the counter was a plump, middle-aged woman with a face like a currant bun.

"Morning, moi luvver," she smiled.

"Hi." Lexy picked up a basket and wended her way around the crowded interior, breathing in the indefinable smell of the small grocery.

"Ah, I can see you're a proper cook, like me," said the woman, as she scanned the items Lexy had put in the basket. "What is it tonight? Lentil soup? And you're making your own bread, are you?"

"Yup."

"Not local, are you?"

"No." Lexy picked up a newspaper.

"On 'oliday?"

"Sort of."

The shopkeeper raised her eyebrows.

"Got somewhere to stay?"

"Er…"

"There's a nice guest house down Mill Road. My sister runs it. I'll get you details if you like."

"No, thanks very much, I'm sorted." Lexy put down the paper.

"Somewhere round 'ere? Where's that then? I thought my sister 'ad the only guest house round here." The curranty eyes bored into hers. Lexy felt like asking her if she fancied a job as a private investigator's assistant. She'd make a bloody good one. "I'm staying with friends."

"Oh – in Nodmore?"

Lexy shot a look through the glass door at Kinky, willing him to make a scene. He lay on his side, basking in the sun, eyes half closed.

"Just up the road, actually. A… er… relative of theirs died recently. They've come down to sort out the estate, and I'm staying in her cottage, making sure everything's ticking over." There – will that shut you up, you nosy bat?

"Died, you say? Who was that, then? If you don't mind me asking, that is."

Feeling almost hypnotised, Lexy found herself admitting, "Elizabeth Cassall."

"Oh, yes, 'er up at Four Winds. That was tragic, that was. Woman like that in her prime shouldn't 'ave taken a tumble like she did. If you ask me, there's something more to that business than meets the eye."

"Really? How do you mean?"

The woman's face suddenly took on a distrusting expression.

"I didn't think Elizabeth 'ad no relatives. "

"Distant relatives," said Lexy. "Very distant. Must dash."

The voice called after her. "You going up to Four Winds, then?"

Lexy jumped into the sanctuary of her car.

"'Strewth, Kinky! Do you reckon she's ex KGB?"

The chihuahua pawed at her. She opened a box of dog biscuits. "Special baked bean flavoured ones, just for you. Only kidding."

She tore open a packet of crisps for herself, then, finding she had a signal at last, checked her phone for messages. There was just the one, from Milo. *Where r u?* Lexy tapped in a reply. *Nodmore. Want to meet at the Unicorn tonite?* She didn't want to tell him exactly where she was staying – although anyone in Nodmore village would likely be able to supply that information for him tonight after that interrogation in the village shop – but it would be nice to have some company for a couple of hours.

The reply came almost immediately. *Be there at 8.*

Was that a promise or an order? Lexy sat back with a grin.

She watched idly as the door of the thatched cottage opened. A man stepped out and stooped to pick up two bottles of milk. He stood up, coughed, then defiantly took a puff of the cigarette in his hand. He glanced over at her car, and Lexy got a sudden jolt. It was the man Elizabeth had painted. The picture hanging on the upstairs landing. She'd caught his decadent expression to a T. Was he someone she knew well?

He turned and disappeared into his cottage. Lexy made a

mental note to find out who he was. Someone in the pub would know.

Lexy drove back towards the cottage, her mind turning over what the woman in the shop had said.

There's something more to that business than meets the eye.

Did she know something? Perhaps there was talk in the village.

She turned on to the tarmac lane that led to Pilgrim's Farm. The gate was still firmly fastened, and a farm worker was carrying out some fencing work next to it.

Well, he would be as good a start as anyone, if she was going to start asking around about Elizabeth. And he could open the gate for her. She stopped the car and wound down the window, smiling brightly.

The man was bluff and burly, with a bushy moustache, a large drinker's nose, and a ruddy complexion. He was dressed in a frayed waxed jacket, worn corduroys and green wellington boots.

"Can I 'elp you?" He sounded like the only way he wanted to help Lexy was out of his sight. To her surprise he wasn't a local – sounded more like a Yorkshireman.

She held the smile. "I'm just on my way up to Four Winds Cottage. Would you mind getting the gate?"

A frown settled on his brow, making him look like a satyr.

"And what business might you 'ave up there?"

"Er…" Lexy wasn't expecting that. "… I'm just looking after things for the new owners."

"'Ow do you mean, new owners?"

She was getting a bit fed up with this. "The woman who used to own it left it to a family called Paterson in her will."

The man visibly paled under his wind-blasted patina. "Elizabeth l-left the cottage to someone?" he stammered.

"That's right," said Lexy, briskly.

He stared at her for a moment longer.

"Apologies. Let me introduce m'self." He offered a meaty hand. "Bruce Gallimore. Owner of Pilgrim's Farm." In spite of

62

his obvious unease, he indicated the buildings and paddocks behind him with a grandiose gesture.

Lexy blinked. This was the father of lithe, charming Tyman? Although now she looked closer, she realised she could see Ward Gallimore in the narrow, suspicious eyes.

"I'm Lexy Lomax."

"Will you be up at the cottage long?" Bruce enquired.

Now Lexy was really curious. What was up there that the Gallimores didn't want her to find?

"Just a couple of nights."

The wiry black eyebrows shot up. "A couple o' nights?"

"Yup."

Bruce Gallimore pulled at his moustache and glanced up the hillside in the direction of the cottage. "Bit remote up there. No phone signal. You'd be better off in't village. There's a guest house out on Mill Road."

Lexy set her jaw.

"Yeah. I know. Someone's already told me," she replied. "But I'm fine up at the cottage, thanks."

His face set.

"That was a strange business with Elizabeth, wasn't it?" Lexy remarked.

The narrow dark eyes burned into hers. "Nowt strange about it. It were just an accident. That's what the verdict will be."

"Bizarre accident, though," said Lexy. "Falling backward over a balcony isn't something that occurs all over the place, is it?"

"It 'appens."

"Do you think she tripped, then?"

He gave her a hard stare. "It don't matter what I think. Fact was, it were an accident. I won't keep you, any road." With that, Bruce turned and unlatched the gate, pulling it open for Lexy.

He thought different then, did he?

She drove through and stopped next to him.

"I met your sons earlier," she said. "Up at the cottage."

Bruce frowned, pulled a mobile from his pocket, and turned

it on. It rang immediately, a jangle of hideous electronic noise.

"Mind you don't frighten the sheep with that."

But he was already talking. "Aye. Well, I know now. I'm on my way."

"See you, then." Lexy drove away, slowly enough to catch Bruce saying, "… and she's coming up there now. So you make sure Tyman's…"

Tyman's what?

She cruised along the tarmac lane, past the fancy sheep.

The Gallimore family had something to hide. Something to do with the cottage. Maybe something linked to Elizabeth's death.

7

Lexy turned up the path through the trees, puzzling over Bruce's phone call. He had been warning someone, presumably Ward, that Lexy was on her way up. And telling him to make sure Tyman… what? Kept out of the way? Got out of the cottage? At the thought of this, Lexy suddenly put her foot down and the Panda lurched forward, propelling Kinky into the footwell.

"Better stay there, pal," she said. "Rough ride coming up."

The car bounced over potholes and through puddles. It took all her strength to hold on to the steering wheel. She strained her eyes for a first view of the cottage. If she saw Tyman sneaking out…

But Four Winds stood serene and empty in its clearing. Not a hint of a Gallimore.

Nevertheless, as soon as the Panda had shuddered to a halt Lexy was out, running all the way around the place checking windows and doors.

She unlocked the front door, dashed down the hall and checked every room, her blood inexplicably up. But there was no sign of any disturbance. She slowed, taking deep breaths.

Perhaps what Bruce had actually been about to say was make sure Tyman sorts those sheep out. Or make sure Tyman gets back down to the farm, and doesn't spend any more time exchanging pleasantries with the unwelcome newcomer.

Shaking her head, Lexy went back to the car. Poor Kinky was still sitting in the passenger footwell. He didn't look best pleased to be back at Four Winds Cottage. He got out slowly, sniffing the air. No doubt he could smell the lingering aroma of Django, the German Shepherd.

Lexy went in, plugged in the fridge, and put the food away.

The bread and soup would have to wait. She had a far more

pressing task. She needed to search Four Winds Cottage from top to bottom for whatever it was the Gallimores wanted to get their hands on.

Lexy started upstairs, in the fateful front bedroom. She'd already checked the patio and windows. Now she carefully went through the dark wooden wardrobe, tallboy and dressing table. Kinky sat in the doorway, watching her solemnly.

All contained clothes, good quality, nothing flashy. Lexy went through all the pockets she came across. All empty. No shopping lists, receipts, jotted down phone numbers, suicide notes...

Even the underwear drawer, that most obvious place of all for a woman to keep secrets, contained... underwear. Mostly the serviceable type, but there were, Lexy noticed, a couple of black lace numbers. Looked like Elizabeth still had her moments. And why not? Although it wasn't the *why?* that interested Lexy so much as the *with whom?*

She checked out the photo of the stern-looking young man in army desert fatigues on the tallboy. Took it out of the frame. Nothing written on the back. No date. Looked a little faded. Lexy got the feeling it hadn't been taken during one of Britain's current desert conflicts. She replaced it, wondering who this soldier might be. He seemed out of place in this laid-back, feminine house.

Lexy pulled back the quilt on the bed, and looked under the pillows. Nothing. She got down on her hands and knees and peered under it. Nothing.

"What do you reckon, pal?" she asked the chihuahua. Again, he was sniffing the bedroom carpet with peculiar concentration, tail well down.

It couldn't have been vacuumed for at least six weeks, ever since Elizabeth's fall, in fact. Here and there lay tiny scraps of dried grass, and a couple of those little goose-grass burrs that stick resolutely to clothing, shoes and hair, hitching a hopeful ride to the next growing spot. At first Lexy assumed she'd brought them in the day before. Then it struck her that goose-grass would have pollinated a good month or more ago. These barbed seed heads had dried and turned brown – meaning they'd been there for a while.

She collected them up, noting their position, then searched the landing and stairs. She found two more burrs, and several pieces of grass. The trail led through the living room, which yielded another three burrs, tangled in a furry rug by the patio door.

Lexy considered. Someone had come in from outside, having first brushed up against goose-grass growing along the footpath. The burrs had attached themselves, with their usual blind hope, to trouser bottoms or shoe laces. Had this unwitting carrier then made his way up to Elizabeth's bedroom?

Could have been Elizabeth, of course, although judging by the clean state of the house, she didn't seem the type to walk through it in outdoor shoes.

Or it could have been her killer.

Lexy felt a thrill of fear, mixed with exhilaration.

Of course, she thought, plummeting back to earth again, it might just have been Milo's police colleagues who had been there carrying out their investigation. But they would have approached the house from the front, and were unlikely to be garnished with burrs of goose-grass.

"Let's work on the assumption that someone planned to do away with Elizabeth," she said to Kinky. "Someone who's been secretly observing her routine for a while. He gets into the cottage on the morning in question, sneaking in through the patio doors while Elizabeth is in the kitchen."

She traced the imagined footsteps, talking all the while. "He nips upstairs to the front bedroom, slips on some gloves…" She mimed this. "Quietly opens the windows wide… " She unlocked and pulled them open. "Then waits behind the door, here." She stood in position. "When he hears her come up the stairs, he makes some kind of sound to lure her into the room…" She cast

67

around. There was a book on the bedside table. Lexy slid it across the carpet so it hit the opposite skirting board with a thud.

"Elizabeth comes hurrying in to see what the noise is. She goes straight over to the window, puzzled because it's open, hears a sound behind her, turns to see a figure advancing on her, then before she's had a chance to draw breath, let alone scream – quick shove, over she goes."

Kinky was unable to comment on this theory.

"Say," Lexy pressed on regardless, "for argument's sake, it was one of the Gallimore sons who sneaked in that morning…" Why did an image of Ward pop into her mind? "… and shoved Elizabeth over the balcony for reasons of his own. Who could know it was anything other than an accident? There wouldn't be a murder weapon. Unlikely to be any witnesses. Could almost be a perfect crime."

She fell into silent thought, picking up the binoculars from the dressing table. What were they doing here, so out of place in a bedroom? Then Lexy remembered Tyman mentioning the barn owl Elizabeth had pointed out to him. She must have been a bird-watcher. Lexy took a squint through them.

Forget the birds – they showed Pilgrim's Farm in unexpectedly good detail. Lexy had a clear view of the front door, the stables in the yard, and an open hayrick, in and around which cows were munching. Perhaps Elizabeth had still been keeping an eye on the animals, despite the misunderstanding over the pigs.

Perhaps she had discovered something going on down there.

Lexy frowned. All roads of speculation seemed to lead to the Gallimores. But then their behaviour at the mention of Elizabeth had been almost a caricature of guilt. No wonder the people in the village were talking.

She went into the guest bedroom and repeated her search. The blanket chest contained… blankets. The chest of drawers contained winter woollens, and in one lower drawer she found a couple of swimming costumes.

Lexy removed all the clothing and checked the drawers inside and out. Nothing. She replaced everything with a sigh.

She went over the carpet on her hands and knees. No goose-grass burrs in here, or any other scraps of vegetation. Whoever had tramped it up here had only brought it into the front bedroom. Lent further weight to her ambush theory.

It was a similar story in the two back rooms. The sofa bed in the third bedroom yielded no secrets, nor did the clothing on the rail in the boxroom.

Thoughtfully, Lexy returned downstairs. She wondered whether she dared confide in Milo about her theory of a murderous intruder. He wouldn't be best pleased that she was querying the official investigation. Lexy didn't doubt that the police had done all they thought necessary in a case like this, but she knew how busy Lowestoft CID had been during the summer. Milo had told her himself. Trouble was, when the investigation had taken place, Elizabeth's bequest hadn't come to light.

She yawned. The day had turned into a real scorcher. She still had the studio to go through, and she ought to do a proper job on the living room, to say nothing of the kitchen.

She opened the back door and breathed in the enticing scent of the hillside. What was the rush? She was going to be here for a couple more days. Plenty of time to investigate to her heart's content.

"Why don't we cut ourselves some slack, Kinkster?"

The dog gazed anxiously up at her.

"R&R, mate. You look like you need it, and I certainly do."

Lexy nipped back upstairs and helped herself to one of the swimming costumes. She grabbed a towel from the bathroom, made sure she had locked up everywhere, and minutes later she and Kinky were heading up the forbidden hill.

She might be trespassing but what the hell, she was good at keeping a low profile. Just have to make sure Kinky didn't take off after any sheep. Not that she'd seen any up there yet. Probably keeping in the shade on a day like this. Lexy followed the track up the hill, then carefully descended the steps to the beach.

It was a particularly deserted stretch – too far from Clopwolde for people to lug beach paraphernalia and kids. Good-o – all the more peace and quiet for her.

In the shelter of the cliff, Lexy quickly changed into the swimming costume. Bit tight, but no one was there to point and laugh.

She waded into the waves, enjoying the gradual acclimatisation. The sun had managed to warm the normally icy North Sea to a bearable temperature, and Lexy swam strongly, relishing the sensation.

Back on land Kinky was digging in the soft sand at the base of the cliff, directly under a large sign that said No Digging. It was good to see him enjoying himself.

After a quarter of an hour Lexy emerged from the waves, trying with difficulty to keep her footing on shifting pebbles. Not exactly the Birth of Venus, more like a contestant in a log-rolling contest.

She lay down on the towel and closed her eyes. Just for a minute.

Lexy woke up three hours later on the hard shingle, numb, sunburnt and encrusted with sea-salt.

Kinky, his whole body stiff with sand, had dug enough holes to destabilise the entire cliff.

Painfully, they trudged back together.

Lexy hosed the chihuahua down outside the back door, then stripped off her damp clothes in the kitchen, threw them in the washing machine and headed for the bath.

At seven-thirty, wearing clean jeans and a t-shirt, her denim jacket tied around her waist, Lexy set off. A brisk half-hour walk should get her to the pub in time. There was no question of driving; she needed a drink.

She followed a well-trodden, steep footpath that led straight down through the trees towards Pilgrim's Farm. It opened out into a meadow halfway down and Lexy couldn't help but notice goose-grass growing at the side of the path in a tangled hedge-row. Another tick in the box for her hidden assassin theory. She just wondered what Milo would make of it.

The Unicorn was a dark and ancient hostelry, full of low beams and hidden alcoves. Two elderly men playing cribbage in a corner looked up briefly and dismissively as she entered.

The only other customer was a man who sat at the far end of the bar, pint at hand, whisky chaser waiting ready, head bent towards the busty, attentive barmaid leaning on the counter talking to him. A man Lexy recognised. The one from the thatched cottage. The chap Elizabeth had painted.

Lexy took two steps towards him, and he glanced up with those decadent black eyes that Elizabeth had captured so well. Up close, she saw that his face was ravaged by hard living.

The barmaid gave Lexy an enquiring look.

She was about to slip on to one of the bar stools and order a drink when she felt a light touch on her shoulder.

"Jumpy," said Milo. He had materialised from one of the alcoves.

"Sunburn."

"What would you like?"

"Pint of cider, please."

He raised his eyebrows. "You driving?"

"No, I walked."

"I could have picked you up."

"It's OK. Didn't take long."

Milo turned to the barmaid, and Lexy's eyes slid back to Elizabeth's oil painting subject again. He was still looking her over, amused now. Lexy quickly turned away before he leapt to the wrong conclusion about her interest in him. He seemed like a man who would very swiftly leap to wrong conclusions.

Milo led the way back to the alcove carrying the drinks. He'd got himself a modest half of cider. Lexy could almost feel the man at the bar smirk before he turned back to the intimate chat he'd been enjoying with the barmaid.

Kinky stationed himself on the seat beside her, and she secured his lead around her wrist.

"So, you managed to find somewhere to stay?" Milo took a sip of his drink.

"Yeah – little bed and breakfast. Thought it would be for the best."

"Think you had the right idea. I saw your husband yesterday in his marquee, and he certainly has a panoramic view of your cabin."

Lexy gave an involuntary shiver. "Did you actually see him in action? Doing the genial host act?"

Milo nodded.

"Jerk, isn't he?"

Milo nodded again.

"You still working on that case?" he asked. "The girl with the supernatural fixation about that fall up at Four Winds Cottage?"

"Uh-huh." The fall girl. Is that what Rowana had made herself into? Taking the blame for someone else's murderous act?

"It's only up the road from here, isn't it?"

"That's right." She avoided his eyes. Too late.

He put down his drink, comprehension dawning. "That's where you're staying, isn't it?"

Lexy rolled her eyes. "I wasn't intending to. I just went up there for a quick look, I knew it was empty and I…"

"Broke in?"

"No. I had a key. Decided on the spur of the moment to stay there."

"Who knows you're there?"

Lexy pulled a face. "Yesterday – no one. But as of this morning – probably the whole village."

He frowned.

"Well, first," said Lexy, "I ran into the two sons who come from the farm at the foot of the hill."

"The Gallimores."

"Yes – do you know them?"

"They're known to us." He took another sip.

"By us you mean the police?" Lexy's heart began to race. "Care to elaborate?"

Milo hesitated.

"Don't worry – I won't tell the chief constable."

His lips twisted. "Gallimore senior – what's his name – Bruno?"

"Bruce."

"That's it. Arrived here over a year ago. Came from France, where the two sons were born and brought up, although I think he was originally from Yorkshire."

That figured.

"His wife had been killed in a high wire accident. Came to the attention of the French police, which is how we got to know about it."

"High wire?"

"She was a circus performer. Gallimore ran a circus out there."

"You're kidding." Lexy tried to imagine Bruce in a ringmaster's outfit; white breeches, red coat, black boots, top hat, big whip in his hand. It wasn't an image that sat easily with the curmudgeonly farmer. He had the right moustache, though, luxuriant enough to wax into a theatrical curl either side.

"So what was the story with the high wire?"

Milo shrugged. "Don't know the details, other than there was some kind of argument up there, and she fell and broke her neck."

As he watched Lexy take this in, her smile evaporating, Milo's expression slowly changed, too. "Now you're going to tell me the Gallimores are involved in another falling incident, aren't you?"

Lexy took a big gulp of cider. "I don't know. Maybe."

"I don't believe I'm hearing this. The Elizabeth Cassall case is over. Finished with."

"But listen – this might be important."

Milo closed his eyes, appeared to count under his breath. "OK. You've got five minutes. Then if you mention that woman again, I'm out of here."

"Deal." Lexy leant forward. "When I met Tyman Gallimore, Bruce's younger son, up at the cottage this morning, and told him I was a friend of the Patersons, and that they were the new owners and…"

"Hang on. Who are the Patersons?"

"Rowana's family. You know – witch-girl. And her dad, and older sister, Gabrielle."

"Her family owns the place now?"

"Well, Rowana does, actually. Elizabeth left it to her in her will."

Milo's brow creased. "But I didn't think Elizabeth had any living relatives. She was an only child, parents both dead, husband dead…"

"Husband? Didn't know she was married." Lexy thought back to the photo on the tallboy. "Was he in the army, by any chance?"

Milo nodded. "Killed in the Gulf War."

So that was him. "Tough."

"Yes." Their eyes met briefly. Milo had been there. His policewoman wife had been killed on duty less than a year ago.

"So these Patersons?" he urged. "Where do they fit into the family tree?"

"Oh, they're not relatives of Elizabeth. That's the odd thing."

Milo stacked three beer mats neatly together. "Go on," he growled.

"Elizabeth used to be a friend of Rowana's mother, apparently. Must have been a very good friend, because in her will, Elizabeth left everything to her. The cottage and all her savings. And in the event of her death…" Lexy shrugged. "Everything went to her daughter, Rowana."

"How did you find all this out?"

"From Rowana herself, when she came to see me. You see, her family had this confectionery shop in London, which the Patersons had run since the year dot. Except that six weeks ago they got evicted, because it turned out Mr Paterson hadn't been able to afford the rent any more. Something to do with the shop coming into the ownership of a big property corporation."

Milo pursed his lips and folded a paper napkin into a tight square.

"Obviously it was traumatic for them," Lexy went on, "and they had been desperately thinking of ways to raise money and salvage the situation. In the end, they realised that it would take nothing short of a miracle. So Rowana thought she'd have a go at summoning an ancient pagan goddess to help them out."

Milo rolled his eyes.

"Give her her due, she got all the equipment," Lexy continued. "Altar, candles, herbs and stuff, then one night, when the other two were away, she set up a magic circle in the greenhouse..."

"The greenhouse?"

"Don't ask. Carried out a summoning spell, invoked a goddess and entreated her to bestow riches. Abracadabra, the following morning, a friend of her mother who just happened to have left Rowana a country cottage and thirty grand in savings in her will went plummeting to her death."

"The following morning?" Ice-grey eyes met hers. Milo took a plastic pen out of his pocket and began absent-mindedly clacking it between his teeth.

Lexy watched him, chin in hand. "So, are my five minutes up yet?"

"Shut up, and... keep talking."

"Rowana said the will was a complete shock to her. She'd never even heard of Elizabeth Cassall. I mean, you can understand how she might have thought the whole thing was somehow down to her magic-making, poor kid. She's beside herself. Convinced she was responsible. Didn't even want to come here and see the place."

Milo unfolded the napkin and drew a circle in the middle. Wrote the letters RP in the centre. Rowana Paterson.

"Presumably her dad and sister felt differently?" he said. "After all, here was their opportunity to get back on their feet."

"According to Rowana, they'd never heard of Elizabeth either, but I get the impression her dad didn't say it very convincingly. Think her sister is the only one genuinely overjoyed about it all, especially as Rowana has said she'll donate the lot to starting up a new confectionery business."

Lexy felt in her bag. "Now here's the really weird bit. I found this in Four Winds Cottage."

She handed him the photo.

He studied it and gave her a sharp look. "The Patersons?"

"The very same."

He turned it over. "Taken last year, in London – that's the Eye in the background."

Lexy nodded. "And without their knowledge, by the looks of it."

"Implying what? That Elizabeth was secretly stalking them?"

"It kind of ties in with their claim that they've never heard of her."

Milo contemplated the photo in silence for a moment. "But surely the father must have known Elizabeth if she was such a good friend of Rowana's mother?"

"You'd have thought so."

"So where do you come into all of this?" Milo's voice was weary.

"I told you. Rowana hired me to investigate whether her psychic meddling had caused Elizabeth's death."

The detective raised his eyebrows.

"Which, obviously, it didn't." Lexy took another large swallow of her cider. "The kid just needed someone to confide in, put her mind at rest. She gave me the key to the cottage. I mean, I had to at least come here and have a look, didn't I?"

"Yes, you did, didn't you?"

"Makes a difference, that will, doesn't it?" said Lexy.

"Maybe."

"But it doesn't explain the odd behaviour of the Gallimores." Lexy moved on to her pet subject. "Now, this, I think, is even more bizarre."

Milo shut his eyes. "I want to go home now."

"Listen, like I was saying earlier, when I met Tyman today, he was utterly... well, flabbergasted when I told him Four Winds Cottage was in new ownership."

Milo gave her a *so what?* look.

"He let slip that his family had been banking on buying the cottage. They expected it to come on to the market after Elizabeth's death. Then, when I asked him about Elizabeth, Tyman told me that he was the one who found her. Shortly after she fell over the balcony."

"I know that. He made a statement."

"But I got the feeling he wanted to tell me something else. I dunno, like there was something more to it." Lexy was annoyed that she couldn't explain it better. "He said he felt guilty about it."

Milo's eyebrow crooked up.

"Then Ward Gallimore appeared." Lexy pulled a face. "Wasn't giving much away, but I could see he was also in deep shock when his brother told him the cottage was in new hands. I mean, he practically dragged Tyman away – like they had some urgent thinking to do. It was obvious they wanted that cottage pretty badly."

"Badly enough to kill the occupant, you mean?" Milo gave a short laugh.

"You had to be there. When I met the father, he was exactly the same about it. This automatic assumption that they would be able to buy the place because Elizabeth had died. It just made me wonder."

She paused, looking at the detective hopefully. "Perhaps they discovered Elizabeth had no relatives. Thought that if she was out of the way, they could get in there."

"That's pushing it a bit far."

"Interesting choice of verb, that. Freudian slip, was it?"

"Very funny."

"Anyway, it then got me wondering whether ownership of the cottage would mean that the Gallimores owned the whole of Freshing Hill. Which means that they could subsequently sell it on for development, or something, for big money."

"You and your imagination."

"It's a perfectly reasonable theory. And that's another thing. I spoke to the woman in the village shop today. She reckons that there was more to Elizabeth's death than meets the eye, too."

"Lexy – this is a village. If Elizabeth had died peacefully in her bed aged one hundred and two, the woman in the shop would say there was more to it than meets the eye. Where's your evidence?"

"No smoke without fire."

"Is that it?"

"Well, I bet the Gallimores won't waste any time approaching the Patersons about buying the place."

"Doesn't prove anything." But Milo's eyes were thoughtful.

Lexy frowned. "You know what they… uh-oh."

She snatched the photo from the table and thrust it in her pocket. Rowana Paterson had just pushed open the door to the pub. She hesitated in the doorway, looking around. Saw Lexy and her mouth fell open in surprise.

Lexy frantically beckoned her to the alcove.

"What are you doing here?"

Rowana shot a look at the policeman.

"It's OK," said Lexy. "This is Milo. He's my… partner." She tried not to look at his startled eyebrows. Milo, this is Rowana Paterson."

Milo crushed the paper napkin in his fist.

"Hi," said Rowana, still eyeing Milo dubiously. She turned to Lexy. "Dad got this sudden urge to come over and have another look around the grounds up at Four Winds."

"What – now?"

"Yes. My sister's here, too. They're just parking the van." Rowana looked anxiously behind her at the door. "The reason we came here first is because I wanted to go to the loo. Then Dad decided he wanted a beer. They'll be here in a minute. So, what are you doing here?" She dropped her voice. "Investigating?"

"Yeah," Lexy murmured back. "And the thing is, Rowana, I'm staying over at the cottage."

The girl gasped. "Seriously?"

"I thought it would be better to be on the spot. I hope you don't mind."

"Of course not. But isn't it really scary there on your own? And you stayed overnight?" Her voice had risen.

"It's fine. It's fine. Really. Only trouble is…"

Rowana gave a start. "They're here."

She squashed herself further into the alcove. Milo cleared his throat. Lexy was practically sitting on his lap now. Kinky balanced precariously between them.

"Nice place, isn't it?" A man's voice, quiet but melodious. "Be great to have a local like this. Look at those little alcoves."

Lexy and Rowana ducked.

"Did you find anything out about… you know what?" whispered Rowana.

Oh, yes. The Goddess Helandra and her part in Elizabeth's downfall. "A couple of things. We need to talk, but not now, obviously."

"They're getting a drink," said Milo, from the corner of his mouth.

"Right," Lexy muttered. "That'll give me a chance to nip back up to the cottage and move my sleeping bag out from the middle of the living room, before your dad looks in and thinks he's got a squatter." Wouldn't want him to think that.

Milo shifted against Lexy. "I'll drop you there."

"I don't know why on earth he wants another look," Rowana said. "It's not like we're going to be living there. I'd better sneak over and join them before…"

"So you're selling it?" Lexy interrupted.

"Yes, we're… "

"Rowana! What are you doing?"

Lexy and Rowana raised their heads.

Standing in front of the alcove, carrying two drinks, was an exceptionally pretty girl, who knew she was exceptionally pretty. The photo in Lexy's pocket didn't do her justice. Sapphire eyes flicked over Lexy's faded jeans, ancient denim jacket and scarred chihuahua, then turned to the policeman, and opened a little wider.

Rowana appeared dumbstruck.

"Hi," blabbered Lexy, brain in overdrive. "You… you… must be Gabrielle. This is a bit of a coincidence, but when your sister came in just now, I recognised her from a photograph in my friend's cottage. Isn't that funny? I recognise you all, actually. I'm a friend of Elizabeth Cassall. Or rather I was, before she died, that is."

She tried not to look at Milo, who was pressing a hand against his forehead.

A man joined Gabrielle, slim and careworn, with a lock of hair that fell anxiously over his face. He'd caught Lexy's last few words.

"Were you really?" he said. She clocked where the uppity daughter had inherited her sapphire eyes.

"Yes. We met down here. Me and Elizabeth. I've been staying in her cottage. To look after the plants and so on. Keep things ticking over 'til you got here. She had no one else, you see." The fixed smile on Lexy's face was beginning to hurt. "I hope you don't mind?"

Rowana edged out of the alcove, freeing Lexy and Milo from their close encounter.

"Staying there?" frowned Gabrielle.

"Not at all, in fact that's terribly kind of you. I'm so pleased that Elizabeth had a friend who was prepared to do that." The man smiled at Lexy. "Sorry, I should introduce myself – Steve Paterson. And these are Gabrielle and Rowana, my daughters."

"I'm Lexy. Lexy Lomax, and this is my er… friend, Milo."

Milo stood up and shook Steve Paterson's hand.

"And this is Kinky."

The chihuahua waved his tail politely.

Gabrielle was still frowning. "How come Elizabeth had a photograph of us?"

Lexy could see she was going to be trouble.

"A photo?" Her father straightened, an odd, guarded expression in his eye.

Rowana looked like she might faint.

None of them noticed when the pub door opened again.

8

It was only when Tyman Gallimore was halfway to the bar that Lexy glanced over. Her eyes bulged. Behind him were Bruce and Ward, engrossed in muttered conversation.

"Interesting development." Milo had followed her gaze.

Tyman looked around. He spotted Lexy and stopped dead. Bruce and Ward almost shunted into him, and for a split second they all appeared comically frozen.

Tyman defrosted first.

"Hello again, Lexy. Didn't expect to see you here." He eyed the three Patersons.

"Hi," Lexy stretched her smile to manic proportions. "This is Steve, Gabrielle and Rowana." She introduced them with a flourish, as if they were old mates. "The Patersons. The new owners of Four Winds! And this is my friend Milo," she added.

Bruce came forward, took in the Paterson family with shrewd eyes, and introduced himself and his sons in turn. He then produced a large wad of notes from his pocket.

"Right, now we've done with the formalities, can I get you all a drink? Seeing as we're neighbours, of sorts."

Lexy sent a look of despair to Milo. This was so not what she needed. The Gallimores thought she was a friend of the Patersons, and the Patersons thought she was a friend of Elizabeth. One wrong word and the whole charade would collapse sobbing on the floor.

Milo gave an imperceptible shrug. Seemed she was on her own. Terrific.

"Certainly need a drink." Tyman dragged a nearby table towards the alcove, and sat next to Lexy. "Our Anglo-Nubian goats went on the rampage earlier. Ate their way out of a paddock, destroyed two ornamental cherry trees and when we caught up with them they were intimidating the pochards."

"Pochards?" enquired Gabrielle.

"A not very intelligent duck." Ward sat down next to his brother.

"Aye – it were a right bugger's muddle." Bruce returned with the first of the drinks. "Beats me why we keep goats. Give us a hand, boys, pass these down. Ruddy things are always breaking out and causing mayhem. Too clever by 'alf, your goat." Lexy noticed that Bruce had bought her another full pint of cider, even though she'd asked for only a half.

"They have their uses though, don't they?" Tyman turned to his father with an unexpectedly bitter look.

"Shut it, Tyman." Ward was smiling, but not with his eyes.

Lexy wondered what that was about. What dodgy use could a goat be put to? She didn't even want to go there.

Rowana, who had been gradually backing away, disappeared in the direction of a sign saying Ladies. Lexy contemplated going after her, but she was too worried about what might pass between the Gallimores and the remaining Patersons in her absence.

Bruce watched Rowana go, then his eyes flicked to Gabrielle. He leaned back and murmured something to Ward. Clearly something lewd. His son gave him a pitying look.

Meanwhile, Milo had turned to Tyman. "Have you lived at the farm for long?" A conversational gambit. He knew exactly how long they'd been there.

"About six months. Dad's been here longer, setting it all up."

"Aye, I moved over from Normandy," said Bruce. "Had a little farm there, and all. Always had an interest in farming, haven't we, boys?"

"Not always," remarked Ward.

"What's your line, Steve?" Bruce hurriedly turned to Rowana's father. He clearly didn't want to reveal his circus-owning past.

"We're in the confectionery trade."

"Oh, aye? What does that involve? Manufacture? Supply?"

"We had a shop in London," said Steve. He brushed the lock of hair from his tired-looking eyes. "Bloomsbury."

"Very nice, too. Property prices still holding up there, I hear. Speaking of which, I, er, I take it you're going to sell Four Winds Cottage?"

He certainly didn't waste much time on foreplay. Lexy shot Milo a knowing glance.

"We're thinking about it." Steve looked vague.

"We'll have to do more than think about it, Dad," Gabrielle muttered.

"It's just that I might be interested, myself," said Bruce. "You know, quick cash sale, before it goes on the market. Save you hanging around."

"Brilliant," Gabrielle beamed at her father. "The perfect solution."

"What did you have in mind for it?" enquired Steve, a frown creasing his forehead.

"Er…" Bruce exchanged a quick glance with his sons. "Nowt particular. Just thought it would, you know, make a nice little holiday 'ome, or summat."

He hadn't been prepared for that question. So why, one had to ask, did they really want to buy it?

"Well, if we decide to sell it," Steve said, "I'll let you know."

For some reason, Lexy felt like clapping. She threw back the remains of her first pint of cider and started on the second.

"If?" Gabrielle ejaculated.

"Can't say fairer than that." But Lexy caught the desperation in Bruce's eye.

He turned to her next.

"You'll not be staying at the cottage any more though, pet?"

"Won't I?"

"Well, we've had a spate of break-ins recently. Wouldn't want to think of you up there alone."

"I'll make sure I leave some lights on overnight," she said.

"Not tonight, you won't." He looked triumphant.

"What do you mean?"

"Didn't you know? Electricity went off an hour ago. That's

why we came out, eh, lads? No sense in sitting in the dark. Usually takes them all night to get it back on."

A likely story. They must have messed with the junction box. Cut a wire, or something. Well, sod that. They weren't messing with her.

"There's loads of candles at the cottage." There were three small penguin-shaped candles at the cottage. "And I've got the dog. May be small but he's dead hard. I'll be perfectly all right." Lexy downed some more cider and wiped her mouth, smiling around.

Bruce Gallimore closed his eyes as if in pain, and Ward gave Tyman a grim look.

"Oh!" said Gabrielle, who had lost interest in the conversation some while back. "I think I recognise that bloke at the bar." Her voice dropped to an excited whisper. "He's an author, or something. He got drunk in the West End last week and decked a footballer – it was in the papers."

"I think you'll find he's an artist, not an author," said Ward. "Archer Trevino."

So that's who he was. Lexy looked at Elizabeth's oil-painting man with renewed interest. If she remembered right, there was something of his in the Tate Modern. Another place she used to go to escape from Gerard.

"Yes, that's him," said Gabrielle. "He got arrested. They must have released him."

"Obviously." Ward eyed her with amused disdain.

"He's our local celebrity," said Tyman. "He and Elizabeth were friends."

Friends? Elizabeth didn't just know the hell-raising artist, she hung out with him.

"Oh, does that mean you know him, too?" Gabrielle turned eagerly to Lexy. "Like, through Elizabeth? You could introduce us."

It was a bloody shame she couldn't do magic herself, Lexy thought. Because if she could, she'd turn Rowana's airhead sister into the pub cat.

"I wouldn't think he'd be in the mood to be introduced to strangers at the moment. Not after what happened at the cottage."

Mercifully, Ward Gallimore had stepped in. He didn't seem to have noticed Gabrielle's assumption that Lexy knew Elizabeth.

Gabrielle gazed at him. "Oh. Right."

"Perhaps some other time."

"Yes, of course." She still gazed at him. Obviously not used to being chided, but finding she liked it. "What was your name again?"

"Ward."

"That's a funny name. Is it short for something?"

Ward gave his father a weary look. "Hereward."

Hereward the Wake. The Anglo-Saxon rebel involved in leading resistance to the Norman Conquest. Good name for someone brought up in France.

Gabrielle broke into a peal of laughter, although Lexy doubted whether it was in appreciation of the irony, unless she'd got her very wrong.

She saw Archer Trevino look up from his pint. His look became a stare, and the stare became fixed. Who, among them, had he recognised? Whoever it was, he didn't want to stick around and say hello. Seconds later he'd abandoned the stool, pint, chaser and barmaid and slammed through a door at the back of the bar.

"Not like 'im to leave a drink unfinished." Bruce, who had witnessed this disappearance too, leaned back to peer out of the mullioned pub window. "He's off down t'road like a whippet wi' the runs."

"That's one of his paintings over there." Tyman had been scanning the far wall of the pub.

Milo and Lexy used the excuse to get up, go to the other end of the bar, and have a look.

It was a series of silvery grey lines, with pink, red and brown splatters, entitled Dawn Explodes over Dingle Marsh.

"More like Herring Gull Explodes over Dingle Marsh," muttered Milo, "but then I've never seen the point of modern art."

"I was right, wasn't I?" Lexy whispered. "About the Gallimores falling over themselves to buy Four Winds Cottage. And they don't want it for a nice little holiday 'ome, or summat." She imitated Bruce's broad accent.

"They seem keen, but I wouldn't read too much into it," he said. He leant towards her. "Listen, *partner*, did you say Steve and Gabrielle were away from home on the morning Elizabeth died?"

Lexy thought back. "Rowana said her sister was out with a boyfriend and her dad was away for the night when she did her magic ceremony thing."

"That right? Wonder where he was?"

They looked over at Steve, who was nursing a pint, a faraway look in his eyes.

Lexy frowned. She didn't want Milo wasting time on the Patersons when it was the Gallimores he should be concerned about.

"I'll try to find out," she told Milo, "but it won't be easy. It's not the kind of thing you can come out and ask someone, not unless you've got a sheriff's badge on your lapel."

"You saying I should ask him?"

"No. No – I'm just asking you to bear with me. Although, you don't seriously think… not Rowana's father?"

Milo glanced over at Steve, then back at Lexy. "Why not? You said yourself he must have been desperate. Livelihood gone, two daughters to provide for…"

"He just doesn't seem the type."

"Believe me, there is no type."

"Right. OK. I'll see what I can do. Better get back in case someone else puts their foot in it."

"Lead the way."

Lexy struggled back round to her seat. Tyman winked at her. He was feeding Kinky crisps. There was another round of drinks waiting, and Steve was speaking animatedly to Bruce.

Fortunately, the subject of conversation was merely the old car in Elizabeth's shed. Steve must have seen it last time he was up there. "She's in pretty good condition, considering," he was saying. "And the upholstery isn't bad, either. Elizabeth had the good sense to keep it under cover. Do you know…" He turned to Gabrielle and Rowana. "… I really think I might be able to get her going. She'll be worth much more if I can."

"We haven't got time for you to be renovating old cars," Gabrielle snapped.

"Actually," Steve went on, not seeming to hear her, "I could do with a hand from Russell. For a merchant banker, he knows his motors. He fixed that clutch pedal on the van without batting an eyelid. Any chance of getting him down here tomorrow, or the next day?"

Gabrielle looked as if she had swallowed something inedible.

"Dad," Rowana hissed. "Gabby isn't seeing Russell any more. He's going out with somebody else. Don't you remember the ring? And the engine grease?"

"Of course. Sorry, sweetheart – slipped my mind. Seems a shame though. Could do with him right now."

"Well, I'll give you his phone number if you like. Just tell me when he's coming and I'll find somewhere else to stay, so he doesn't have to see me." Tears glistened in Gabrielle's eyes.

Obviously a sore point.

"If you ask me, that old rust-bucket'll need more than a mechanic," said Bruce. "Needs a skip, more like."

"Yes, well, the cowl does not make the monk," Steve replied.

Everyone contemplated this in silence.

Lexy saw Bruce nudge Tyman. The latter turned to Rowana.

"So, Elizabeth was a distant relative of yours, was she?"

Rowana gazed at him, reddening. "N… not exactly."

"She was a good friend of my second wife, Jackie," Steve stated quietly.

"Oh, aye?" Bruce drained what must have been his third pint.

A certain tension hung over the table.

"We had no idea about this, but she left the cottage and… well, everything she owned to Jackie, and by the terms of the will, if Jackie died, it all went to Rowana." Steve smiled at his younger daughter. She didn't smile back.

"So, your wife…?" Bruce's wiry eyebrows were interrogative.

"Died. Yes. Sixteen years ago."

"Tragic." Bruce rubbed his chin. "Very tragic. Lost my wife, too. Know how it feels…"

Lexy and Milo exchanged a glance.

"Aye, well," Bruce went on, contemplating his empty pint mug. "These things 'appen. If they don't kill you, they cure you." He turned to Ward. "Get 'em in, lad."

More drinks arrived.

The conversation turned to rare sheep breeds, a subject clearly close to Bruce's heart, and a safe one given the minefield of choices.

During the course of the conversation, Lexy felt herself slumping in her seat. Next to her, Steve gave a complicit smile.

Ward's dark head was bent towards Gabrielle. "… yes, it must have been tough losing your business like that. No wonder you're…"

Tyman was chatting to Rowana. She looked like a cornered bird. She jerked her head towards the Ladies.

"'Scuse me," Lexy murmured, squashing past Steve.

"Well, what did you find out?" Rowana demanded through the cubicle wall.

"You can relax." Lexy buttoned her jeans. "I don't think there was anything supernatural about Elizabeth's death." She pushed the flush button.

"Really?" Rowana was waiting for her by the row of sinks. "How do you know for certain?"

Lexy pumped soap on her hands, watching the girl in the mirror.

"Because I reckon someone from this world was involved."

Rowana visibly paled. "So it wasn't an accident either? I knew it wasn't just a coincidence! You think she was… murdered?"

They were on dangerous ground here. What was Lexy going to say? Yeah, Rowana, I reckon the boys from the farm killed her. You know, the ones out there buying us drinks. And, get this, my friend Milo, who is actually a cop, is starting to think it was your dad who did it.

"Hold your horses," she said. "It could still be a coincidence. Might well have been a burglar she surprised. I mean, Bruce was saying there'd been some break-ins in the area." He might even have been telling the truth, Lexy thought. There were always break-ins, in every area. You only had to pick up a local paper to see that. "So, I'm just collecting evidence at the moment." She gave an easy smile. "What you need to do is stop feeling guilty."

Rowana looked sceptical. Lexy was going to have to do more than just reassure the girl that the Goddess Helandra didn't do it. She was going to have to prove that someone else did.

She ran a hand through her hair. "Better go back."

"Do we have to? I'm fed up with Simon trying to chat me up."

"His name's Tyman. Is he hassling you?"

"No, not really. He's just being… talkative."

"Keep calling him Simon. He'll get the message."

Ward and Gabrielle were still deep in conversation when Lexy and Rowana got back.

"Same again?" Bruce jumped up, his hand in his pocket. "I were just about to get another round in."

"I'll just have a half this time." Lexy made sure she sat between Tyman and Rowana. She felt as if the manoeuvre hadn't gone unnoticed by him. In fact, he was watching her intently.

"Er… you haven't got any big black dogs on the farm that run along the beach between here and Clopwolde at dawn, have you?" she asked. Bit of an inane question, but it was hard to know what to say to someone she'd recently decided might be a murder suspect.

He looked startled, as did Rowana. "No. Why – have you seen one?"

Ward glanced over, his dark eyes wary.

"Three times. I'm told it's a local ghost dog called Old Shuck."

"Yeah. I've heard of him. But you think this creature's for real?" Tyman looked genuinely concerned.

"It has drumming feet."

She saw Ward's lips forming a sarcastic curl. He turned back to Gabrielle.

"A hoofed dog?" Tyman raised an eyebrow.

"Hmm – doesn't seem right, does it?" Lexy felt herself blush. "Which made me wonder if it's something else."

"Don't think there's anything on the farm that meets that description," said Tyman. "I mean, we've got some pretty rare breeds, but none of them that I'd call ghosts." He grinned. "Not a bad idea, though – a herd of ghost cattle would be dead cheap to feed. Dead – get it?"

"Ha-ha," said Lexy. "So, what made you go in for rare breeds?"

"It was Dad, really. He was brought up among old British sheep breeds when he lived on the Yorkshire moors, and he always had this thing about wanting to make sure they didn't die out. He's basically a traditionalist, and it's rubbed off on Ward and me. I like the idea of a working farm that preserves the old values."

Tyman knew his stuff, and waxed lyrical about Pilgrim's Farm. Lexy could imagine how good he would be with visitors to the place. In fact, she was finding it difficult to maintain antipathy towards him, despite her suspicions. She wondered if the other two, Bruce and Ward, were the real movers and shakers in this mystery surrounding Four Winds Cottage.

"Ought to be going now, girls." Steve drained his glass. Gabrielle glanced at Ward, and gave her father a disappointed look.

"Me too." Lexy looked around for Kinky. He was gazing at Tyman, a shard of potato crisp on his nose.

"Sure you don't want to book in the guest house, lass, now

you're in the village?" Bruce was still trying.

"No, I'll be fine at the cottage."

"Rather you than me."

Lexy shrugged. "The worst thing that's going to happen tonight will be Kinky bringing up cheese and onion flavoured crisps all over the living room rug."

The farmer guffawed, but his face was uneasy.

"Are you absolutely sure you're going to be all right?" Steve touched Lexy's arm. "I don't like the thought of you being up there on your own with no lights, or anything."

He was so kind and concerned that Lexy felt unexpected stab of envy of Gabrielle and Rowana, for having a living, caring father. Their eyes held for a second longer than they should have done, and she realised that it wasn't only the father-figure that she found attractive about Steve Paterson.

"Honestly, I'll be fine," she reiterated.

"Well, if you're sure…" He and his daughters moved off, Milo silently following behind.

The Gallimores stood by the door, saying goodbyes to everyone as if they owned the place.

It was dark outside, and the wind had got up again, setting Rowana's long hair whipping around her face. Gabrielle had tucked her strawberry blonde barnet into a hood.

"We're parked down the road," said Steve. "Good to meet you, Lexy. Thanks for keeping things going at the cottage. We'll be over there tomorrow morning, so we can talk then."

"Sure," said Lexy. She watched them go, until the sound of a throat being cleared behind her reminded her that Milo was still there.

"Would you like… ?" he began.

The pub door opened again, spilling light across the pavement, and Bruce and Ward came out, to be met with a ferocious blast.

"By god, it's a regular cocking hurricane out 'ere." Bruce clamped on his flat cap. "Hope you shut that chicken shed, lad. If they get out, ruddy things'll be sailing through the air like cruise missiles."

"Don't worry, they're safe and sound." Ward turned to Lexy. "Need a lift?"

She started in surprise. "No, it's OK, thanks. Milo's dropping me off."

Ward shrugged and turned back to his father. "Where's Tyman?"

"In the khazi."

"I'm dropping you off, am I?" said Milo, at her shoulder.

"Do you mind? You were going to ask, anyway." Lexy stumbled against the kerb, letting go of Kinky's lead. The dog waited patiently while she fumbled in the gutter.

"Suppose it's better than you going back with the Gallimores like that."

"Like what?"

"Like you've had one cider too many."

"Well, excuse me. I didn't realise you were counting."

"All that bravado stuff about staying in the cottage."

"That wasn't the cider speaking, I assure you."

"So you really are staying there? Up at the old Bates place?"

"Don't you start." Lexy began to follow him to the car.

She glanced back. Bruce and Ward were standing a little way up the road by a Land Rover, talking in low voices.

"Can you wait for me?" Lexy pressed Kinky's lead into Milo's hand, and with the policeman's expletive ringing in her ear, she turned on her heel and ran quietly back, keeping to the shadowy doorways. They were standing with their backs to her. Bending double, the cider making her bold, she crept up to within hearing distance.

"… sooner or later she's going to find out. Same as Elizabeth did. I tell you, we've got to do something." That was Bruce.

"Like what?" Ward hissed.

"Longer she stays up there, the worse it gets for us."

"I know that. It's not like we haven't tried everything possible."

Their voices became lower, and, frustrated, Lexy crept even closer.

"… this is going to have to go to plan B, then, isn't it?" Ward's voice was grim. "We'll just have to deal with her the hard way. It's the only option."

Lexy froze, the wind whipping past her.

"I don't like it, son, but I think you're right. Any road, keep Tyman away from her. You know what he's like."

"Shut up – he's coming now."

Lexy pressed back into a doorway as the pub door opened once again, and Tyman came out, pulling his jacket around him. The Land Rover doors slammed shut and tyres crunched on loose gravel.

Forcing her legs to move, Lexy scuttled back down the road.

"At last," said Milo. "Said your fond farewells to the Gallimores, have you?"

"What?" She stared at him through the dark.

"Hallelujah. Now perhaps we can go." He fired the engine.

Lexy sank into the passenger seat. Did she hear Bruce and Ward right? Was Ward really threatening to do away with her if she didn't leave the cottage? Surely not. But what else could he mean by 'deal with her the hard way?' She stared at her wide-eyed reflection in the passenger side window.

Sooner or later she's going to find out. Same as Elizabeth did. What did Elizabeth find out? What was up at Four Winds Cottage? Lexy's skin began to crawl.

And why did they want to keep Tyman away from her? It was the second time Bruce had warned Ward about that.

As the car wound along the dark lanes, Lexy tried to control her thudding heart. She took some deep breaths. In out, in out. Right. She needed to do something about this. Needed to tell Milo. And she needed to explain the situation in a coherent, sensible way. He already thought she was drunk. In fact, she was drunk. More drunk than she would have expected to be after a couple of pints of cider. Must have been strong stuff. She tried to form the right words in her mind. They bustled around like startled sheep. Sheep jumping over a…

"Here you are then."

"Wha… we're here already? That was quick."

"You were asleep."

Lexy struggled upright in her seat. "Was the gate open at the farm?"

"Yes."

"How did you know the way?"

"I'm a policeman."

"D'you want to come in for a minute?"

"You're inviting me into a house you've broken into?"

"Milo – the owner of the freaking cottage knows I'm here. So do the Gallimores. It's not like I'm doing it behind anyone's back."

He gave her one of his weary looks and opened his door.

The darkness was absolute, and up on Freshing Hill, Four Winds Cottage was living up to its name. Lexy felt her way along the garden wall, her eyes nearly shut against the gale, calling to Kinky to follow her. She heard Milo stumble and curse. Probably tripped over the poor mutt.

Feeling in her pocket, she located the key and unlocked the front door at the third attempt.

They tumbled in, and Milo struggled to get the door shut after them. Lexy tried the hall light. It didn't work.

"Arseholes," she muttered. "Well, they're not getting me out of here."

"What are you on about now?"

"Nothing. I'll tell you later. Stay there and I'll get the candles."

"What – there's still no electricity?"

"Yup."

"Wind must have brought a line down. It happens all the time round here."

Lexy felt her way up the stairs. "I think we'll find it's only affecting Four Winds Cottage."

She groped for the candles in the guest bedroom and came back down. "Got any matches?"

"Somewhere," She heard Milo's jacket rustle. "Here you are."
A scrape and a flash.

"Can you light this?"

The wick sizzled and flared.

Milo's face appeared in the circle of light.

"Is this candle an owl?"

"No. It's a penguin."

"Oh, yes. I see that now."

"Come into the kitchen." Lexy led the way.

She pulled up the blind and peered out in the direction of Pilgrim's Farm, expecting to see all lights blazing. To her surprise, there was nothing of the sort there, just a dull glow.

She frowned. Perhaps there really had been a power cut. The wind was pretty mad, after all.

"I'd offer you a cup of tea, but…"

"Got anything else?"

"Wine?"

"Go on then."

Lexy fetched the bottle of elderberry wine from the pantry.

Milo uncorked it, poured two glasses and raised one to his lips.

"Not bad. Now – are you going to tell me what's going on with the Gallimores? What were they saying outside the pub?"

All of Lexy's previously composed sentences decomposed.

"Those bastards are out to get me."

"The Gallimores?"

"They want me out of here. Like they wanted Elizabeth Cassall out. Because she found something out about them."

"What was in that cider?"

"Look – you know what I was saying earlier? In the pub?"

"What – this great idea of yours about them having bumped off Elizabeth so they could get their hands on this place?"

"Well – for starters, what they were saying outside the pub was that sooner or later, I'd find out, just like Elizabeth did."

"Find out what?"

"I don't know, do I? That's the thing. And they said, the longer I stay up here, the worse it gets for them."

"You sure you heard them right?"

"Oh, yes – I'm sure. And get this. Ward said if I didn't get out, they'd have to go to Plan B. He said, 'We'll just have to deal with her the hard way.'"

Milo gave a short laugh. "What are you trying to say? That he's going to come up here and take you out?"

"Yeah. And I don't think he's planning on taking me out on a picnic."

"You really are living in La-La Land, Lomax."

"Well, it's possible, isn't it? They want the cottage really badly for some reason. They've already tried to buy it from the Patersons, and they want me out of it right now."

"OK. Why would they want it that much?"

Lexy threw back her elderberry wine with a grimace. "There must be something in here that incriminates them in some way."

"Don't you think they would have removed it long before you arrived here?"

"Not if they assumed they would be able to buy the place as it stands. Anyway, perhaps it's something not immediately obvious, something that they have to, you know, search for."

"Like what?"

"Who knows? But it has to be bad enough for them to be considering getting me out of the way… permanently."

They stared at each other.

"That's just crazy," said Milo, at last. "What do you think – Ward Gallimore's going to come striding up here and blow you away with a shotgun? Hardly."

"Can't you at least check the case record for Elizabeth's death? Someone might have missed something."

"I knew it. I knew it would come to this. Any idea what you're asking?"

"How difficult can it be?"

"I have to give a reason, you know."

"Don't bother, then." Lexy opened the back door and let herself and Kinky out into the back garden. She breathed deeply. The sky was crammed with stars, double the usual number, and two pale moons hung over the hillside. That cider had certainly got to her, and the elderberry wine wasn't helping. She leaned on the rough stone wall of the house, having doubts herself, now.

When she went back into the kitchen. Milo was rinsing his glass out.

"Sorry," she said.

"Lexy, you're making a mountain out of a molehill here." He dried the glass and draped the tea towel over the back of a chair. "Just leave it. I'll give you a ride back to Clopwolde tonight and we can come and get your car tomorrow."

"What – and let them win? I'm meant to be investigating Elizabeth's death."

"I've had enough of this." Milo headed for the door. "You're forgetting that one of my officers was in charge of investigating that case. If he'd found the least reason to believe Elizabeth Cassall was murdered, do you seriously think he would have ignored it?"

"No. No, of course not. But he might have missed something."

Milo turned, his hand on the door knob. "I'm telling you, Lexy – that woman fell backwards over her balcony accidentally. It's not the first time something like that has happened and it won't be the last."

Lexy shrugged, looked away.

His voice softened. "If it'll put your mind at rest I'll get someone from uniform to go and have a chat with the Gallimores tomorrow morning. We've got a ready-made pretext if they've been talking about break-ins. Give them the not-so-subtle message that we're watching them. But only if you go back home tonight."

Lexy grimaced. "Even if I wanted to drop this case, which I don't, I still wouldn't go back to Clopwolde right now."

"Damn, you're pig-headed. But why don't you want to go home?" His eyes narrowed at her expression. "Oh, yes – the husband. But he can't be that bad, can he? I mean, what's he going to do if he sees you?"

Lexy looked down. "Let's just say he's not going to be very happy. And Milo, he's mixed up with some very dodgy people." She paused, noting the grey glint in the detective's eye. "There's stuff he wouldn't draw the line at. Not just ripping people off. He didn't like being crossed. Over the last couple of years things got quite nasty."

"Didn't you ever think about reporting it?"

"I gave a few anonymous tip-offs to your lot, you'll be pleased to note. Not that they did anything. But Gerard suspected me. I had to keep my head down for a long time, and toe his line." She gave a ruthless laugh. "Funny, though, after all that – the thing that really pushed me over the edge was that lost Lowry painting. Y'know – Gerard stealing all that money that should have gone to charity. That really got me here." She thumped her chest.

Milo smiled through the flickering light. "Well, he reckoned without you."

"Yeah, he did, didn't he?"

"So, he ever hit you?"

The question took her by surprise. "Nothing I couldn't handle." She twisted her empty glass. "Anyway, I'm out of it, now. And perhaps you can understand now why I want to stay out of it while he's in the village."

Milo nodded. It was too dark to see his expression. "Perhaps you are better off here, on balance," he conceded.

"So, you're off?" She kept her voice casual.

"I suppose I'd better get some sleep. As had you."

"Guess."

"I'll see you when you get back to Clopwolde."

"Yup."

"Want me to stay?"

Did he really say that? "I'll be all right."

"If you're sure."

Lexy stood by the door. The engine and headlights came on. Milo was illuminated in the driving seat. He lifted his hand in a single salute, and went, taking the light with him.

"See you," said Lexy softly, feeling her way back to a kitchen of jumping shadows.

Kinky pressed a damp nose against her ankle, making her gasp.

"What are you doing?" she shouted, then immediately bent to stroke him.

"Sorry, mate – I'm really on edge." She sat dolefully for a long while before picking up the candle and lurching into the living room, dripping hot wax all over her jeans.

The candle went out, and with a groan, Lexy lay back on the sofa, fully clothed.

The faces of the Gallimores drifted in front of her eyes. Bruce, Tyman, Ward, Bruce, Tyman, Ward – each wearing a sinister smile.

"Kinky – are you awake?"

The chihuahua grumbled from the other end of the sofa where he'd just settled.

She fell into an uneasy sleep.

9

At four o'clock in the morning Lexy's eyes flew open.

She'd had that dream again. The faceless pursuer. Legs turned to lead. Hot breath on her neck.

She couldn't even blame Kinky this time. He was still curled up at the bottom of the sofa.

She lay there, trying to get her hammering heart under control. This was becoming ridiculous. The same nightmare, twice running. Running. She gave a mirthless laugh which was suddenly cut short.

She'd heard a noise.

So had Kinky. He jumped down, silent but alert.

Lexy crept over to the patio window and tweaked the curtain back. It was still dark outside. She stood straining her ears, listening for something – she wasn't sure what, exactly. The sound she'd heard had been one she thought she knew, but from where? It was out of context in this chilly night.

Nothing more broke the thickly blanketed silence.

Lexy stumbled to the safety of her sleeping bag.

When she next opened her eyes it was daylight, of sorts, an overcast sky, and a fine, misty rain. She had a horrible taste in her mouth, a thumping headache, and the sunburn on her shoulders was as sore as hell.

"Why didn't you stop me drinking pints, Kinky?" she groaned.

She lay back gingerly, assaulted by memories of the previous evening.

The irony was, it was meant to have been a pleasant night out, just Milo and herself. Then, along came the Patersons, and as if that wasn't bad enough, the Gallimores of Pilgrim's Farm.

Lexy cringed as she recalled how worked up she'd been about

the rare breed farmers, and their inexplicable threats outside the pub. How Milo had been trying to talk sense into her. Offering to stay. And then that nightmare again.

She leaned down and picked up her jacket.

God, her head. It took a couple of minutes before Lexy was able to take the photo from her pocket and look at Steve Paterson, smiling kindly down at his daughter.

Lexy groped her delicate way to the kitchen, and reached automatically for the light. It came on. Electricity was back. Well, that was something. She wouldn't have to boil up a billy-can in the front porch to get a cup of tea. At a whine from Kinky, she unlocked and pushed open the kitchen door.

It was unseasonably cold outside. Purple clouds gathered like bruises.

Kinky slunk out.

From her bag, left on a kitchen chair, Lexy's mobile rang. She glanced at the drear weather. Of all days, today wasn't the one she would have expected to get a signal.

She plucked the instrument from her bag before the atmospherics changed their mind.

It was Milo.

"You all right?"

"Yes – fine."

"Electricity back on?"

"Yep."

There was a pause.

"Any problems during the night?"

"You mean, did someone try to break in?" She sat down. "No. But I woke up at four in the morning… " She hesitated. "I heard a sound."

"What kind of sound?"

"I dunno. A cough, maybe." Or gunshot through a silencer. "Close by, outside."

"Man or woman?"

"God knows, Milo."

"Look," he said. "I've been thinking about Elizabeth's death. I mean, there's nothing tangible to support reopening the investigation, but, well, like you, I've just got a bit of a feeling."

Lexy stared at the phone. Result.

"I'll do a bit of digging. Meanwhile…" Lexy heard urgent voices in the background. "Right. Got to go. I'll be in touch. Ring if anything else, you know… suspect… happens."

"I will."

"In fact, call me anyway."

"Sure." Lexy clicked the phone off. Was he going soft?

Moments later, she heard an engine outside. She moved quickly to the window. It was the Patersons, here much earlier than expected. Lexy ran a hand through her hair. She was still wearing last night's clothes.

There was a knock at the front door, and Kinky whistled through from the back, barking loudly.

"Not too early, are we?"

Steve Paterson, who looked as if he'd also slept in his clothes, gave her his grave, sweet smile.

"No – come in. Have some tea."

He went past her, followed by Gabrielle, who was wearing carefully applied make-up. Rowana brought up the rear, looking as if she expected Elizabeth's ghost to pop out of a crack in the floorboards any minute and smother her.

"Are you all right?" she whispered.

Lexy was sick of saying it. "Yeah, fine."

Steve led the way into the kitchen.

"Sleep all right?" he enquired.

"Not really," Lexy said. "Kind of explains my dishevelled appearance."

"I didn't notice anything different," Gabrielle murmured.

Lexy filled the kettle and switched it on, then assembled four of Elizabeth's best china bird-embossed mugs on the table. Robin, sparrow, blackbird and blue tit. She gave Gabrielle the tit.

"I thought we'd go to a hardware shop today, and get a couple

103

of bolts for the patio door, and a few window locks," said Steve. "Don't want any unwelcome guests."

"Any more than we've already got," Lexy heard Gabrielle whisper to Rowana.

"Good idea." Lexy dropped two spoons of sugar into her mug.

"Shall we have a look around?" said Rowana.

"Yeah. See if she had anything valuable." Gabrielle grabbed up her mug and they headed out of the door. "Oh, and didn't you say there was a photo of us here?"

Steve looked up sharply.

Lexy blinked. "Where did I put it?" she murmured. "In one of the books in the other room, I think. I'll dig it out for you."

"OK." Gabrielle disappeared.

Steve was over by the window, looking out at the shed.

"It's a great place, isn't it?" said Lexy.

He nodded, and came to sit at the table.

"Hope you don't mind me being here," she said.

"Not in the least."

"I was only planning to stay until the weekend, if that's OK?"

"'Course it is. Stay as long as you like. Er… did you know Elizabeth well?"

Lexy had been expecting the question. She just thanked her lucky stars it came now, and not at the pub the previous night, in front of the Gallimores.

Even so, it was difficult lying to him.

"I only came to know her relatively recently."

"Did you talk about the past much?" His eyes seemed to be asking more than his words.

Lexy shook her head

"Was she happy?"

"Think so. She seemed content here."

"It had to be an accident, then?"

Lexy was taken aback by the conversational turn. "What – the fall? It seems that way. The coroner's report…"

"Yes, I know what that's going to say. But… what do you

think? As her friend?"

"Me?" Lexy thought how to word it. "She didn't seem to be depressed, if that's what you mean."

"So you don't think it was suicide?"

She shook her head, noting his expression of relief.

Did he know something that might have caused Elizabeth to want to kill herself? Lexy was almost too engaged in this thought to notice he'd spoken again.

"Tell me about yourself." He was considering her, head on one side.

"Not much to tell." But all the same, Lexy found herself talking about her upbringing in a series of caravans and motor vans, and how she and her folks had travelled the lanes and by-roads of Kent and Sussex, hop-picking, fruit-picking, ditching, hedging and anything else they could get.

He in turn gave her a potted history of Paterson's Fine Cakes, and the trials and tribulations of bringing up two daughters on his own. "Different as chalk and cheese they are," he said, fondly. "Rowana's a thinker, and Gabrielle is a do-er."

Lexy wasn't inclined to tell him that, in her experience, Rowana was perfectly capable of doing as well as thinking.

"But then they've got different mothers, haven't they?" she said. "I guess they must each have inherited some characteristics from them."

"Rowana mentioned that, did she?" he said, looking taken aback.

Lexy regretted saying it immediately. Steve thought she and his daughter had only just met the previous night.

"It came up." She managed to change the subject, and it was only when the girls had returned from their exploration that Lexy realised she'd forgotten even to try to discover Steve's whereabouts on the night before Elizabeth died.

"It's a really nice place," said Gabrielle. "Except that neither of us wanted to go in Elizabeth's bedroom. You know, where she fell out of…"

"Find anything interesting?" Steve asked.

"Nothing worth anything," said Gabrielle. "She didn't seem to have much at all. But it has potential to be done up. It could look really amazing if it was decorated properly."

"She's made a little art studio." Rowana's eyes were shining. "And it looked like she was pretty good with oils."

"Just like you, sweetheart." Steve started to smile at his younger daughter, then his expression changed. So did hers. Did her eyes begin glistening? She suddenly ducked out of the room.

"Well, I'm off to Clopwolde to get those window locks and some bits for the van," said Steve, after a momentary silence. "The last thing we need now is for our only transport to give up the ghost."

"Like mine." Lexy glanced out of the window to where the lime green car stood.

"What's wrong with it?"

"You mean other than being a Fiat Panda? It's just a bit erratic at the moment. Refused to start the other night, the next day it went again, except now it just sounds like it's only firing on three cylinders." Bit like she was, in fact.

"Got the keys?" Steve held out his hand. "I'll take a look."

Gabrielle rolled her eyes. "Dad…" she began. "We're never going to get back at this rate."

"Would you really?" Lexy located her jacket and handed them to him. "Thanks ever so much."

Every woman's dream. A keen amateur car mechanic.

She gave Gabrielle her best smile, and began washing up mugs.

The girl wandered over to the window. She glanced down the hill and gave a little start. "I'm going for a walk."

"You do know it's raining?"

Gabrielle shrugged. Donning a bright red mackintosh that she had brought in with her, she set off, leaving by the front door.

"I've never known her to voluntarily take a walk," said Rowana, coming back into the kitchen, her eyes slightly red.

"Perhaps the countryside is working its magic on her."

"What do you mean – magic? Have you found something…"
Wrong word.

Steve put his head around the kitchen door, cutting Rowana short.

"She just needs some new spark plugs," he said. "And an oil change wouldn't go amiss."

"Is that all?" Lexy felt a surge of relief.

"I'll get new plugs while we're out. It won't take me long to sort it out."

"Thanks. That's brilliant." Lexy fumbled for her wallet.

"Pay me when I get back. Can you come along, Rowana? I need someone to navigate." Steve left without waiting for an answer.

Rowana exclaimed in annoyance.

Lexy listened to the van roar away, then sat alone in the kitchen.

It was an odd thing, but she could have sworn Steve had been in Four Winds Cottage before, even though he claimed otherwise. When he first came in, he'd made straight for the kitchen, and he hadn't been looking around him either, like Gabrielle and Rowana. When he excused himself to go to the loo, he'd gone directly upstairs to the bathroom. Might just have been lucky guesswork, but he seemed somehow to know his way around the place.

Unnerved, Lexy stared out of the window, wondering how long Gabrielle intended to stride about in the rain. The girl wasn't exactly good company, but at that moment anyone would do. It wasn't as if Kinky was the life and soul. He was pacing around the kitchen, throwing her anxious glances. No one could accuse him of being relaxed in Four Winds Cottage.

The sound of the garden gate slamming made her look up sharply. Feet pounded up the path.

Lexy grinned. "Here she comes. Rain must have got worse."

Her expression changed at the terrific hammering on the front door.

"All right, Gabrielle, keep your arse on."

Kinky shot into the hall like a greased ferret.

The frenzied knocking came again.

"I'm coming, all right?" Lexy bundled down the hall and turned the handle.

The door was shoved open so hard that it bounced against the wall.

Ward Gallimore burst in, and slammed it behind him.

Kinky barked savagely.

"What the hell are you doing?" Lexy backed up the hall. As if she didn't have an inkling. This was it. He was going to deal with her. He must have been watching the cottage. Seen the others leave.

How would he do it? A knife? A blunt instrument? Well, she wasn't going easily. She tensed, ready to give him a right hard kick where it would hurt the most.

But Ward strode straight past Lexy, giving her an odd look as he did so.

"Bloody bull's escaped," he said through gritted teeth, before turning sharply into the kitchen, and yanking the cord at the window. The blind shot up as if electrified.

A burst of laughter escaped Lexy.

"Where is everyone?" Ward demanded. His dark hair glistened with rain.

"What do you mean?"

"I mean where are the Patersons? I saw them drive up here an hour ago."

"Rowana and her dad went out again in the van. Gabrielle…" The significance of an escaped bull finally hit Lexy. "Oh, hell – she went for a walk."

"Where?"

"Don't know. Down the path towards the farm, I think."

"When did she go?"

Lexy checked her watch. The hands looked meaningless. "About ten minutes ago?"

Ward's face was very close to hers. Close enough for her to feel the drips from his wet hair running down her cheek.

"Stay here," he said. "Don't leave this house. As soon as I've found Gabrielle, I'll be in touch."

Bit belt and braces, but Lexy wasn't going to argue with him. "You can't miss her," she said. "She's wearing a bright red raincoat."

"Right." In two strides he was at the kitchen door, and after a quick look around, he was gone.

Lexy sped upstairs to the front room, grabbed up the binoculars and pulled open the windows, sweeping the parts of hillside that weren't obscured by trees. If she knew where Gabrielle was, she could dash out and get her back.

Lexy had a healthy regard for bulls, having encountered enough of them during her childhood wanderings in the countryside. She'd had a couple of close shaves, too, but that was from bulls confined in fields that she, strictly speaking, shouldn't have been in. She'd never faced one that had got loose. She imagined Gabrielle, standing still and white-faced on the footpath, while in front of her a huge, angry shape pawed the ground and lowered its head. The girl wouldn't stand a earthly. Especially not dressed in bright red. An important little detail, she recalled, that seemed to have escaped Ward Gallimore. Puzzled, she brushed a remaining drop of water from her cheek.

Five minutes of anxious scanning was rewarded by the sight of two figures down near Pilgrim's Farm. It was Ward and Gabrielle. He had his arm around Gabrielle's waist, and she was limping slightly. They disappeared into the farmhouse.

Lexy ran down the stairs and opened the front door, slipping down to the gate with Kinky. She stared down the rutted track that led through the woods, her ears straining for the sound of the Land Rover. It was illogical, but she felt somehow responsible for dumb, irritating Gabrielle. She should have thought to tell her that the land was private, and right now she wanted to make sure she was back before her father, preferably in one piece.

Nothing happened for five minutes, then Lexy glimpsed a movement from the path that led past the cottage. Grabbing Kinky, she dashed back to the front door, and pushed him in, ready to jump inside herself and slam it shut if a Minotaur head suddenly appeared around the corner.

But it was Tyman Gallimore. He had a canvas bag slung over one shoulder, and wore a deep, preoccupied frown. Django followed him in similar mode, but without the bag.

Lexy shut Kinky inside and called to Tyman. He looked up with a startled expression.

"Have you found it?" she yelled, running to the gate. Angry, muffled barks followed her.

Tyman shifted the bag. "Found what?"

"The bull, of course. Ward managed to get Gabrielle back to the farm."

Tyman paused uncertainly. He looked rumpled and exhausted. "What's happened, exactly?"

"You mean you don't know?" Lexy took a quick look around, and opened the gate. "You'd better come in the garden. It'll be safer."

Tyman came in, his eyes narrowed in puzzlement. Django padded in behind.

"Ward came up to the cottage," Lexy said. "About a quarter of an hour ago. One of your bulls has escaped and Gabrielle was out walking. Ward went after her, and I saw him take her back to the farm. I'd go down there, but Ward told me to stay here until it was safe."

Tyman rubbed his forehead. He set his bag on the ground, and Django sniffed at it, then looked up at Tyman and broke into a series of excited yelps.

"Shut it, will you?" Tyman nudged the dog out of the way with his foot, and hoisted the bag up on the wall.

"What have you been doing?" Lexy eyed the bag. A dark stain covered the bottom of it.

"Just seeing to the sheep."

"Lucky you didn't run into the bull yourself."

"Yeah." He squinted down towards Pilgrim's Farm. "Look, I'd better get down there. They'll need help if it's still loose."

"But you can't just walk back – you might get gored. Ward should be driving Gabrielle up here any minute. Why don't you wait?"

"No – I'd better go." He swung out of the gate and strode over to the path that led to the farm. "Just make sure you stay here," he called back over his shoulder. "We'll let you know as soon as things are safe."

Lexy watched after him until he was out of sight. As she turned to go back in, she spotted the bag, still sitting on the wall. Lexy eyed the stain. As if hypnotised, she moved slowly towards it. She'd just have a quick look…

But as she reached out and touched the flap she heard the sound of running feet, and Tyman reappeared.

"Forgot my bag," he gasped, grabbing it.

Lexy turned and walked slowly up to the front door.

"There's something mighty peculiar about all this," she said to Kinky. He looked as if that was what he'd been trying to tell her all along.

She sat at the kitchen table, trying to recall the hazy conversations of the night before.

Keep Tyman away from her. You know what he's like.

Why had Bruce said that? Was Tyman the wild card? The one who would be most likely to crack under pressure and reveal whatever it was they were trying to cover up? If that was the case she ought to get him on his own.

Lexy rushed to the door at the sound of an engine.

A Land Rover came to a gravel-spraying halt at the gate. Gabrielle descended carefully from the passenger seat. Ward leaned over and spoke to her briefly, then turned and drove off.

"I've been rescued from a bull!" trilled Gabrielle, limping up the garden path. "It was really exciting."

"Did it chase you?"

"No. I didn't actually see it," she admitted. "But Ward suddenly rushed up behind me – nearly scared me to death – and told me it was loose. I panicked, of course, and started running, then I fell over a wall."

"Fell over a wall?"

"A low one." She giggled. "I cut my knee, and Ward said we might as well go back to Pilgrim's Farm, as it was nearer, and he helped me back, and patched me up in their bathroom. The farmhouse is awfully nice. There's an Aga in the kitchen, and real slate floors, and the bathroom's got proper antique fittings and a … "

"Was Bruce there?" Lexy cut in.

"Oh, no, he was out trying to catch the bull. We were all on our own." Gabrielle looked at Lexy as if she was going to say something else.

"Does your knee hurt?" Lexy asked, looking at the neat bandage.

"It stings a bit. Ward said he's pretty experienced at bandaging legs, but they usually belong to ducks or sheep. He said… oh, never mind." With a half-giggle, Gabrielle, who was very bright-eyed, limped into the kitchen, and sat down.

"I think I need a drink," she breathed.

10

The front door banged, making Lexy and Gabrielle jump. It was Steve, Rowana and an exhaust silencer.

Gabrielle immediately regaled them with the story of the rogue bull, with full and dramatic embellishments.

Steve's jaw set as he listened.

"Right. I'm going down there to sort this out," he said. "I'm not going to run the risk of my family being gored to death by some crazed bovine, even if it is a rare breed."

"Oh no, Dad – too embarrassing," wailed Gabrielle, obviously regretting her spirited re-telling of the tale. "I'm perfectly all right. It wasn't like anything happened."

Steve was unmoved. "They need to damned well take more responsibility." And off he went in the van.

So – he had a tough side, too.

"Bloody hell, Gabby, you're such an idiot," snorted Rowana. "Why did you tell him all that stuff? You know what he's like."

But her sister was already making for the stairs, climbing a little awkwardly with her bandaged knee. "Let's try and see what happens down there."

"There's some binoculars in the front bedroom," Lexy volunteered.

"Binoculars?" Rowana pounced on the word. "Do you think Elizabeth was watching the farm?"

"Reckon so," said Lexy.

"Why?" demanded Gabrielle.

"I think she was concerned about how they were treating the animals."

"So she was a bunny hugger."

"Anything wrong with that?"

"Suppose not."

"I think I'd be pretty proud of Elizabeth if she was a friend of my family."

"But that's just it. She was only friends with my mother." Rowana followed Gabrielle and Lexy into Elizabeth's bedroom.

"So this is where she… ?" Gabrielle stared over at the window.

"Yup." Lexy watched Rowana go pale.

Gabrielle grabbed the binoculars. "He's just driving through the farm gate."

"Hope it was open." Rowana stood behind her, hands knotted together. "Why can't we have someone normal for a father? He'll probably pick a fight with one of them and get himself beaten to a pulp."

"Looks like he's run over a hen." Gabrielle focused the binoculars.

"Terrific," said Lexy.

"Oh no, it's all right, it's a cat."

"So that's all right is it?"

"No – I mean it's a cat, and it's all right. Touchy, aren't you?"

Lexy gritted her teeth.

"Now he's knocking on the door – someone's let him in. Might be Ward." Gabrielle flushed pink.

Rowana noticed it too. "So what happened when you went back to Pilgrim's Farm?" she enquired, her voice casual. "Anything interesting?"

Gabrielle shot her a calculating look. "Maybe."

"So?"

"Let's just say that Ward Gallimore didn't only bandage my knee in the bathroom."

Boy, was she pleased about something.

"What else did he bandage?"

"God, Rowana, I meant that after he bandaged my knee, he took hold of me and kissed me."

"I don't believe you!"

Gabrielle giggled. "I can't help it if Ward fancies me. It's a free country."

"Even so, you can't get involved with him!" It hadn't been quite what Lexy had meant to snap.

Gabrielle jumped down her throat immediately. "Why not? You jealous?"

Get real. "No. It's just that…" Lexy wasn't quite sure how to put this. "He… well, you don't know him. You don't know what he's after."

"Think I can guess."

"What I mean is…"

But Gabrielle had turned back to watch the farm again. "Hey! There's someone down there looking at *us* through binoculars! Hope they can't lip read." A silly smirk spread over her face. Was she actually vain enough to think that Ward was seeking her out like some lovesick Romeo?

"May I see?" Lexy took the binoculars. She was right. A dark figure by an outhouse in a paddock had lenses trained on Four Winds Cottage. Was it Ward, Tyman or Bruce? The figure was in shadow, too difficult for her to make out, but someone was definitely keeping an eye on them. Lexy was willing to bet that ogling Gabrielle wasn't their main incentive. So, what were they up to?

Several minutes passed. Gabrielle, bored of holding a pose at the window, began opening drawers and cupboards. "Would you look at this!" She held up a blue, flowery nightdress.

"Not everyone shares your impeccable dress sense," said Rowana.

"Yeah, I noticed."

Was that directed at her? Lexy bit back an urge to retaliate.

"So, how come you have a chihuahua?" Gabrielle was now looking unfavourably at Kinky, who was minding his own business on the bed. "Is he, like, a fashion accessory?"

"Do I look like a fashion victim?" Lexy lowered the binoculars, forcing an easy smile.

"So you never carry him around in a designer handbag?"

"I'm not sad enough to own a designer handbag."

Gabrielle's carefully plucked eyebrows shot up.

"How did you really get him?" Rowana said.

"His owner died," said Lexy. "And just before she went, she asked me to look after him."

"What a drag," said Gabrielle.

"Some might say so."

"You could have taken him to Battersea or somewhere. I mean, it wasn't like his owner was going to know."

"Funnily enough, that was what my ex suggested. But I'd made a promise," said Lexy.

"So?"

"I keep my promises." It was the Romany in her. "Anyway, Kinky grew on me. He's a damned sight more polite and intelligent than some people I meet."

The sapphire eyes grew hard.

"Let's go downstairs," said Rowana. "I've got some chamomile tea."

"And that's meant to tempt me?" Gabrielle was now contemplating an ancient teddy bear that sat forlornly on Elizabeth's pillow.

She checked the label in its ear. "Thought so. It's a Steiff – they can be quite valuable – so Russell says. He was really into collectibles. Sweet, isn't it?"

She hugged the thing. Then, to Lexy's astonishment, her face creased up into tears.

Rowana, clearly used to these mood swings, produced a tissue. "He's not worth it, Gabby."

"I know," Gabrielle flopped on to the bed. "But I can't help it."

Kinky, disconcerted, backed away, and slid inelegantly to the floor.

Lexy turned to the dressing table, both to hide a smile at her clownish dog, and to hide her embarrassment at Gabrielle's scene. Didn't work. The mirror reflected the two Paterson sisters.

"Why do I miss Russell so much?" Gabrielle blubbed, still gripping the unfortunate bear. "I thought I might be getting over him by now, but I'm not." She blew her nose loudly. Not on the bear – Lexy checked. "Stupid, isn't it? I'm in love with a complete and utter dork. And the last thing I expected was to see him with another woman."

"Perhaps he just has irresistible animal magnetism," soothed Rowana.

"Don't be stupid. It's his money."

Well, at least Gabrielle had said it before Lexy did.

"Let's face it, he was always going to have gold diggers throwing themselves at him. The fact is, money makes a man look attractive. Even when he's quite ugly."

"That the sort of sweet nothings you used to whisper in his ear?" Lexy couldn't help herself.

"You don't know one single thing about this." Gabrielle turned livid eyes on Lexy, balling up the tissue and dropping it on the floor.

Lexy held her hands up in a conciliatory gesture.

Rowana led Gabrielle out, throwing a reproachful look behind her.

When Lexy went downstairs a few minutes later, they were sipping pale yellow tea. Rowana pushed a mug towards Lexy.

"Thanks. Sorry about upstairs," Lexy said to Gabrielle. "I shouldn't have said that."

She shrugged. "It's what everyone thought, anyway."

"Oh, thanks, Gabrielle. I…" But Rowana's protest was interrupted by the growl of Steve's van engine again.

Rowana immediately rushed to the door. "Bet he's got a black eye."

Far from it. Her father seemed to have forgotten all about his earlier rage, and was full of the farm. The Gallimores had clearly done a number on him.

"They've got an amazing collection of animals down there, and they make all their own dairy products with goat and sheep's milk. It's quite an industry."

"They milk sheep?" Gabrielle looked disgusted.

"What about the bull?" Lexy ventured.

"Oh, Edgar – he's a real character. A White Park. It's a breed that's been around since Roman times. Anyway, he's safely back in his paddock now. He's not really dangerous, Bruce was telling me, just a bit playful."

Lexy thought back to Ward's desperate hammering on the door that morning. Playful?

"So," went on Steve, "we've all been invited down to the farm tonight for a meal. You too, Lexy."

Lexy nearly choked on her chamomile brew. "Unexpectedly friendly," she managed.

"I expect they feel guilty about the bull," said Steve. "I was rather annoyed when I first went down there."

"Perhaps there's another reason." Gabrielle gave a self-satisfied smile. "We'll have to go back to the B&B, Dad. I need a change of clothes. Shame about that horrible little shower there – perhaps I'll have a quick soak in the bath here before we go."

Rowana was watching her sister with troubled eyes.

"I'll go and have a look at these motors, then," said Steve. "A cup of tea and a sandwich wouldn't go amiss. Normal tea," he added, glancing at Lexy's cup.

"I'll bring it out to you." Rowana began rooting through a carrier bag they had brought with them.

The back door shut. From upstairs came the sound of running tap water.

"I suppose they've invited us down there tonight so that Bruce can do some more work on persuading us… me… to part with the cottage," said Rowana.

"Reckon you're right, there," said Lexy.

"But then, I guess if they're making us a decent offer on this place perhaps we should accept, and move on." Rowana started buttering bread. "After all, selling it is what we're meant to be doing. We won't be able to start up a new business otherwise."

She paused. "Trouble is, I'm not sure I want to give up it now. I thought I'd hate it here because it would be a constant reminder of Elizabeth's death, and my part in it and… "

"Rowana – I've told you – you didn't have anything to do with it."

"I know. But, the thing is, I already feel really at home here. The countryside is beautiful, and there's a kind of peace about it that… I dunno…"

"Appeals to your aesthetic soul?" Lexy supplied, half in jest. She knew where Rowana was coming from.

"Yes, exactly that. And I love it that Elizabeth's made a little art studio."

She'd mentioned that earlier, when she'd had that odd exchange with her dad, which seemed to put her on the verge of tears.

"You paint, do you?" Lexy asked.

"Yes." She shot a look at Lexy. "Promise you won't tell, but I've been offered a place at an art college in London. Just found out before we left the shop."

"Well, that's wonderful!"

Rowana sighed. "Thing is, I can't accept it. Dad and Gabrielle are going to need me when we start the new business."

So that was it.

"They could advertise for someone."

"It would be too expensive to hire a new employee, when we've got me for practically nothing. Anyway, we can't afford the college fees."

"Rowana, you are actually quite well off, compared to most teenagers," Lexy reminded the girl.

"I can't use Elizabeth's money to put myself through college."

"But it's your money now."

"And I said I'd give it to Dad for the business. All of it. Because there's a part of me that will never stop feeling guilty until I know the real reason for Elizabeth's… accident." She gave Lexy an apologetic smile.

Perhaps it was time to level with her.

"Look, Rowana. I want you to stay calm about this, OK?"

Rowena's smile faded. "What have you found out?"

"Nothing definite. But I think the Gallimores might have had something to do with Elizabeth's death."

"The Gallimores?" Rowana looked ready to panic. "But, Gabby… and Ward… and we're meant to be going there tonight."

"Like I said, stay calm." Lexy indicated upstairs towards the bathroom, from where a faint, tuneless singing was coming. "Nothing else is going to happen. It would be too risky for them. I'm just working on the idea that if one or all of them were involved, their incentive was to get their hands on this cottage."

Rowana was watching her, eyes wide.

"Since I first ran into them up here, they made it obvious that they expected to buy the place – they'd banked on it going on the open market after Elizabeth's death. They had no idea that she'd left the place to an old friend. They were completely staggered when they found out."

"As if their master plan had fallen through?" The girl was pale.

"Couldn't have put it better myself."

"But why would they want this place so much?" She gazed around, mystified.

"They own all the rest of the land on this peninsula. Having the cottage would give them ownership of the whole of Freshing Hill."

"What's so great about that?"

"Might make a nice golf course. Bit steep in places, but golfers enjoy a challenge."

Rowana's face creased in dismay. "You mean they'd sell it to a big corporation? This piece of countryside?"

"I'm only saying they might – if they needed the money. It would give them an incentive, wouldn't it? A motive."

"Bruce certainly didn't waste any time last night in offering to buy it," said Rowana in consternation. "Did you see his face when Dad said we'd think about it and let them know if we decide to sell?"

"Black as thunder." Lexy confirmed.

"Well, I'm never going to sell it to them, now. Whatever they offer me." Rowana viciously sliced tomatoes.

"Glad to hear it." Lexy truly was.

"So it's just like I said – they really are going to be working on Dad tonight, to try to get him to persuade me to sell them the cottage." Rowana put her hand to her mouth. "And Ward's doing the same with Gabrielle. He's just using her."

And Tyman would be concentrating on Rowana. Wonder how long it would take her to work that out.

"We can't let the Gallimores know anything's up," said Lexy. "You mustn't give the game away by telling your dad, or Gabrielle, not until I've checked out their alibis."

Rowana clenched her jaw. "OK." She loaded sandwiches on to a plate. "God, poor Gabby, she's been really unlucky in all her relationships."

"Perhaps it's something to do with her motivation."

"What – you mean money?" Rowana considered. "I know what you're saying, but I reckon this thing she had with Russell was different. Although she always put on this cool act about it not being serious, I watched them together, and I think she was starting to get really fond of him."

"Hence the tears earlier?"

"Yes. He was a bit of a berk, but he was a nice berk. At least, we thought he was. And he was absolutely over the moon when Gabrielle agreed to get engaged. Or rather, when she suggested it."

Lexy smiled to herself. "How did she meet him?"

"He used to come into the shop and gaze at Gabby over the macaroons. Like I said before, he's in his thirties, practically bald, bit soft – but he's loaded, he had a Ferrari, and some other little sports car – a Lotus – and he took her to all the best places."

Lexy was about to make a cynical remark, when she remembered a certain teenage girl who used to live with her dad in a caravan, until Gerard Warwick-Holmes came along in his flash 4x4 and seduced her with the promise of the high life.

"Dad and I just thought it was a bit of a joke at first," Rowana continued. "Until Gabby had been out with him about five or six times, then Dad started to worry that it might be getting too serious. So he invited Russell round to the flat for afternoon tea. That usually spelt doom for Gabrielle's relationships. But Russell was completely immune to Dad's eccentricity, and the general peculiarity of our place. In fact, I don't think he even noticed. He and Dad spent the whole time talking about combustion engines.

"After that, Dad seemed quite happy to let things go along – that was until we found we were losing the business and Gabby announced that she was going to marry Russell, and get him to buy us out of trouble. Dad went mental. He's got a really strict moral code." She lowered her voice. "I hate to think what he'd have done if he found out I'd been practising ceremonial magic."

They heard the particular slosh from upstairs that indicates someone getting out of a bath.

Rowana started speaking more quickly. "Gabrielle decided she was going to get married anyway, so she went to Russell's house, with me in tow, trying to talk her out of it. He lives in South Kensington – really posh."

Lexy knew. She used to live there herself until three months ago.

"Anyway, when we got there, we were standing outside, hiding behind a pillar, because his house had pillars, and I was still arguing with Gabby. Then Russell suddenly came out of the door with an incredibly beautiful blonde woman. They jumped into his car, he kissed her, and off they went, straight past us without even noticing."

"How did Gabrielle take it?"

"She was devastated. Russell had given her a ring, you see. She didn't wear it on her engagement finger because of Dad, but apparently he'd made all kinds of promises."

"Typical."

"Anyway, all the way back on the Tube she was trying to get this ring off, but it was stuck tight. We tried everything. I reckon people stayed on past their stops just for the entertainment. In the end we told Dad and he levered it off with engine grease."

Lexy winced.

"She sent it back to him, and told him she never wanted to see him again. The following day we packed up and moved out of the flat to a rented place in Clapham. She changed her phone number so he couldn't ring her. She was like, really, really mad. And upset."

And just ripe to be taken for a ride by a farmer's son with dodgy intentions.

Rowana delivered a plate of sandwiches to Steve in the shed. Lexy carried the tea. Steve was only partially visible under the car.

"You do know it looks like something Noddy might have driven, Dad?" said Rowana.

He poked his head out. "How dare you? It's a Frogeye Sprite."

"It still looks like something Noddy might have driven." Rowana headed back to the kitchen.

Steve watched her through the shed door. "Perhaps I'd better dig out my blue hat with the bell on it."

"Hold me back, someone," said Lexy.

"Cheeky."

She was aware of his eyes on her back as she crossed the lawn to the cottage.

Lexy went into the living room. She needed to try and continue with her search for whatever the Gallimores might want from the cottage. She went methodically through the bookcase. Elizabeth had a good collection of books on flora and fauna. Lexy began checking them at random to see if Elizabeth was in the habit of concealing notes or photographs between pages.

She pulled out a gold and white bound tome entitled *The Language of Flowers*, and flicked through it. It was an illustrated

123

copy of an original Victorian book.

On the inside cover were a few handwritten lines.

Elizabeth,

Nor hath the blossom such strange power,

Because it saith 'Forget-me-not',

For some heart-holden, distant spot,

Or silent tongue, or buried hour.

(Charles D. Roberts).

As you know, I can never truly thank you enough,

Your loving,

Jackie

December 1990

Jackie. Rowana's mother. Must have been written not long before she died. Lexy pondered the words. *Some heart-holden, distant spot, or silent tongue, or buried hour.* Words suggestive of a secret, that had meant something to the two women.

Lexy replaced the book and went into the studio across the hall, where Rowana was sorting through tubes of paint.

"Can you remember much about your mum, Rowana?"

The girl shook her head. "I was only a baby. I've got photos back in London. She looked like me. On the small side, but not so skinny. Same hair. Dad never says much about her. Gabrielle remembers her vaguely. She said she was very quiet. I think she might have been depressed – something to do with her illness. Perhaps she knew about it before my dad did."

"What was it?"

"Breast cancer."

"I'm sorry."

They heard Steve call. Rowana gave Lexy a quick smile, and they went through to the kitchen.

"I've changed your plugs," Steve told Lexy, wiping his hands on a rag.

"Thanks!" Lexy fetched her bag and handed him some of Rowana's cash.

"Dad and I are going back to Clopwolde now, to get some

clothes," Gabrielle announced, appearing on the threshold. "Are you coming, Rowana, or are you going like that?"

"I haven't packed my ball gown, if that's what you mean."

Nor had Lexy, funnily enough.

She looked down at herself. The Gallimores were going to have to take her just as she was.

In her jeans, and on her guard.

11

By late afternoon, the weather had turned fine and fresh.

Lexy sat on the kitchen doorstep in a meditative state. Kinky had unearthed a long-buried knuckle bone from the flower border. It was larger than he was, but he'd managed to drag it to the shelter of a hydrangea, where he was gnawing the revolting thing with relish.

Lexy looked around her. A beautiful tranquillity hung over the whole hill. The only sounds were birdsong, the rustle of breeze in ash and sycamore, the distant boom of the sea, the grinding of a chihuahua's teeth on unyielding bone...

She shook her head. She couldn't get the previous evening's conversation with Milo out of her mind. In particular, his alert, thoughtful look when she had told him that Steve had been away from home the night Rowana had carried out her magic ritual.

Lexy took the photo of Steve, Gabrielle and Rowana out of her pocket yet again and scrutinised it. Why would Elizabeth have this photo? Had she gone up to London and taken it herself? It seemed the obvious answer. But why so secretive? Had she fallen out with Steve when Jackie died?

The sound of an approaching engine made her stuff the photo back into her jacket pocket. Kinky growled and dragged his prize further under the hydrangea, as if he was expecting the bone confiscation squad.

He wasn't far wrong. Lexy watched as a white estate car came to a halt behind the Panda.

DI Milo unfolded his lanky form from the front seat. He was wearing shades, a white shirt and a black tie.

"Everything all right?" he asked.

"More or less. On your way to a funeral?"

"Just got back from one, actually. One of my arson victims."

126

"You confessed to it yet?"

"Sorry?"

"Never mind. Want a drink?"

"I've done some digging." Milo settled back with his glass.

"So has Kinky," said Lexy. They glanced over at the partially hidden dog and bone. "Hope you managed to find something less grisly than he did."

"Depends on how you look at it. I checked out this business with the Gallimores in France. You know – the mother's fall from the high wire."

"And?"

"Unfounded. Just a grievance from the clown she was having an affair with. Nothing proved."

"Their mother was having an affair?"

Milo removed his shades. "Yup."

"With a clown?"

"Yup."

"As in Coco the?"

The detective waited patiently for Lexy to stop laughing.

"We are talking about a circus here. When the mother fell, there were no safety nets in place. That's how she died. Apparently it happened early one morning after an argument with her son."

Lexy sobered up immediately. "Her son? Which one?"

"Tyman. He blamed his mother for the marriage breakdown and they were having a loud barney in the big top. Anyway, the story goes that she suddenly swarmed up the scaffolding tower to the high wire in a rage. She started to cross, lost her balance and fell." Milo stood up and brushed his trousers. "The clown reckoned that Tyman followed her up there and pushed her. Tyman denied it, and had the backing of his father and brother, and a collection of circus people willing to confirm this. No reason to believe otherwise."

Lexy got up too, wanting to detain Milo. She was still trying to assimilate this news. Had the clown lover been right? Bruce's words of warning from the day before rang in her ear.

Any road, keep Tyman away from her. You know what he's like.

Did he know what his younger son was really capable of?

"So, with all that high wire stuff in mind, do you reckon the Gallimores had something to do with Elizabeth's fall?" she said, using the word fall deliberately.

But Milo wasn't to be drawn. "I'm struggling for a motive. I can't find any links between Elizabeth and the Gallimores, certainly nothing that would make one of them want to kill her." He paused. "Except for that one incident with the pigs, and by all accounts, that blew over. By the way, the deeds to Pilgrim's Farm specify that the Gallimores own the grazing rights on Freshing Hill, but they also state that the hill is not to be sold or used for any other purpose than grazing. So there's no obvious financial reason why they would want the cottage badly enough to actually do away with the occupant."

That put paid to her golf course theory.

Lexy frowned down at the neat farm buildings below. She still didn't trust the Gallimores. The bark of a dog in the yard travelled across the clear air to them. A ferocious returning growl emanated from under the hydrangea.

"Did you know that Four Winds was built by one of the former owners of Pilgrim's Farm?" Milo continued. "It was sold to Captain Robert Cassall in the 1980s. You know, Elizabeth's husband, who was killed in the Gulf War."

Lexy thought again of the photo of the stern young man in army uniform in the front bedroom. "Poor Elizabeth."

"She doesn't seem to have had the best of luck all round. You staying here again tonight?"

"Too right I am."

"Call me, won't you, if there's any problem."

"OK." If she could get a signal.

"Right – I'm off, then."

"Will I see you... ?" The roar of an engine made her break off.

"Who's that?" Milo was on his feet and off round the corner.

"… later?" Lexy followed him gloomily.

Gabrielle was just alighting from the van, wearing a dark red and gold sarong which made her look sickeningly glamorous, a fact of which she was very well aware.

"Hello, again," she simpered at DI Milo. "Are you coming, too?"

"Coming where?"

"We've all been invited to Pilgrim's Farm for dinner." She made it sound like the Queen's Garden Party. "Lexy, too."

Lexy gave her a withering look. Milo was going to find it just a little odd that she was waltzing off to dinner with the same family she'd just been accusing of threatening to bump her off. And of killing Elizabeth, for that matter. Unfortunately now wasn't the time to start explaining that the only reason she was going was to find out where all three Gallimores were at nine o'clock on the morning Elizabeth died.

Milo shot a look at her. "I've got a heavy workload tonight."

He replaced his shades, and made for his car, nodding at Steve and Rowana.

"Bye," said Lexy.

He turned to her, but she couldn't see his expression.

"Goodbye, Lexy," he said.

"Thanks for the…"

But his car door slammed, and he was gone.

"Oh, crap," said Lexy.

"Right, are we all ready?" said Steve.

"Hang on," said Gabrielle. "We need to get the suitcases in."

"Suitcases?"

Steve gave Lexy an apologetic smile. "Gabrielle's twisted my arm. We're going to stay at the cottage for the next couple of days, until we go back to London. After all, who's going to object?"

"Oh. Right."

"We need to save as much money as possible." Steve lugged a

backpack, a sports bag and a large pink suitcase from the back of the van, together with some plastic carriers.

Lexy helped carry it all in. If the Gallimores didn't like *her* being in the cottage, how were they going to take to this?

"We can walk down the footpath to the farm, now that the bull's under lock and key," said Gabrielle, clearly eager to be off. "I know the way."

"What, and walk back up in the pitch dark?" said Rowana.

"Oh, Ward will give us a lift."

She was confident.

"Come on, Kinky," said Lexy to the hydrangea.

She was greeted with silence.

She bent down and peered under the foliage, then jerked back. "Oi – don't you growl at me, you little…"

"What's the problem?" inquired Steve.

"He dug up a bone earlier. Haven't been able to part him from it ever since."

Steve bent down to look. "Blimey, that is a big one!"

"Er… what are we waiting for?" Gabrielle's voice broke in.

"Can't leave him here," said Lexy. "Going to have to get it off him."

"OK, in that case – you distract him, and I'll grab it." Steve crouched low and flexed.

Kinky started snarling.

"Trick is not to let him know we're scared," said Lexy, shuffling around on her knees so that she was behind the dog. His eyes bulged ominously, and he tried to drag the bone further out of sight.

"He's the size of a fridge magnet," said Steve. "What's to be scared of?"

He clearly wasn't familiar with the breed.

"Ready?" Lexy tweaked Kinky's tail.

The dog whirled around, letting go of the bone.

Steve grabbed the large slippery mass and ran backwards with it. Kinky snapped madly after him.

"Wha-a-y! Can't stop!" Steve fell flat on his back. The bone, obeying the laws of gravity, kept right on going, straight through the kitchen window.

The deafening crash of breaking glass temporarily paralysed everyone.

"I'll mend that," said Steve, when the shock waves had receded.

"God, it doesn't matter now – we're going to be late. Get up, Dad!" Gabrielle was the only one who hadn't seen the funny side, apart from the irate chihuahua, who was scrabbling at the kitchen door.

Lexy put him in her car, and swept up the glass, while Steve quickly tacked a piece of polythene across the gap. "I'll get some glass and do it properly," he promised.

Lexy regarded it ruefully. Even the most incompetent burglar could break into Four Winds Cottage tonight.

"Got the wine?" Gabrielle set off, picking her way in gold-sandalled feet.

"Yes – I'll carry it, shall I?" muttered Rowana.

"Won't you be cold?" Lexy called after Gabrielle.

"Who cares?" Gabrielle turned and smirked.

"Put a cardigan on," Steve said.

The girl groaned but complied.

"That sarong is beautiful, by the way," Lexy felt bound to say. She didn't like Gabrielle's manners, but her clothes really were lovely.

"Oh… thanks," said Gabrielle, looking down at herself, as if she hadn't realised what a stunning garment she was wearing.

"See – I told you," said Rowana. She turned to Lexy. "Gabrielle made it herself."

Lexy was impressed, and said so.

Gabrielle and Rowana led the way down the hill, Steve and Lexy following a little way behind, a disgruntled chihuahua some distance after them.

Steve raised his eyes at Gabrielle's swaying back. "You got kids?"

"Managed to avoid it so far." During the course of her marriage, Lexy had become increasingly disinclined to inflict Gerard's offspring on the world.

"Best way. Nothing but trouble." But he was smiling.

Lexy forced a grin too. Yeah.

"What's that glinting in the sunlight?" he said, squinting towards the farm. He started in surprise. "Someone's watching us!"

"What, again?" Gabrielle threw back her shoulders, allowing the breeze to ripple through her hair.

"What do you mean, again?"

"Oh, nothing. Hurry up, can't you?"

Steve shrugged it off, but Lexy was puzzled. One of the Gallimores was watching them, just like they had earlier. But which one? And why?

They swished through the long meadow grass, abuzz with grasshoppers and crickets, until the farm came into clear view. This approach was lined with more neatly fenced paddocks, each containing a pair of spotted, striped or mottled pigs.

The farmhouse itself was made of old stone, painted white. A whiskered piebald horse with one blue eye and one brown watched them unevenly from a stable in the yard.

Django also watched them – from behind the bars of a large kennel. If Kinky could have crowed, he would have.

Rowana pulled a bell cord next to the farmhouse door. A jangling sound came from inside, followed by footsteps. Tyman Gallimore appeared.

Lexy found she was looking at him in a somewhat different light since Milo's little disclosure about the circus, let alone any other suspicions she might have been harbouring against him.

He led them through a wide hallway, then opened a set of double doors into a vast living room illuminated with evening sunlight. The décor was distinctly masculine. A chestnut-coloured leather three-piece dominated the sitting area, arranged around a huge, glass-topped table which was weighed down with a pile of *Fancy Duck Breeder* magazines. The room was decorated with horse brasses, fishing rods and black and white photos of the farm in its earlier days when it was populated by bog standard livestock.

Bruce Gallimore stepped through a set of French windows at the far end of the room with a glass of champagne in his hand.

"Welcome to Pilgrim's Rare Breeds Farm!" he boomed.

Lexy could see Gabrielle looking beyond him. She was wondering where Ward was.

Steve went forward to greet Bruce, almost tripping over a large shaggy rug that looked as if it used to be a rare breed itself. Lexy heard Kinky growl. He could chase this one all he wanted.

Then she noticed the large blue Persian cat that was regarding them dispassionately from the back of the sofa. It fixed Kinky with a basilisk stare, and the chihuahua turned to stone. But only for a moment. The next he had launched himself at the sofa. Lexy caught the flying dog in mid-leap, smiling brightly around.

"Play nicely," she muttered into his ear. "Or you'll never see the bone again."

"Oh, don't worry about Chutney," said Bruce. "He can look after hisself." The cat certainly looked like a regular bruiser. He had remained in place despite Kinky's attempted coup, and now took his time about jumping down and stalking across the room.

Bruce turned to Tyman. "Well, fetch our guests a drink, lad."

They actually had a cocktail bar in the corner. Lexy wondered where they were hiding the snooker table and jukebox.

"Who's drawn the short straw tonight?" Bruce beamed around them.

Everyone looked blank.

"I mean, who's the driver? Can't be you, pet." He addressed this to Gabrielle. "You 'ad to do the honours last night."

"We walked, actually," said Steve. "From the cottage. That's where we're staying for the next couple of nights."

There was a thud and a gurgle from the bar. Tyman had knocked over a bottle of vodka.

"All of you?" Bruce ejaculated. "Well… I…" He seemed to be lost for words.

"What would you like?" Tyman called. He sounded slightly hysterical.

Lexy nodded to herself. She had been right. The Gallimores weren't happy about the Patersons' invasion. But why?

She accepted a champagne cocktail and wandered around the room with Gabrielle and Rowana, looking at a series of pictures of sheep from the naïve school, the sort with huge square bodies and tiny little heads.

"I don't remember seeing any of them on the farm," Gabrielle frowned.

Bruce and Steve stood by the open French windows. Steve was talking about Land Rovers. Bruce was staring at him.

A small, rotund woman with a very red face bustled in.

"I'll start laying the table then," she puffed.

"Oh, aye. Right you are, Mrs Mangeot," Bruce murmured.

"She's the Suffolk version of a Swedish au pair." Tyman, obviously recovered, had come up behind them. Gabrielle gave a little snort of laughter and Steve slid her a warning look as he continued his monologue on the hazards of big end replacement.

Lexy studied Mrs Mangeot with interest. If she was the Gallimores' housekeeper, she just might have some idea of their whereabouts on the morning of Elizabeth's fall.

The woman whipped a tablecloth out of a drawer and flicked it over a long oak table, then suddenly let out a yelp.

"Are you all right there?" Lexy asked.

"Just remembered I left the asparagus steaming," said the woman. "They'll end up in a pulp if I don't go and rescue them."

"Want a hand?"

"Bless you." Mrs Mangeot opened a large canteen of cutlery on a sideboard. "Here you are, dear – we're having artichoke to start, then fish, dessert and cheese board. Back in a minute."

She disappeared into the kitchen, from which emanated a variety of fragrant aromas.

Lexy took a handful of cutlery and started laying it out. How many would there be? She did a quick headcount, wondering whether Ward would be joining them. It was a question that was also exercising Gabrielle, judging by the number of times she'd glanced at the door.

Mrs Mangeot came back through, bearing bread baskets piled high with sesame rolls. Setting them down on the table, she told them to sit down, as the starter was about to be served.

It looked as if Lexy would have to slip into the kitchen after dinner if she wanted a quiet word with the woman.

They all looked at one another, wondering who was going to sit where. Ward strolled through the kitchen door just in time to join the musical chairs manoeuvre. Gabrielle, pink and determined, managed to claim the chair next to him. Lexy ended up between Bruce and Tyman.

Tyman poured Chablis into delicate crystal glasses. Bruce swallowed his in two gulps. He had clearly downed more than one glass of bubbly before they arrived, and throughout the rest of the meal he regaled them with bawdy tales.

Tyman gave Lexy a helpless look. "No stopping him when he's in full flow," he whispered.

"That woman's a bloody diamond," said Bruce, as they spilled out on to the large patio after the meal. He was looking at Mrs Mangeot's wide backside, as it disappeared into the kitchen. "I ought to make an honest woman of her."

Ward gave him a tight smile. "I think Mr Mangeot might have a thing or two to say about that."

"Lucky man, Mr Mangeot. What d'yer say, Steve?"

"Very fortunate," said Steve.

"Can't beat a woman who can cook," went on Bruce. "Fancy a cigar?" He produced a wooden box and thrust it at Steve.

"Don't try to poison the guests, Dad," Tyman muttered.

"Less of your cheek, lad. These buggers cost me a tenner apiece."

"In that case…" Steve took one decisively. The patio was soon full of smog. Lexy assumed it wouldn't be long before the subject of Four Winds Cottage came up again. She just hoped Steve hadn't changed his mind.

"Fancy a tour of the grounds?" Ward asked Gabrielle.

"I'll come, too," said Rowana, ignoring Gabrielle's pointed look. She turned to Lexy. "Can I take Kinky?"

The dog was about to disappear into the kitchen. Lexy gave a short whistle. She clipped his lead on and handed him over. The dog threw her a resentful look as he was dragged through the French windows.

Lexy made for the kitchen door herself.

"Sorry about Dad being a bit, well, agricultural at dinner." She hadn't noticed Tyman standing in the corner by the bar.

"He is a farmer." Lexy could hear plates being stacked in the kitchen. She took another step towards the door. "Mrs Mangeot promised me a recipe. I'm just going to…"

"Even so, he didn't have to do the donkey joke. But he's been under a lot of strain lately. We all have."

Lexy turned. "Really?"

12

"Farm problems. Anyway, I'm not going to bore you with that."

"I don't mind, honestly." She sat down on the sofa to emphasise that point. The large blue cat appeared as if by magic, and settled itself on her lap.

"They seem a nice family, the Patersons." Tyman picked up a bottle of wine and two glasses, and came to sit beside her.

"Even Gabrielle?"

He gave her a lopsided smile. "I still can't get over her kid sister inheriting Four Winds like that."

"No – I don't think she can, either." Lexy sat back, tried to look relaxed. "Listen, Tyman, did Elizabeth ever mention Rowana's mother, Jackie, when you spoke to her?"

Tyman poured the wine, and handed a glass to Lexy. "Don't think so, but then she didn't talk much about her personal life. Although, she did say she had a husband who died."

"Yes, I heard that. Sad. Wonder if she ever found anyone else."

"Well, there was Archer Trevino, of course."

"The painter? Yes – you said he and Elizabeth were friends."

"More than friends. I think they'd been seeing each other on and off for years – one of those temperamental artist relationships."

Interesting. Was he the one who had taken that photo of Elizabeth in her artist's smock? From the expression on her face it must have been one of their good days.

"Did she have any other close acquaintances?"

"A lot of the villagers knew her, but I wouldn't say she was close to any of them. She kept herself to herself. She was very anti blood sports, and all that. Probably lost her as many friends as it won her around here. There's certainly a few people who would have been glad to see the back of her."

"Enough to have helped her on her way?"

He stared at her aghast. "You mean… pushed her over the… ? God, no – of course not. Where did you get that… ?"

Lexy decided it was time for a swift change of subject.

"So, how did you end up at Pilgrim's Farm? Where were you before?"

Tyman seemed to calm down. "Long story. Sure you want to hear it?"

"If you don't mind telling it."

"OK. You asked for it." He took a deep breath. "Right. Dad is originally from Yorkshire, as you may have gathered. He travelled a lot in Europe when he was young, and that was where he met our mother. It was in Normandy, actually. He was running a little circus out there."

"A circus?" Lexy had prepared herself to act surprised.

"Probably sounds more exotic than it was. Just a troupe of acrobats, stunt riders and… clowns. My mother was French – she came from a very old, correct Normandy family…"

Lexy nodded to herself. She knew that Tyman must have got the Bayeux Tapestry look from somewhere.

"… and she shocked them all by becoming a funambulist."

"A sleepwalker?"

"Tightrope walker." Yes, of course. Silly her.

"She joined Cirque Gallimore, they got married and Ward and I came along and grew up to the life." He swirled his wine around his glass. "Weird mix of northern English and French, travelling around Europe with a big top."

"Must have been an interesting childhood."

"Suppose so. We didn't know any different. It was very close-knit – we looked after one another."

Did you, now? "So – what happened?"

"Dad happened. He got bored, started investing in other stuff – rare breeds, and farming – and some other rather more dodgy money ventures, which eventually resulted in him having to leave France in a hurry."

"How much of a hurry?"

"Same day hurry. Ward and I followed… later. Had something we needed to get sorted out."

She could guess what that was. The inquiry following the death of… "And your mother? What about her?"

Tyman's face set. "She was killed in an accident."

"I'm sorry."

"Why? You didn't know her."

Lexy was taken aback by his vehemence.

"No, but I know what it's like to suddenly not have a mother any more."

"You lost yours, too?"

"Literally. She went to China when I was a kid and never came back."

Lexy's hand went automatically to a chain around her neck, upon which hung a small silver oak leaf.

"You mean she stayed out there?"

"I don't know. She went on a protest mission, a few people trying to save the panda."

"Brave of her."

"Yup. She was always doing that sort of stuff, but usually nearer to home."

"Would have got on well with Elizabeth."

"Yeah." They exchanged a smile. He seemed such a nice lad. Lexy had to keep reminding herself about Milo's account of the high wire incident. And Bruce's warnings to Ward to keep Tyman away from her. As if he heard her thoughts, Bruce looked in through the French windows. The smell of cigar skulked in with him.

"All right, lad?"

"Yes, fine," Tyman almost snapped.

Bruce withdrew.

"When she didn't come back," Lexy continued, "I thought it was because she didn't want to be with my dad and me any more.

I just assumed she'd got a taste for it, and she was out on the high seas chasing whaling boats, or something. But Dad got on to the British Embassy in China, and he chased around contacting people and organisations for years, trying to find someone who might know where she was. In the end he convinced himself she'd been killed out in China. Said that was the only thing that would stop her coming back to him."

"He obviously had a lot of faith in their relationship."

Lexy nodded. It had been a faith she couldn't understand or share. Her mother, Angelica, had been the original free spirit.

"Dad was never the same again," she went on. "Then I walked out on him when I was sixteen after a row. I found out last year that he was ill. All those cigarettes he smoked. I went straight to the hospice, but I didn't get there in time."

She didn't know why she had told Tyman all this.

"Similar thing with my mother," he said. "She split with my dad and I blamed her for everything that was wrong in the world. Then she went and got herself killed in some stupid accident, and I…" He stopped, looking choked. "She must have died thinking I hated her."

"A parent is never going to think that," said Lexy.

"Hope you're right."

So did she.

He finished off his wine, watching her. "Anyway, when Dad came over here he started looking around for a place to set up a new rare breeds farm, and, well, here we are."

"Must be hard work."

"We've got people who come and muck out, and do the feeds and so on. But we do a lot of the graft ourselves, and it is tough. Hence the housekeeper, in case you thought we were unbelievably lazy."

"The idea never crossed my mind."

Tyman topped up their glasses again.

"Why do you want to buy the cottage so badly?" Lexy regretted the question as soon as it blurted out of her mouth.

"What do you mean?" Tyman's face had reddened. He took a glance out at the patio, to where his father sat with Steve.

"Just curious, that's all. I mean, were you thinking of buying it to let? To generate a bit more income?"

"We're not exactly strapped for cash. No – we just thought it would be easier if we owned that whole parcel of land."

Parcel of land. Was that how they viewed that beautiful hill?

"So what would you do with the cottage?"

"I dunno. Perhaps Ward or I would take it over."

"You wouldn't knock it down, or anything?"

"Of course not." He stared at her. "Why are you so interested?"

She shrugged.

Tyman's face suddenly cleared. "Don't tell me – you want to buy it yourself? Is that what all these questions are about?"

"No," protested Lexy, half laughing. "I haven't got a penny to my name. Couldn't raise a mortgage if I wanted to."

They regarded one another in silence.

"Who are you, really?" Tyman asked.

"Just who I say I am," Lexy smiled. "A friend of the Patersons."

"What do you do? When you're not looking after cottages for friends, that is."

She hesitated. "This and that. Whatever I can get."

"Woman of mystery, then."

He was closer than he thought.

"You certainly ask a lot of questions," he added.

"So do you."

At that moment Rowana slipped through the French window, Kinky surging ahead of her. She gave Lexy an interrogative look.

Lexy pushed the cat from her lap, giving a small shrug and shake of the head. She was no further forward. Tyman was far too jumpy when the subject of the cottage came up, let alone Elizabeth's death. He had been more forthcoming when they had been speaking alone up at Four Winds.

Rowana unleashed Kinky. He made a beeline for the kitchen, ignoring Lexy. Must have seen her and the cat together. He wouldn't forgive that in a hurry.

"Drink?" Tyman indicated the bottle of wine.

"Can I have a Coke?"

Tyman got up, and Rowana perched next to Lexy.

"Gabrielle and Ward are getting on like a house on fire, unfortunately," she muttered. "Have you managed to find out anything from Tyman?"

"Not yet." Lexy stood up. "I'll go and have a snoop around upstairs. Try to keep him talking for a while."

She slipped out of the door before Rowana could object, and ran lightly up the stairs. There were several varnished oak doors along the landing.

One was slightly ajar. After a quick glance at the stairs behind her, she pushed it half open. It gave a slight creak. Gritting her teeth, Lexy took a look inside the room.

It contained a double bed with a rumpled checked quilt, and built-in wardrobes. Over the back of a wooden chair a pair of jeans and a checked lumberjack shirt had been thrown. Lexy recognised them as the ones Ward had been wearing earlier when he had run into Four Winds Cottage like a madman.

She slipped in, pushed the door to, and went over to a laptop computer by the bed. It had been left on standby. She pressed a couple of buttons, and scrolled through Ward's emails. They were mostly to do with farm business, with a couple of personal ones from friends in France. Nothing about the cottage. She didn't really know what she was looking for. She started to open the top drawer of the desk then pushed it back quickly at the sound of approaching voices.

Someone was coming up the stairs. Bugger. The voices became louder. The door creaked. Lexy did the only thing she could think of and dived under the bed.

A second later the door was pushed wide. She recognised Ward's brown shoes. The other pair belonged to Gabrielle.

"This won't take a moment," she heard Ward say. "I just need to find it."

Lexy heard the sound of cupboards being opened and shut. She just had to hope that whatever he was looking for wasn't under the bed. My, how they'd laugh.

She could feel sweat trickling down her forehead.

Gabrielle's pretty sandalled feet moved around the room, coming to a halt by the window.

"You've got a nice view out over the stables."

"I prefer the view in here."

Ward's shoes moved towards Gabrielle.

Lexy cringed. What a line! It was all the worse for knowing that he had an ulterior motive.

Then she heard Tyman's voice, outside in the hall.

Ward backed away from Gabrielle.

There was a knock on the door. "You in there?"

Ward grunted an affirmative.

Tyman's boots appeared. The brothers didn't believe in taking their footwear off in the house. Lexy thought back to the trail of dried grass and burrs leading to Elizabeth's bedroom.

"Sorry, mate – didn't realise you had company." There was a grin in Tyman's voice. Behind him, the four stout blue legs of the cat appeared.

Lexy almost screamed. Who else was planning on coming in? The Four Horsemen of the Apocalypse?

"Not a problem," replied Ward. "I'm just looking for a book I want to lend Gabrielle."

In spite of her plight, Lexy wondered what on earth it would be. Ward didn't look as if he read chick-lit.

"I seem to have misplaced Lexy," Tyman was saying. "She came up to the bathroom a while ago."

"Well, she's not in here," replied Ward. "Perhaps she decided to give you the slip."

"Yes, well, we wouldn't want that, would we?" said Tyman.

There was a brief pause. Lexy wondered what he meant.

"I doubt she's gone far," said Gabrielle. "Shall we help you find her?"

"No, I'm sure she'll turn up." Tyman's boots withdrew.

"Ah, here we are. *Tom Jones* by Henry Fielding. I knew I had it somewhere," said Ward.

"Big, isn't it?" replied Gabrielle. "Well, I suppose he's led a very interesting life and all that. Can't wait to read it – hope there's lots of scandal."

"I don't think you'll be disappointed."

Ward moved towards her again.

Lexy groaned inwardly. There was a huge dust bunny inches away from her nose and she was terrified of inhaling it and giving vent to an explosive sneeze. She was also starting to feel intensely uncomfortable. She shut her eyes. The thought occurred to her that Ward and Gabrielle might suddenly descend on the bed. There wasn't much room between floor and mattress as it was. With the bed weighed down by those two she wouldn't stand a chance.

To make matters worse, the cat spotted her. It padded over towards the bed, put its head down and peered at her.

"Sod off!" Lexy mouthed, making silent flapping movements at it. It didn't.

"Look at that cat," Gabrielle said. "Looks like he's seen a mouse."

"No mice in this house." Ward paused. "Now, come here a minute."

It was more than a minute. Lexy lay on her side, trying to avoid the unblinking yellow eyes, and the sight of Gabrielle's feet extended on tiptoes. Just as she couldn't take any more, she heard Ward break off with a groan, saying, "Come on, we'd better get back. Don't want Tyman telling everyone he found you in my bedroom." He began walking towards the door.

"God, no." Gabrielle swiftly followed. "My dad would go mental."

Lexy heard their steps recede, and lay back in relief.

"Mind out, pussy cat." She rolled out from under the bed, dusted herself down, and ran back down the stairs.

Everyone was in the living room.

"Ah, here she is!" boomed Bruce. "The amazing disappearing girl. Did you get lost, pet?"

"No." Lexy replied. "Just been trying to find my dog."

"There you go." Bruce gave Tyman a satisfied nod.

"I think he's in the kitchen," said Ward.

"Might have known. Is it OK if I go and…?"

"Just through there." Bruce indicated the way.

Lexy swept into the gleaming kitchen. Kinky was lying in what was obviously the Persian cat's basket, right in front of the range. The bowl beside the basket was empty. Revenge had been sweet.

Lexy hoped he hadn't used the litter tray as well.

"Cheeky little monkey, isn't he?" Mrs Mangeot appeared from another door, wearing a jacket and hat, and carrying a straw bag.

"Can't take him anywhere."

"Well, I'd best be on my way," she said. "Thanks for stepping in earlier."

"No problem. It was a great dinner. Really delicious. Er… Mrs Mangeot?"

"Yes, dear?" The woman was beaming at the praise.

"It was an awful business about Elizabeth, wasn't it?"

"Dreadful day, that was." Mrs Mangeot set her bag on the worktop. "Tyman came rushing down from the cottage, white as a sheet. His dad had just come in from the pigs. Eating his breakfast, he was. I always get their breakfast."

"You must have to get here very early."

"Not too bad. Half eight I get in. Breakfast is always ready at nine. Proper farmer's breakfast, bacon, egg and sausages, because they've all been up and about since six o'clock, tending to the animals."

"But Ward and Tyman were late?"

"That morning, yes." The housekeeper considered. "Tyman had gone up the hill to see to the sheep, but he was usually back in time for breakfast. Ward was checking the animals in the quarantine unit out in the far paddock. He does that every morning. He got back here just before Tyman came bursting in."

"Must have been a shock?"

"Well, he slammed through that door." She pointed to the one Lexy had come through. "Shouting like a lunatic, he was. Scared the living daylights out of me. 'Elizabeth's fallen from her balcony! She's dead!'

"He ran straight over to the phone, saying he couldn't get a signal up at the cottage, and started to call 999, then Ward grabbed him and fairly dragged him into the other room, to make him calm down and explain it properly. He's much more level-headed, Ward. My heart was jumping in my chest. Poor Elizabeth's dead, I kept thinking. It was Mr Gallimore who called the ambulance a couple of minutes later, and then they all jumped in the Land Rover and drove up to the cottage to meet it."

Lexy nodded, trying to take this all in. Bruce had an alibi. He had been eating breakfast when Elizabeth plummeted. Ward appeared to have one, too. Just left Tyman, right on the spot. And whatever he'd done, they had covered it up together. Lexy's face was grim. She'd known from the moment Tyman had spoken to her about the accident, when they'd first met up at the cottage, that he had been holding something back.

Mrs Mangeot was looking quizzically at her. She'd just said something.

"Sorry?"

"I said, was Elizabeth a friend of yours?"

"She was a friend of some friends," Lexy said, pulling herself together. "I'm up at the cottage looking after things."

"Yes, I know, dear. Maureen from the shop told me."

She would have.

"Very special lady, Mrs Cassall was," the housekeeper went on. "Animal lover just like me. I was so upset when the news hit me

I couldn't stop crying for a week. And they haven't even had the decency to release her body yet for burial. All this inquest business. Why it takes so long is beyond me."

"You think it was just an accident?"

"Of course I do. She was never the sort to take her own life, and I'm just as sure no one took it for her, whatever they might be muttering about in the village."

"What are they saying?"

"Some reckon it's something to do with my Gallimores." Mrs Mangeot's already sizeable chest expanded as she drew in an indignant breath. "And I'll tell you exactly what I've told them – there's no nicer, kinder couple of lads than Ward and Tyman, and their dad's as soft as a kitten, despite all his bluff ways. That lot 'ud have trouble putting a blooming hen to sleep, let alone pushing a woman over a balcony."

Lexy tried not to look too slack-jawed at this.

"Anyway, I'd best get on." Mrs Mangeot picked up her bag, and with a smile at Lexy, disappeared through the door.

Lexy's returning smile faded quickly. From what she'd just learned, the Gallimores were in it up to their necks as far as Elizabeth's death was concerned. Was that why they were so desperate to buy the cottage – because of the forensic evidence that might be still in there if the embers of the inquiry were raked up again by some meddling busybody like herself?

Or was it something more obvious they wanted from the cottage – something she'd so far missed? Something was nagging at her. She needed to find out more.

Lexy clicked her tongue, and Kinky scrambled sleepily out of the basket and followed her to the living room.

Steve, Bruce, Gabrielle and Ward were sitting together. Rowana was sequestered in a corner with Tyman. Lexy went straight over to them. Now she suspected that Tyman may have been involved in some kind of cover-up over Elizabeth's death, she didn't want him so much as talking to Rowana. And she was going to do her damnedest to halt this sham romance that his brother had going with Gabrielle.

Tyman and Rowana were looking at a wooden plaque nailed on to a beam. It depicted a devilish face surrounded by leaves and foliage.

"Know what it is?" Tyman was asking her.

"Green Man." Lexy pushed between them.

"Oh – you... er... know about him, do you?" Tyman turned to her, looking disconcerted at her severe face.

"Brought up with the story. He's Jack in the Green, the Lord of the Wild." She glared at him. "The old fertility god that people used to worship before Christianity."

Rowana slipped away.

Tyman, still eyeing Lexy askance, nodded. "When the pagans were forced to build churches on top of their sacred groves, they often used to put an image of the Green Man in the rafters. Just to remind them of the old days." He paused. "There's one down in Nodmore, as a matter of fact."

"Oh, yeah?"

Across the room Gabrielle was chatting about Tom Jones. "It's amazing how his appeal has lasted over generations."

"I'm fascinated by all that pagan stuff," Tyman went on, in lowered tones. "On the last day of August, which is tomorrow, coincidentally, the locals from around here used to get up before dawn and climb to the King Oak on Freshing Hill to gather a last garland of green leaves and bring it down to their homesteads. It was a good luck ritual before winter."

"There's a King Oak on the hill, is there?" Interested in spite of herself, Lexy fingered her silver necklace again.

"Yes – a huge one, about five hundred years old. Must have been planted deliberately, because there are no others of that size and age."

He took a swift look around the room.

"Fancy going up there tomorrow? At dawn?"

13

"You serious?" Lexy was on the verge of scornful laughter.

"Why not?"

She thought quickly. Yes, why not? She wanted to get him somewhere on his own, didn't she? Even though the thought was anathema to her.

"OK."

"What are you two whispering about?" Gabrielle checked her reflection in a mirror as she, Ward and Steve began to move toward them.

"We were talking about the Green Man," said Tyman. "I was telling Lexy about the carving in Nodmore church."

"Green Man?" Steve looked intrigued and Tyman launched into his explanation again.

Lexy saw Gabrielle tug at Ward's sleeve, and they drifted off. Rowana watched them, chewing a fingernail.

"Don't worry." Lexy had said that to Rowana before, the day the girl had first come into her cabin on Clopwolde quay. On balance, Rowana had a great deal more to worry about now than she'd started with. Funny, that.

Lexy exhaled. She wanted to get back and start putting her myriad thoughts in order. Thankfully, Steve was making going home noises.

"Very kind of you to have invited us," he said to Bruce.

"My pleasure." But the look on Bruce's face told Lexy that the words were empty. He hadn't managed to persuade Steve to get Rowana to part with the cottage.

However, Bruce wasn't disgruntled enough to make them walk home.

"Won't hear of it. No trouble to take you back. One of the lads will drive, eh, Ward?"

Gabrielle's prediction had been correct.

Ward nodded and produced a set of keys from his pocket.

Bruce and Tyman accompanied them into the moonlit yard. Tyman drew Lexy to one side.

"See you at quarter to six tomorrow morning. At the back gate of the cottage."

"I'll be there."

Ward stood by the open door of the Land Rover, his deep frown illuminated by the interior light.

Gabrielle dived into the front passenger seat, meaning that Lexy, Steve and Rowana had to squash in the back, being thrown against each other as they sped up the track. Lexy wasn't finding it too much of a problem being thrown against Steve.

Before they knew it, they had been deposited outside Four Winds, and the Land Rover was bouncing back down the track, the headlights wildly illuminating the woods. Lexy wondered if Ward was watching them from the rear view mirror. If so, would he clock the triumphant expression on Gabrielle's face?

"Well, say what you like about them," Gabrielle proclaimed to her father. "I think the Gallimores are really nice. And generous."

"They weren't being generous," snapped Rowana, as they turned to go into the cottage. "They were just showing off how rich they are, with their artichokes and housekeepers."

"Not forgetting the Chablis, and ten quid cigars," said Steve. "They were certainly trying to push the boat out – probably because Bruce is so keen to buy the cottage."

"Good. That means he'll pay over the odds. Did you manage to do a deal, Dad?" Gabrielle asked.

Steve glanced at Rowana.

"I don't want him having it," she said.

"Well, that's bloody ridiculous," said Gabrielle.

"Oi – language," said Steve.

"After four hours of Bruce Gallimore effing and blinding, you're having a go at me for one word?"

They went into the kitchen.

Lexy switched on the kettle. "Tea, anyone?"

"I'll have a coffee," said Gabrielle. "Two sugars."

"Coming right up." Over her head if she wasn't careful.

"It's just that I feel attached to this place somehow," Rowana said, as if trying to soften her earlier words. "Almost as if I don't want it to go out of the family. I certainly don't want it going to the Gallimores."

Steve looked stricken. "Sweetheart, I really like it here, too." He paused, looking around. "In fact, I love it. But we – you've – got to sell. We've got no choice. Not if you… we… want a new cake business."

Rowana sighed. "I know. But not to them."

"What is your problem?" snapped Gabrielle.

"Listen," said Steve, "I feel the same about not wanting Bruce Gallimore to get his hands on it. I reckon he's got some plan or other for this hill. But being practical, he will give us a good price for it."

"No! I'm never going to sell it to him. I don't even want to talk about it." Rowana left the kitchen abruptly.

"I'm off, too," said Gabrielle, stirring the coffee that Lexy had silently placed on the table. "But I'm not sleeping in Elizabeth's room where she… Rowana… wait…" She followed her sister, slopping coffee.

"Look, I'm going to nip along to bed, too," said Lexy. With the Patersons suddenly moving in, it all felt rather awkward, like she was a house guest who had overstayed her welcome.

Steve pushed back his shock of hair. "Stay a minute."

She looked at the kitchen clock. She had to be up soon. In five hours, to be precise.

"OK. I'll just finish my tea." She sat opposite him. Raised voices came from upstairs.

He rolled his eyes. "What would you do?"

"What? About the cottage?"

"Yup."

Lexy thought for a moment. "I'd leave it to Rowana to decide.

She's quite a sensible kid." Apart from an unfortunate habit of dabbling in the occult.

"I knew you'd say that."

"So why'd you ask?"

"Perhaps I still needed to hear it."

Kinky whined and raked Lexy's knee softly.

"You knew Elizabeth, didn't you?" Lexy asked.

"I think you've already guessed the answer to that."

Lexy's heart started thumping.

"I knew her a long time ago." Steve's voice was low, eyes automatically reaching to the ceiling, the bedroom where the girls were.

Lexy dropped her voice too. "So why tell everyone, including your daughters, that you'd never met?"

"It was a complicated situation. I met Elizabeth through Jackie. Then Jackie and I had a… kind of parting of the ways with her. I mean, I haven't seen her since Jackie died. Elizabeth never told us she'd left everything to Jackie in her will, let alone that it would go to Rowana if Jackie died."

"So you haven't seen Elizabeth since 1990?"

"No. Why d'you ask?"

Lexy chewed her lip. She reached in her pocket and pulled out the photo of the three Patersons, and handed it to him.

"Where did you get this?"

"It was in the piano stool." She jerked her head towards the living room.

"The piano stool." His lips twisted.

"Along with this other photo." She found the one of Elizabeth in her bag. Steve took it, looked at it for a second and put it down, his eyes averted. He placed the other one on top.

"The date on that photo of you three is last year," said Lexy. "Do you think Elizabeth took it?"

He looked at it again. "Could have done. Poor Elizabeth. I didn't realise…"

"Realise what?" Lexy knew she was pushing it. Steve's face tightened.

"Like I said, it's… complicated. Elizabeth did Jackie a big favour. And Jackie did Elizabeth one back."

Mutual favour between the two women?

"Anyway, it's all in the past now, and I want to leave it there." Steve softened this with a smile. "And enjoy the present."

Kinky gave a louder whine, and a more painful scrape down Lexy's shin.

"Jesus."

"Probably wants his bone back." Steve jerked his head at the sink, where the knuckle bone had landed and still lay.

"That was quite some shot of yours."

"Not bad, huh?"

They both started laughing, faces leaning in together.

Steve took hold of Lexy's hand and their eyes locked for a moment.

Kinky gave another insistent yelp.

Gritting her teeth, Lexy took her hand back, pushed herself up and replaced the photos in her pocket. "Look, Steve, I'm going to have to hit the sack." Before she did something she might regret.

She was aware of his dark blue eyes on her as she shook out half a packet of Doggy Chomps for Kinky.

"Want me to lose that bone?" he asked.

"It did seem to bring out the worst in Kinky. But what're you going to do? Bury it?"

"Funny girl. I'll sling it over the cliff tomorrow."

"Good idea. Thanks. Just make sure there's no one down below."

She shot him a quick smile, then dived out of the kitchen, shepherding Kinky before her.

"Blimey, that was a close one, pal," she muttered. "I nearly jumped on him. Don't know what came over me." The dog gave her a reproving look. "It's not like I need any more complications in my life right now." Fanning herself, Lexy nipped upstairs to the bathroom.

On the landing, she could hear muffled voices. Gabrielle and Rowana were still up. They had obviously decided to share the guest bedroom.

"Well, you seemed to enjoy the evening." Rowana sounded resentful.

"Oh, yes. Especially certain parts of it," Gabrielle purred.

"Which parts?"

Lexy was only too aware of which parts.

"Ah, that would be telling." Gabrielle's voice lowered.

Lexy found herself creeping along the landing.

"Which you clearly want to do."

"All right. The part I spent in Ward's bedroom."

"Gabby!"

"It's OK. I didn't go that far. But I think he likes me."

"But surely you're not serious about him? I mean, for a start he's so old. He's got to be thirty."

Lexy rolled her eyes. Cheers, Rowana.

"So what? I like older men." The bed creaked. "If I can't have Russell, I can at least console myself with someone else. And you can't tell me that Ward isn't a good catch."

"What do you mean?"

"I mean I wouldn't mind being a farmer's wife."

"Gabrielle, you're mental! You only met him today. You can't be thinking of marrying him already."

"Why not?"

"Well, he's…" Rowana spluttered. "I mean, you hardly know him. He might have… bad habits."

Gabrielle broke into giggles. "What do you mean? You're not jealous, are you?"

"No!"

"I was hoping you might have got chatting to Tyman, but the squatter got her claws into him first."

"Squatter?"

"Her with the tattoo. Our unwelcome guest."

Bit harsh.

"Actually, she's really nice, she's a friend of Elizabeth, and she's got every right to be here, in my cottage."

That was more like it.

"Your cottage. I was wondering when you'd bring that up. OK, Rowana, you're the one who got lucky with the will. But that's not going to stop me making my own luck."

"What – by marrying a rich bloke? If you want money, why don't you earn some yourself?"

"Listen to you."

"Hey – I didn't want this cottage, or Elizabeth's money. We might have been desperate, but we would have survived."

"I don't just want to survive. I want to have fun. Not spend the rest of my life icing other people's wedding cakes."

"So, your game plan is to marry the first man that comes along with a bit of money. No matter whether you love him or not?"

There was a silence.

Gabrielle's voice trembled now. "I'm no good at anything, Rowana. You know that. Apart from icing cakes. And I hate cakes. It's all right for you, you're good at other stuff, like painting."

"Try something," came Rowana's voice. "You never know."

"Like what?"

"I dunno. You're pretty good at making clothes, when you can be bothered."

"Big deal."

"Don't knock it. You heard what Lexy said about your sarong."

Gabrielle seemed to consider this. "I suppose she must have been telling the truth, because... she's got no reason to like me."

It was a good point, well made.

Lexy heard a creak from the stair. She scuttled back to the bathroom, and dived in, shutting the door behind her and locking it.

Then she turned around.

Steve was already in there, unbuttoning his shirt.

"Hello," he said.

"Ah – sorry." Lexy dragged the bolt back, trapping her finger. "I forgot something. I'll pop back later. When you're done. Sorry."

She darted out, then trod more slowly down the stairs, clutching her bruised digit. She waited in the hall until she heard Steve leave the bathroom, then crept back up. It was warm and steamy from the shower. She ran it hot herself and stepped under, trying not to think about him in his open shirt. With his flat stomach.

What she really ought to be doing was running the damned shower cold.

Lexy set her alarm clock for five-thirty, put it under her pillow and clicked the table lamp off. Kinky was already asleep, curled up at the end of the sofa, so she couldn't stretch her legs out. She lay awake in the darkness.

Only four and a half hours until she had to get up.

After what seemed more like four and a half minutes the muffled alarm woke her. Lexy snapped it off. Every part of her was shouting 'bad idea', and the temptation to stand Tyman up was almost overwhelming. But she had a duty to seize every opportunity she could to discover what had happened to Elizabeth, not least because she didn't want to consider the prospect that Steve had something to do with it. She slid out of her sleeping bag.

Kinky grumbled through the darkness.

"You stay there, pal," she whispered. "I won't be long."

Ten minutes later she was dressed. She quietly unlocked the kitchen door, and made her way out through a chilly pre-dawn mist across the lawn to the back gate.

It would probably be Tyman standing her up, she thought. But when the gate came in sight, he was waiting silently beside it.

In the half-light Lexy could make out that he was wearing a green camouflage jacket. He was carrying something over his back in a long holder. A telescope?

He held open the gate. "Morning."

"Morning." It went against the grain to be friendly to him, but she had to try. "Are we going spotting?"

He patted the holder. "Well, you never know what you might see." He touched her arm. "I wasn't sure whether you'd turn up."

"I always keep my word."

"That's good to know."

"So, what do we do?" Lexy rubbed her arms. She was only wearing her denim jacket over a t-shirt and it was freezing. If she'd had any sense she'd have packed a jumper. No – if she'd had any sense, she would have turned Rowana Paterson down flat at that first meeting. Then, instead of standing here, she'd be safe in her bed in her fisherman's cabin at Clopwolde quay.

Then she remembered Gerard.

She couldn't win.

"We go up the hill to the King Oak at the top of this main path and gather in the last green leaves."

"Right, the King Oak it is," Lexy said, taking a step forward.

Tyman took her arm. "The villagers always used to race up there."

"You didn't tell me that before."

"Didn't want to put you off."

What did he think – she was some sort of out of shape townie? "You haven't."

"OK. I'll give you a one minute start."

Lexy was tempted to say she didn't need it. But the footpath was only just visible, and he knew the terrain a lot better than she did.

He let go of her arm.

"Right. Go!"

Lexy hared up the path, pushing her way through the overgrown bracken. He'd never catch her – not weighed down by the jacket and that 'scope.

But it seemed like only seconds had passed before she heard

him pounding along the path behind her.

For a moment Lexy couldn't believe it. How had he got there so fast? Was he superhuman? Her legs suddenly felt almost too weak to support her. Then she realised that she was right back inside that nightmare of hers again. Except this time it was for real. And her pursuer was no longer faceless.

He was going to catch her. The blood roared in her head as she struggled on. He was almost on top of her.

Lexy opened her mouth to let out a shriek, but his hand clapped straight over it, cutting off the noise, and she was yanked off the path into the wood, half-carried, half-dragged over a fallen tree trunk, then forced to the ground.

He lay behind her, pinning her against the tree trunk, his hand still over her mouth.

Lexy struggled wildly.

"Sssh," he hissed, gripping her free arm which was flailing uselessly, and locking his leg over hers.

Effectively overpowered, Lexy lay still, her heart crashing against her ribs. What a complete, naïve, sodding idiot she was. She should have known something like this was going to happen. This was Tyman's way of sorting out the problem she posed. He was going to quietly dispatch her and then bury her in the woods.

He pushed Lexy over on to her back. She recoiled in shock.

It wasn't Tyman.

14

It was Ward.

Her first thought was that the two them must have planned this together and she'd walked straight into it. Run straight into it, actually. Ward really was going to deal with her this time.

She gave one last, violent jerk, using all the strength she had left.

He cursed and rolled back, releasing her.

"What the f… ?" she spluttered.

"Sssh," he murmured, placing a warning hand on her arm. Moments later they heard the sound of running feet. Tyman was yelling for Lexy. He sounded almost panic-stricken.

Lexy stared at Ward. Somehow, the expression in his eyes stopped her shouting out.

Tyman's voice receded into the distance.

"Is this some kind of stupid bloody game with you two?"

Ward shook his head.

"What, then?"

Ward made a hand sign, so slight that Lexy almost missed it. He'd crossed himself.

"He can't be trusted."

Lexy remembered Bruce's words outside the pub. *Any road, keep Tyman away from her. You know what he's like.*

"How do you mean, can't be trusted?" she demanded.

"I'm just saying it's best you stay away from him."

"What's he going to do, then?"

Ward's mouth set. "He can be… unpredictable. He's a bit unbalanced."

"Tyman's unbalanced?" she almost shouted. "What does that make you?"

"I know how this looks," he said.

"I don't think you do."

Ward squinted through the trees, now silvered with dawn light, and got up. He grabbed Lexy's wrist, heaving her unceremoniously up beside him. "Come on – I'm taking you back to Four Winds."

"Oi!" She jerked her hand away from him. "I only came up here with your brother because I wanted to talk to him."

"What about?"

She was too furious to be evasive. "Elizabeth Cassall. And her accident."

Instantly, his eyes became guarded. "What's that got to do with Tyman?"

"That's what I want to know."

Ward grasped her shoulders. "Listen – we don't know who you are, or what you're doing at the cottage, but you ask a lot of questions. Too many. Do yourself a favour – leave it alone."

"Or what? I get pushed over an upstairs balcony?"

He dropped his hands. "Is that what you think happened to Elizabeth? That Tyman shoved her out?"

"Well, did he?"

"Of course not, idiot. She fell by accident."

"Like your mother fell off a high wire by accident?"

She thought he was going to hit her. "Who told you about that?"

"Tyman, actually."

Ward's mouth set. "So, you know the truth, in that case."

"I only know what he told me."

Ward took another look around and grabbed her arm. "Come on. Enough said. I'm getting you out of here."

She tried to shake him off. "I don't need an escort."

"No? Well, you're getting one. Move it." He gave her a little push and she stumbled.

She turned and squared up to him.

"Just do it, will you, or I swear I'll carry you down there over

160

my shoulder." He gave another quick glance behind.

Lexy stared at him incredulously. He made a move towards her.

"All right, all right – I'm going. God." She set off swiftly down the path, unable to believe the colossal nerve of the bloke.

In the distance they heard Tyman give another shout.

Lexy glanced back. "Sure you're not just jealous of little brother?"

"Just go!"

Lexy found herself jogging down the hill with Ward at her heels like a camel herder.

"Sounds like he's in a right state."

"Good," muttered Ward. "He deserves to be."

"So I'm meant to thank you for this, am I? What was he going to do, anyway?"

He hesitated before answering. "Like I said, he's unpredictable."

"So you've had trouble with him before? Him and women?"

The grey stone walls of Four Winds came into sight, tinged with rose from the sunrise.

Ward was silent. They slowed to a walk.

"You can't protect him forever." Lexy bent forward to relieve a stitch. "And if he so much as looks at Rowana again, I'm straight on to the police."

She strode across the lawn to the kitchen door without turning, aware all the same of him standing there waiting until she was inside.

"Bastard. Couple of bastards."

Lexy examined the bruises she had acquired when Ward had bundled her over the fallen tree. She turned at the clicking of claws on linoleum.

"Kinkster." She knelt down to stroke him. "I've been taken for a ride." A rough one, perhaps, if Ward hadn't intervened. Tyman obviously had only one thing on his mind, and it hadn't been collecting green leaves from the King Oak.

Lexy pulled a face. Even after all Ward had said, it was still hard to believe. Tyman just wasn't the type. But as she had this thought, she imagined Milo admonishing her. *Believe me, there isn't a type.*

She supposed she ought to feel lucky that Ward had been on hand. Had he overheard the whispered arrangement she and Tyman had made the previous night, and decided to follow his brother? It struck Lexy that it was the second time Ward Gallimore had acted as her protector. First the escaped bull, now this. The joke was, he'd been the one threatening to deal with her. The hard way.

Then in another twist, she had Mrs Mangeot ready to swear blind that the Gallimores were shining examples of humanity incapable of harming a fly.

Lexy rubbed her chin. Ward made the sign of the cross before he'd accused his brother. Some kind of Catholic protection against lies, like crossing fingers. She snorted. Sex didn't come into it. He'd been keeping her away from Tyman for an entirely different reason. It all came back to Elizabeth's fall. Tyman knew something, and Ward was very concerned he was going to spill the beans.

"Blimey, what happened to you?" Lexy hadn't heard the kitchen door open. Rowana stood there wide-eyed, in blue pyjamas, looking about twelve years old.

"Don't ask," said Lexy, pushing herself up and making for the kettle.

"You're all damp. And you're scratched and bleeding."

"Yeah. Kinky's a demanding dog to walk."

"You didn't take Kinky. You were with Tyman."

Lexy spun around.

"I saw you meet him at the gate this morning at ten to six."

Lexy shrugged. "What can I say? What were you doing up, anyway?"

"I couldn't sleep. I heard a noise, so I got up to look out of the window." She eyed Lexy. "What were you doing?"

"Old pagan custom," said Lexy.

"Oh, yes?" Rowana looked disapproving.

"No. Straight up. It really was. Bringing in the last of the summer's green leaves. You have to do it at dawn on the eve of September."

"I saw you run off, then he ran after you."

"That's part of the tradition, according to Tyman."

Lexy went to the larder and tore open a packet of Doggy Chomps for Kinky. The smell made her feel queasy, and she realised that the events on the hill that morning had shaken her up more than she thought.

"Thing is, I went because I thought that if we were on our own he might open up about Elizabeth."

"And?"

Lexy shook the chunks into a dish, grimacing.

"He didn't."

Rowana pulled a face. "Things are pretty bad on the Gabrielle front. I reckon she's losing her marbles. She's now decided she's going to marry Ward."

Lexy just stopped herself from saying "I know."

"Can you believe it? She hasn't even... you know... done it... with him yet."

"Rowana, I doubt that Ward Gallimore has the least intention of marrying your sister, whether or not they do it first."

"You don't know how determined she is."

Any further conversation with Rowana was curtailed by Steve coming into the kitchen in overalls.

"Morning, sweetheart." That was for Rowana. He gave Lexy a searching look as he took in her appearance. "You all right?"

"Fine. Just look a bit of a mess. I went for a walk earlier and tripped over. I'll... er... go and clean up." She brushed past him out of the kitchen and escaped to the bathroom.

When she came back down, her hair washed, towelled dry and sticking up all over, Gabrielle appeared and began banging cups and saucers around.

"What's the matter with her?" Steve mouthed.

Rowana shrugged and sloped out of the kitchen, her face preoccupied.

A buzz came from Lexy's bag. Her phone. The elusive signal was back. Quickly she checked her message box. There was a text from Milo.

Need to see u

She tapped a message back.

Still at 4 Winds.

The reply came straight back.

B there 10 mins

Now what? At least he was still talking to her. Lexy downed a cup of tea and went to wait by the gate. Milo's white estate appeared promptly. He leaned over and held the passenger door open.

"Want to get in?"

"You sound serious. Where are we going? Down the station?" Lexy clicked to Kinky, and he scrambled through to the back seat.

"Away from here." Milo looked over at the van. "Are the Patersons still around?"

"Yup. They've decided to stay for a couple of days."

"Cramping your style a bit?"

"No – it's nice having the company." If a little dramatic.

They bumped down the track through the sunlit trees.

"What's up, then?" Lexy asked.

Milo shot her a look. "Your husband. He got drunk last night in the Jolly Herring and started asking about you."

"Oh, crap." Lexy wound her window down. She still felt queasy and the thought of Gerard wasn't helping. "So it's not just coincidence he's in Clopwolde."

"Apparently not."

"Anyone let the cat out of the bag?"

"Nope. It was just Lonny and his mates down there. He called me. Gerard was offering large sums of money to anyone who could tell him where you were."

164

"That's not good. What happened?"

"I went down there and warned him off."

"No!"

"Yes. First he tried to bribe me, then he threatened me. Obnoxious pillock. I was one centimetre away from arresting him." He turned his cool grey stare on Lexy. "How did you put up with it for all those years?"

She looked away. "It wasn't as bad at first. He was OK when things were going well and he had lots of TV work. Then the booze and coke kicked in. I told you the rest yesterday. It's not easy trying to get away from someone like that."

"I wonder how he tracked you down?"

"Probably got a private investigator on the job." Lexy's mouth twisted. "Don't know why I tried to kid myself I could ever hide from him, anyway."

Milo slowed. They were approaching the driveway leading from Pilgrim's Farm. The Gallimores' Land Rover was blocking the path.

He drew to a halt behind it. Bruce, who hadn't even noticed them pull up, was leaning out of the window yelling to Ward, who was in the adjacent field. Lexy sank down in her seat.

"… and remember to lock up that Old Spot boar, or we'll be up to our tits in swine again. Talking about infatuated males, where the 'ell is Tyman?"

"No idea. Haven't seen him today."

Lexy couldn't help snorting.

"Well when you do, tell him to get that other matter sorted out, once and for all – and I don't care how he does it. D'you hear?"

"I imagine the whole county can hear."

Milo turned quizzically to Lexy. She held up a hand. She wanted to see whether Bruce expanded on 'that other matter'.

He didn't. He started the Land Rover, and shot off down the track, without so much as a glance in his rear view mirror.

Milo let the clutch out, and Ward looked up.

"Dare I ask what you're doing in the footwell?" Milo touched the brake again.

"Dropped my phone. Keep driving."

"Not hiding from the Gallimores then?" The car rolled along the track and Lexy watched Milo make a curt nod in Ward's direction.

"How was dinner last night, by the way?" he said.

"Look, I'm sorry about that. The only reason I accepted the invite was because I wanted to do some more digging. I wanted to find out where they all were at nine o'clock on the morning Elizabeth died."

"And did you?"

Lexy struggled back up on the seat. "Yes – as a matter of fact. I spoke to their housekeeper, and she said that Bruce was having breakfast at the time, and Ward had been checking their quarantine area out the back of the farm."

"Quarantine area?" Milo frowned. "Suppose they must import animals." He touched his indicator and turned into the lane. "So only Tyman was on the scene."

Lexy nodded. "Seems that way."

"Think he did it?"

"I think he knows something. I think they all do, actually. Tyman's very tense about it. I was going to tackle him about it earlier this morning."

Milo raised his eyebrows. "How early?"

"We'd arranged to walk up the hill."

"I see. And?"

"We got parted and I ran into Ward." That was one way of putting it. "He was trying to convince me that Tyman was mad, bad and dangerous to know. But I got the impression that he was using that as an excuse to put me off any further contact with him, in case he gives something away."

"You mean, if there's something dodgy about Elizabeth's fall, something to do with the three of them, he's the one most likely to break down and confess?"

She nodded. "Think he's quite vulnerable. Last night we got

talking about his mother, and the accident on the high wire."

"Oh, yes? What was his version of events?"

Lexy thought back. "He never said," she admitted. "He got me talking about my mother instead."

"Good at diversionary tactics, then."

"And I went right along with it."

"Never mind – you're not the first investigator to get caught like that."

"Next time I'll have to apply the thumbscrews."

"Always works for me."

"Where are we going, anyway?"

"Thought we'd grab a coffee from the machine in that shop in the village."

The currant-eyed woman looked up with sharp interest as they came in. While Milo worked the coffee machine, Lexy approached the counter.

"Hi, there."

"Hello, luvver. Still 'ere, then, are you?"

No, this is a cardboard cut-out. Lexy forced a smile. "It's taking a while to sort out."

"Met them neighbours of yours down the farm yet?"

"What – the Gallimores? Yes." Had she ever.

"Made an offer for the cottage yet, 'ave they? Some of us 'ere reckon it was pretty convenient for them Gallimores, Elizabeth 'aving that accident."

Milo came up behind them.

"Two coffees, thanks. And a *Guardian*."

The electronic till warbled. "There you are, sir." Maureen handed Milo his newspaper and change. As they left the shop, her sideways glance at Lexy seemed to say "You mark my words."

Lexy felt dazed. How the hell did she know?

"What was she on about?" Milo glanced over at Lexy as she buckled her seat belt.

"She knew the Gallimores have been trying to buy Four Winds Cottage."

Milo frowned. "You haven't been saying anything, have you?"

"Well – duh. I've hardly been broadcasting it."

"Perhaps someone overheard them talking to Steve in the pub."

He drove to a car park that overlooked the shingle beach.

"Go on down," Milo said. "I'll be there in a sec. Just got a call to make."

Lexy and Kinky went down the steps to the beach. Kinky ran ahead, clearly delighted to be somewhere that wasn't Four Winds Cottage.

Lexy stared out to sea, her eyes a narrow slit as she thought about Gerard. How had she put up with him for all those years? The womanising, the fragile ego, the alcohol... Lexy could almost smell the alcohol again.

She was suddenly aware of someone descending the steps behind her, whisky-laden breath preceding him on the breeze.

Lexy turned sharply. It was Archer Trevino. He bowed extravagantly as he passed, and gave her the full force of those wicked black eyes.

He would have been very attractive once, Lexy thought, watching him walk slowly along the beach, smoke unfurling from the cigarette clamped between his teeth. He stopped once and coughed.

"The tortured artist," Milo murmured, coming lightly down the steps.

"Wonder why he took to daytime tippling?" Lexy perched on the concrete sea wall behind them, untwisted a roll of sugar into her coffee and stirred it in with a wooden spoon. "Speaking of which, what am I going to do about Gerard?"

Milo propped his lanky frame beside her. "I'm wondering if the best thing is to face up to him."

Lexy shook her head. "You don't know him."

"I can be there."

"Thanks, Milo. But you can't always be there. I honestly think it'll be best if I stay put until the antiques fair is over."

"And hope no one succumbs to the reward he's offering for information."

"None of the Clopwolde quay lot know I'm here."

"Word travels."

"Thanks. How much is he offering, anyway?"

"Five hundred."

"Huh! Thought I was worth more than that."

"Pretty tempting, even so, for anyone with no scruples."

He dropped her back at Four Winds at midday. The sun was illuminating the hill, and Lexy leaned back against the warm, rough wall of the cottage, shutting her eyes. She didn't like it that Milo was getting dragged into her messy marriage situation. What if he ended up arresting Gerard? The whole complicated story about the stolen money might have to come out.

A high hammering sound penetrated her thoughts. It was coming from the shed, and was accompanied by whistling. She smiled to herself. The sound of a man happy in his work.

Kinky, on the other hand, had assumed his usual Four Winds demeanour, and was slowly circling the garden, tail down, nose to the ground. Every now and then he looked over at her anxiously, as if to check she was still there. It occurred to Lexy that the chihuahua had rarely let her out of his sight when they'd been at the cottage, except when she went up the hill that morning. "Shame you weren't with me then, mate," she murmured. "You would have given both those Gallimore brothers a run for their money."

She squinted. Something was glinting in the sun. Shading her eyes with her hands, Lexy looked towards Pilgrim's Farm. Someone down there had the binoculars out again! Lexy's face set. Right. Two could play at that game.

She swung round to the back garden, and through the open kitchen door. Gabrielle was still there, sitting at the table with a glass of water in front of her. She looked unusually serious, as if she had been doing some unaccustomed deep thinking.

"Hi," said Lexy, striding past her. "How's it going?"

"No, thanks," the girl murmured.

Rolling her eyes, Lexy went up to Elizabeth's room, which Steve appeared to be occupying now, given the jeans, spanner, screwdriver and tape measure on the bed. A book lay open on the pillow. Lexy glanced at it. *Miller's Antiques and Collectibles.* Bit of light bedtime reading.

She took up the binoculars, and focused on the farm. It was Tyman. She could just about make him out, his sights fixed on Four Winds Cottage. As she watched, muttering under her breath, she saw him lower them and walk across the yard. Moments later Ward appeared and Tyman handed him the binoculars. He got into the Land Rover, and began to back it out. Were they watching the cottage in shifts? And what was Tyman up to now?

Following a sudden impulse, Lexy clicked her tongue at Kinky, who had followed her up there, sped down the stairs, grabbed her jacket and bag and made for her car.

Steve was walking awkwardly across the lawn carrying a car bonnet. "You off somewhere?"

"Yup. Just remembered something I need to do." Lexy yanked open the car door.

"Something important, by the looks of it."

"Not really. Just need to get my post from back home."

She bundled Kinky unceremoniously into the car, and accelerated off, giving Steve a wave.

He waved back, watching her leave, smudges of oil on his cheeks and forehead.

Tyman had left only a few minutes ago. She ought to be able to catch him up. He might be going on a perfectly innocent trip to the shops. But it was there just the same. The feeling that he might be driving to some destination that would give her that vital clue, the one she needed to figure out why the Gallimores were acting like Four Winds Cottage was a time bomb.

The Panda jolted down the hill, Kinky bouncing balefully around on the passenger seat.

Lexy caught up with the Land Rover on the outskirts of Clopwolde village. She hung back, aware that the lime green car wasn't exactly inconspicuous. She also felt extremely reluctant to get too close to the place. The antiques fair would be in full flow that day, and Clopwolde wasn't big. If someone local had decided to take Gerard's bribe money, it would be an easy thing to let him know that the girl with the chihuahua was at large.

However, Tyman turned up a road that led to an out-of-town supermarket. He was going shopping after all. Typical.

Nevertheless, she decided to wait and see where he went next.

Lexy watched him drive into the car park, gave him a minute, then drove up there herself, pulling up behind an ostentatious, gas-guzzling 4x4 BMW.

She got out and watched him go in, then took her phone from her bag and checked the messages. There was a voicemail from Edward.

'Come and rescue me, sweetie, for pity's sake. I can't take much more of this antiques debacle. Peter's being unbearable. Your kittens are darling, by the way, thank you very much for asking. Now – call me before I have a hissy fit'.

"Oh, crap."

Lexy pressed a couple of buttons. She was taken straight to Edward's voicemail.

"Hi. Really sorry I haven't been in touch. Things got a bit complicated here. I'll come over this afternoon."

She flipped the phone shut, and leaned against the Panda, closing her eyes. No wonder Edward sounded aggrieved. She hadn't given one thought to poor Princess and her kittens in the last couple of days. Although it could be argued that she'd had a lot on her plate. Nevertheless, it was still inexcusable, when her friend was putting up the whole feline dynasty for free in his best wardrobe. She'd better get him a peace offering. Something in chocolate. And perhaps some...

"Well, well, well."

Lexy's eyes snapped open.

"What have you done to yourself, Mrs Warwick-Holmes?"

Her arm was twisted painfully, almost forcing her to her knees.

His face was pouchy under the spray tan, the pale blue eyes bloodshot. She could smell last night's brandy on his breath, mixed with the pungent scent of aftershave and hair gel.

"I see you haven't changed," she gasped through the pain. She could hear Kinky's savage growls through the closed car window.

He released her arm with a jerk and stood back, looking her up and down. "Classy look you've got there, Alexandra. Really classy."

"Ta. Wish I could say the same for you."

"Got any other tattoos hidden away? Butterfly on the ankle, perhaps? Or perhaps you've gone for a tastefully pierced navel?" He grabbed at her t-shirt.

Her knee jerked up, just like mother had taught her when she was a kid, and Gerard Warwick-Holmes doubled over.

Lexy jumped into the Panda, locked it, and rolled the window down an inch, waiting for her husband to recover.

"I want a divorce," she said.

His face loomed at the window, eyes watering. "No chance. Never. Now, where's my money, you bitch?"

"Er... let's think. Are we talking about the money you got for selling that lost Lowry on the black market? The one you found in an old man's loft when you were doing a clearance sale after he died?"

"Where's your problem? The daft old bastard didn't know he had a Lowry. And the private buyer was more than happy to pay cash. Win-win, I'd say."

"Not exactly. If you care to remember, in his will Mr Gillespie left all the proceeds from his clearance sale to charity."

Gerard gave a shout of laughter. "What – did you seriously think I'd donate half a million quid to saving the bloody whale or something?"

"No. I knew you wouldn't," said Lexy. "So I did it instead."

His eyes narrowed.

"I made an anonymous donation to a local bird reserve."

"Please tell me you're joking." His fingers pressed down on the top of the window.

"Well, I can't show you a receipt, or anything, but if you pop along there, you'll be able to see that a big project is now going on to preserve one of the last remaining breeding habitats of the Costello's warbler in Britain. And between us, it's all thanks to you."

Gerard spluttered.

"Oh, and the good news is that two pairs successfully nested there this year."

"You crazy… do you know what you've done?"

"That man trusted you with his property, Gerard. You betrayed him. I just put it right."

"So what does that make you – a bloody saint?"

"Hardly. But at least I'm trying."

Lexy let him force the window down another inch before she started rolling it back up. He snatched his fingers away at the last moment.

"You're going to pay for this," he howled.

"I've got a fiver here – will that do?" She was stupid to provoke him.

He strode to the BMW, opened the back, and got out a long-handled wrench.

Lexy fumbled with the ignition key.

"Open up," he bellowed. "That's stolen property you've got in there."

"I just told you what I did with the money," Lexy yelled back. The engine made a choking sound. "Not that it was yours anyway, which was the whole point, in case you'd forgotten."

"The dog's mine, though." Gerard's face exuded triumph. "He belonged to my mother. She left him to me when she died."

"You didn't want him!" Lexy turned the key again, her throat dry. The car shuddered into life.

Her husband swung the wrench back. "Well, guess what? I do now. You going to open this door?"

"What do you think?" She fought with the gear stick.

The Panda's windscreen shattered like pond ice, covering Lexy and Kinky with glass. "In the back," she shouted, and the dog skedaddled between the two front seats.

Lexy finally yanked the gear into reverse and floored the accelerator. She skidded backwards across the car park. He ran after her. She threw it into a forward gear – first or third, impossible to tell – punched out some of the glass, and hacked down the lane, engine screaming.

Minutes later, Lexy came to a halt up a quiet side street.

"You OK, boy?"

She twisted round, and Kinky stared up at her from the rear footwell, still decorated with lumps of toughened glass.

She pulled him up and brushed it off, then got out. A lapful of glass cascaded across the road.

Lexy surveyed her windscreen and swore. She began punching the remaining glass out.

"Want a hand?"

A woman had come out of the house opposite. A practical-looking woman with sensible grey hair, a broom and a pair of gloves.

Lexy let her do it.

"What happened?"

My husband smashed it with a wrench. "A stone, flung up by a lorry, out on the main road. I stopped as soon as I could."

"Happened to me once." The woman leant on her broom. "On holiday in France. Gives you a real shake up, doesn't it?"

Lexy nodded.

"You insured?"

Lexy gave her wry smile. "I'll sort it later. At least I can see to drive now."

"It's a bit dangerous like that, love."

"I've only got to go down the road."

"I couldn't get all the glass out, but I think I got most of it."

"Thanks," Lexy got into the freshly swept driver's seat.

"Don't forget your dog."

"Oh, yeah." Lexy quelled a hysterical laugh as she leant over and opened the passenger door.

"Want me to lift him in? Doesn't bite, does he?"

Kinky looked like he was in shock. The woman placed him on the passenger seat, and Lexy drove slowly off.

She hesitated at the end of the road, looking in each direction for a black BMW.

Tyman Gallimore and his Land Rover had gone right out of her mind. She knew where she was heading.

"Sweetie, is it honestly worth getting the thing fixed?" Edward surveyed the Panda dubiously.

"Well, on the up side, it still goes," said Lexy. Just. "And I really need to get back to Nodmore."

"Why?"

"Well, you know – this job I've got going on."

"You ought to join the AA." Peter, immaculately dressed as ever, came down the front steps with a tray of tea.

"Yeah, I know. I will."

"No, you won't," said Edward.

Lexy kicked the Panda's balding front tyre.

Edward sighed. "Are you OK, sweetheart? I sense you're a little tense. Has someone been upsetting you?"

You could say that. "No – not at all."

"Well, aren't you the lucky one?" Edward's lips pursed.

"I have apologised a thousand times," said Peter.

Edward ignored him. "I'll go and ring my little man at the garage about this windscreen. At least one can depend on him." He headed for the huge studded wooden front door. "Come along, Kinky. We'll find you a nice biscuit."

The chihuahua's drooping tail flipped up and he trotted after Edward.

175

"What did you do?" Lexy asked Peter.

"Oh – it's this antiques fair. Causing ructions. Last night I had to cancel a big dinner date I had with Edward and assorted friends." He grimaced in the direction of the house. "Didn't go down too well. Thing is, I was asked to stand in for a friend who was ill. I mean, what can one do? And then this morning I had to get up at the crack of dawn to cover for bloody Gerard again. Can you believe it?"

Lexy flinched. "Gerard?"

"You know. Warwick-Holmes. *Heirlooms in the Attic.* Meant to be hosting the show – introducing the talks, doing fundraising auctions, that sort of thing, but he keeps going AWOL. His mind obviously isn't on it. The Committee are going to contest his fee. Well, you can't blame them – he's broken the terms of his contract. Personally, I think it's the old… " He did a drinking charade. "Whatever it is, he seems to have his own agenda here."

Ain't that the truth?

Peter laughed. "Nearly got himself arrested last night down the Jolly Herring, while I was trying to have a quiet drink. By that nice, tall policeman of yours, funnily enough."

Lexy tried to look surprised. "He's not my nice, tall policeman."

"'Course he is, dear. Anyway, suffice to say Gerard is a liability. We'll all be unutterably glad to see the back of him."

"I can understand that. He's… er… definitely going at the end of the week, is he?"

"Don't put doubts in my mind. I expect he's got another show to go on to, although I'm bound to say I'll be tipping off a few organisers after his performance this week. Anyway, what are we standing out here for? Come and see the main attraction."

"Aren't they just adorable?" said Edward

The three of them gazed upon the unbearably cute black kittens nestled against a fulfilled-looking Princess.

"Edward," said Lexy, after a while. "You do know, don't you?"

He turned his genial face to her. "That they're not Rexes.

Yes, lovie."

"But they're not ordinary moggies, either," Peter pointed out. "Not with their heritage. They'll be a cut above average, both in looks and intelligence."

"It just means it's going to take me a bit longer to pay you back," Lexy sighed.

"It also means that Peter and I will be able to keep our new little family. The kittens won't have to be sold." The two men, temporarily reconciled, it seemed, smiled dotingly. "With your permission, of course."

"Edward, if you weren't gay I'd give you a big French kiss. Of course you can keep them. And Princess, too, if you like. I mean, what with Kinky, I could never give her a home."

Edward beamed like a hundred watt bulb. "Let's call that a done deal, then."

But a shadow had passed over Lexy's face at the thought of the chihuahua. Gerard just might be mad enough to track her down to Four Winds Cottage and try to take him.

The worst of it was that, technically, Kinky did belong to her husband. He really had inherited the dog from his mother. During her final illness, the old woman had asked Gerard and Lexy to look after Kinky, and they had faithfully promised. But when the chihuahua had arrived at their South Kensington house in a wicker dog carrier a few days later, Gerard had wanted to take him straight to Battersea Dogs' Home without so much as opening the thing.

Lexy had intervened. She'd never been keen on little dogs, but to her, a promise really was a promise. Anyway, Kinky might be small, but, as Lexy discovered, he had the heart and stomach of a Great Dane. She would never let her unforgiving husband get his filthy hands on him.

"Edward," she said.

"Yes, honey?" Edward couldn't drag his eyes from the kittens.

"Could I ask another enormous favour?"

"You know you can."

"Could you look after Kinky for me for a few days?"

That got his attention. Edward blinked. "Are you going away?"

"No. Er… yes, actually." Good idea. "This thing I'm working on – it would be really useful for me to get up to London. Could be tricky if I had Kinky with me."

"Well, of course we can look after him." Edward glanced at Peter. "Just need to make sure he doesn't come in here."

"You can leave him shut in the kitchen," said Lexy. "I'll give you some money for his food. Just make sure he's kept here at all times. Take him out in the garden for a quick walk a couple of times a day and he'll be perfectly happy."

That wasn't entirely true. Kinky would be bloody furious if he was shut in Edward's kitchen for the next four days. But at least he would be safe.

She fished in her bag. "Here's his lead."

"You're leaving him here now?"

"If that's all right."

"Something's the matter, isn't it, lovie?" Edward scrutinised Lexy. "I know it is."

"Not at all. It's just that things are kicking off with this case." She pretended to check her mobile. "In fact, I need to get off as soon as my windscreen is fixed."

Peter straightened. "You're driving to London in that wreck this evening?"

"Plenty of life in the old Panda yet," Lexy blustered.

Again Edward and Peter exchanged looks.

Lexy hated lying to her closest friends in Clopwolde, but she didn't want them to know her marital link with Gerard Warwick-Holmes. She just couldn't bear to go into all the explanations. It had been bad enough admitting it to Milo.

"I was just about to get some shopping, before I… er… pop down to the show again," said Peter. Edward regarded him dangerously. "So I'll buy the dog food."

Lexy handed Peter a fiver.

The phone beside the bed rang and Edward picked it up.

"It's the windscreen man. He's on his way. But then I said he was reliable."

He flounced out, and Lexy and Peter followed, exchanging wry looks.

They waited in the large, immaculately clean kitchen while the car was being fixed. Edward fussed around, pressing biscuits, cakes and chocolates on Lexy.

"What have you done to your arm, sweetie?" he said sharply. Lexy looked down. A set of bruises was developing in a ring around her upper arm, just under her tattoo, where her husband had gripped her so painfully earlier.

"Those look like fingermarks. Has some brute been man-handling you?"

She shrugged. "Just a misunderstanding. Kind of thing that happens all the time in my line of work."

"I wish you'd get a safer job."

"Hey – I can roll with the punches."

"Listen – why don't I come up to London with you, and help you out with whatever you're doing. Please," he added silently, jerking his head back at Peter, who was assembling a collection of Cath Kidston shopping bags from a cupboard.

"Who's going to look after Kinky?" Lexy said.

He gave her a frustrated glare.

15

An hour and a half later, Lexy arrived back at Four Winds Cottage. She felt bereft without the chihuahua.

Steve was sitting on the front lawn, cleaning a pile of rusty bolts with a wire brush.

"Gabrielle was scared I was going to rope her in when she saw me doing this," he smiled. "She decided she had a prior appointment in Lowestoft."

Lexy winced. "I know which I'd prefer. Where's Rowana?"

"Hiding, I think. How was Clopwolde?"

"Uneventful." If you don't count being attacked by a raving lunatic with a long-handled wrench.

"Anything good in the post?"

"What?" Oh – yes, the post. "No. No premium bonds or exotic job offers."

"You know, I never asked you." Steve squinted in the sun as he looked up at her. "What exactly do you do?"

Lexy thought. "I'm a house-sitter."

He smiled. "I should have guessed, really."

"I look after people's pets while they're away."

"I know the kind of thing. Amazing what people will pay to have Fido looked after in the comfort of his own home, isn't it?"

Is it? Lexy made a mental note to look into that.

"Speaking of which," he continued, "where's Kinky?"

Lexy looked round automatically before she spoke. "He's… with friends."

"Oh?"

"This couple I know. Love him to bits. Sometimes I leave him there for a night or two. When I've got things to do."

"Have you got things to do, then?" Steve attempted to brush

oil from his face. He made it a whole lot worse.

"One or two."

"Don't give much away, do you?"

"That's because I haven't got much to give away. I do a bit of house-sitting and…" I investigate mysterious deaths. "… when I visit new clients, like I'm doing tomorrow, I like to keep Kinky out of the way in case he tries to kill their pets. Doesn't create a good impression first off."

Steve laughed. "I got rid of that bone of his, by the way. Nice up there on the cliff, isn't it?"

"Gorgeous. But I forgot to tell you that it's private ground. Hope the Gallimores didn't see you up there – they seem to be morbidly paranoid about their sheep. Not sure what they think we're going to do with them."

"I didn't even see any," said Steve.

Lexy went into the cottage, and walked up the hall, sniffing the air. What was that smell. Oil paint? Coming from Elizabeth's studio? For a mad moment she wondered if she was having some kind of ghostly olfactory episode. She put her head around the door.

On the up side, there wasn't a pale outline of Elizabeth Cassall daubing at the canvas.

But on the down side, there was a new painting sitting on the easel.

A painting of Old Shuck.

Lexy approached it disbelievingly. It was the shaggy black creature to perfection, running hell for leather, exactly as Lexy had seen it on three separate occasions. Who… ?

She heard the sound of crockery being stacked in the kitchen. Twisting away from the painting, she strode down the hall. It was Rowana.

"Did you do that painting in the studio?" Lexy asked, without preamble. She half-expected the girl to say 'What painting?', but Rowana nodded. "I was going to tell you – it was really weird, but when I was looking out of the bedroom window earlier,

I saw that dog, or whatever it was, running through the trees on Freshing Hill."

Freshing Hill? It was getting closer.

"At least, I thought I saw it – it was there one moment, gone the next," Rowana went on. "So I thought I'd paint it, while I still had an image in my mind. It was probably a trick of the light or... what's the matter?" She was looking at Lexy curiously. "Hang on a minute – it's that dog you were talking to Tyman about in the pub, isn't it? Old Shuck? The ghost dog?"

"Maybe." Lexy didn't want to alarm her. "How big did you think it was?"

"'Bout as big as a wolfhound. Big shoulders. And shaggy, with a huge head, kind of facing down. Just like I painted it. It *is* the one you saw, isn't it?"

Lexy nodded.

They stared at one another.

"Well, if we've both seen it," said Rowana, slowly, "either that means we've both seen a ghost... or, whatever it is, it's real."

"Of course it's real," snorted Lexy. "It's someone's dog that's got loose."

Rowana arched her eyebrows. "Not everything can be explained," she said.

Lexy went into the cool of the living room. Her green sleeping bag was slumped on the sofa like a large dead caterpillar, and yesterday's clothes were strewn across the rug where she'd left them. As she bent to pick them up, a sudden wave of exhaustion hit her. She'd only had a few hours' sleep the night before, followed by all that malarkey up the hill at dawn, to say nothing of the pleasure of getting reacquainted with Gerard. And now this with the damned black dog again. Added to which something was still lurking at the back of her mind. Something someone had said. Was it Ward or Tyman? She'd have a think about it. She sat down on the sofa, kicked off her trainers and settled back.

The room was full of evening shadows when Lexy awoke. So

much for thinking. She stretched, rubbing her eyes. She could hear voices in the kitchen – Gabrielle must have come back.

She padded over to the patio door and pushed it open, breathing in the perfume of the late summer garden.

She stepped outside in her socks, and crossed the patio on to the lawn.

A movement caught her eye. Lexy looked up just in time to see a dark shape disappearing up the sheep path. She drew in a sharp breath. Old Shuck again? How much closer was he going to come? Well, this time she was going to confront the creature, even if she had to chase it all the way to Clopwolde and back. In her socks.

Lexy climbed over the garden wall, and walked quietly up the track into the wood, listening intently. The only sound was the liquid song of a blackbird.

She advanced a little further, then halted, standing dead still on the narrow gloomy path. In mid-verse the blackbird stopped short, issued a loud, harsh warning and swooped away.

The wood was smothered in silence.

Lexy looked around. Someone was watching her. She could feel it. She looked sharply into the thick undergrowth. God, where was Kinky when she needed him?

A twig snapped.

"Right. Who's there?" The shake in her voice took all the authority out of the demand.

There was no reply, just that same silence, as if the whole wood had drawn in a deep breath.

Lexy was filled with a sudden, nameless panic. She flexed, silently counted to three, then whirled around and darted back down the path to the low grey stone garden wall. She vaulted over it and collapsed on the lawn.

After a few seconds she sat up, shaking her head in quiet embarrassment. So, she was going to chase Old Shuck to Clopwolde and back, was she? Looked like she'd underestimated him, then.

Rowana was leafing through a magazine in the living room when Lexy came back through the French window. She stared at Lexy's red face, grass-stained jeans and dusty socks.

"Did you fall over again?"

"Yup."

"You were right about chihuahua walking being demanding."

"I was on my own, actually. Kinky's staying with some friends for a couple of nights."

Steve was making his way across the lawn towards them, temporarily driving all thoughts of Old Shuck from Lexy's mind.

"What's for dinner?" he enquired, stripping off his overalls on the patio.

Lexy blew her spiky fringe off her forehead. "I could make us something," she offered. "Soup and home made bread?"

"Sounds like a little piece of heaven. I'll just be in the shower."

Lexy shot a brief glance at him as he went past. If Rowana hadn't been there she'd have reminded him to lock the door this time. In no uncertain terms.

She went through to the kitchen and began measuring out flour.

Lexy was outside gathering herbs when Steve came down, damp and clean, pulling on a t-shirt.

"Want any help?" he asked. "I can't do the technical stuff, but I slice vegetables pretty well."

"You could start on the spuds. They're in a bag in the kitchen."

"Right on to it, ma'am."

"Where are you going with that?" Gabrielle had swept out of the spare bedroom and met Lexy on the landing carrying a tray of dough.

"Airing cupboard. I need to let it rise."

"Oh, right. Can you come and look at something?"

"Sure." Lexy balanced the dough tray on a pile of bed linen in the airing cupboard, then followed Gabrielle, wondering what on earth the girl might want her to see.

She had laid out a dress on the bed.

"This is nice." Lexy dusted off her hands and picked it up. An emerald green satin cocktail number, beautifully sewn, with a subtle silver design at the neck, sleeves and hem. "More than nice, it's absolutely gorgeous." She looked for the label. "Where did you get it?"

"I made it."

Lexy regarded the girl in astonishment. "Where did you learn to do this?"

"Taught myself. I always liked doing it, ever since I was a kid." She shrugged. "I've never really shown my stuff to anyone. I wasn't sure if it was good enough."

"Well, I'm no expert, but if this dress is anything to go by, I think you've found your vocation here."

Lexy left Gabrielle staring into space. She could almost hear the possibilities ticking over in her mind.

It might have been the effect of the meal, but everyone was yawning by ten o'clock that night, and by eleven all three Patersons had gone to bed.

Rowana had been the last to go up. She checked outside the patio door. "Oh, look – it's nearly a full moon."

Lexy stood outside, looking up at the constellations, trying to remember which was which. There was a time when she'd known the night sky like the back of her hand. When she was a kid, living in the wilds.

Her head cocked to one side as she listened to the sounds coming from the dark woods surrounding the cottage. The soft hoot of a tawny owl. The yelp of a fox. The indefinable rustlings of mice and voles. And something else. Lexy moved along the wall of the cottage. A figure, with a torch, quietly making its way up the path. One of the Gallimores? It was too dark to see. Whoever it was, Lexy intended to find out. She might have screwed up with Old Shuck, but this would be different.

She rushed back into the cottage, grabbed a torch from the hall cupboard, and shrugged her jacket on. She stopped with a frown halfway through. Was that a car engine? This time of night?

She let herself out on to the patio again. It was half past eleven. The yellow, waxing moon hung in the sky, illuminating her path across the lawn. She climbed over the low wall and walked quietly up the path, which was only just visible in the moonlight's glow.

The inexplicable terror that Lexy had experienced earlier in the wood was forgotten in her desire to discover the identity of the night walker. There had been no doubting the reality of *that* figure.

Treading warily, she stopped every minute or two to listen. The stranger was still up ahead – Lexy could hear the rustle and crunch of leaves underfoot.

The moon, which had picked out the path ahead with silvery light, passed behind a cloud. Lexy slowed, waiting for her eyes to adjust to this new, velvety darkness. She didn't want to use the torch and lose her night vision.

It became harder going. Once or twice she found her feet tangled in the undergrowth as she wandered off the track.

She looked up, trying to see a patch of sky. Was the moon going to come out again? At what point had the trees started pressing in on either side of her?

She listened again. All was silent now, apart from the odd stirring in the undergrowth – the sound of small furry things going about their legitimate business. Sounds she'd heard many times before. But she couldn't hear her quarry any more.

Then Lexy heard a louder rustle coming towards her, and a heavy exhalation of breath. Sheep, perhaps, coming down into the wood to shelter for the night. Or a muntjac deer. Or…

She stumbled against something. She'd reached the same fallen tree Ward had pinned her against earlier. Meant she'd strayed off the path again. Nothing else for it. Lexy fumbled in her pocket for her torch.

Then she froze.

16

Ward Gallimore's voice had pierced the night.

"Get out of the way, Tyman!"

"No!" his brother yelled back. "Don't shoot! Don't... "

But a shot rang out anyway, mind-blowingly loud. Lexy didn't know if it was her reflexes that hurled her down by the fallen tree, or a bullet. Either way she was on her back in exactly the same place as she had been much earlier that day. Except this time Ward Gallimore wasn't lying on top of her.

He was trying to kill her.

He was striding straight towards Lexy, the gun barrel in his hand gleaming softly in the moonlight.

She tried to scramble up, clutching at the fallen tree, but her legs weren't having any of it. Lexy braced herself. But instead of an explosion followed by nothingness, there was a heavy thud and a shout of pain.

Ward had fallen, landing face down a few feet away from her. He twisted on the ground, clutching his ankle.

Lexy eyed the dark shape of the gun which had tumbled to the ground beside him.

Ward raised his head a few inches and looked over at her.

"Lexy," he gasped. "You... all right?" He fell back with a groan.

Anger helped her to struggle to her feet this time. "You try to blow my frigging head off, and you're asking me if I'm all right?" Her voice was several octaves higher than usual. "Or were you just checking I was dead? Well, sorry to..."

She was interrupted by Tyman, who was running towards them, holding a torch with a powerful beam that almost blinded Lexy.

"You haven't... ?"

"She's all right." Ward spoke through clenched teeth. "I missed her by a few inches."

"Perhaps you should practise more." Lexy advanced a few steps, her eyes searching for the gun on the woodland floor. "You two really have got some weird game going on, haven't you?" Then she found her legs buckling under her again.

Tyman grasped her arm. It was like some bizarre re-run of the charade that had taken place that morning. Except this time Tyman was playing Sir Galahad.

As he pulled her upright, Lexy felt blackness rushing to meet her. He put an arm out to steady her.

"Lean on me for a moment, get your balance."

She didn't want to, but Lexy found herself clinging tightly to his arm.

"We need to get out of here. Can you walk?"

Lexy nodded.

Tyman raised his voice. "I'm taking Lexy down to the cottage."

"No." Ward's voice was harsh with pain. "Leave her… here… with me." He fell back again.

"What's the matter with you?" Tyman shone the torch on his brother. Ward was curled up on the ground, his face a study of pain. "My ankle," he spat. "I need help. Go on your own. It'll be quicker."

"No way."

Lexy looked from one to the other. She had an overwhelming feeling that she was in danger from one of the Gallimore brothers. She just didn't know which.

Ducking forward, she sprinted off.

Ward gave a harsh yell. "Don't let her go!"

Lexy stumbled through the undergrowth until she found the path, rimed by silver moonlight, then she ran flat out, her breath coming in great sobs.

Running footsteps began to gain on her. That wasn't just a dream she'd had – it was a bloody premonition.

Just as she thought her heart and lungs would explode, Lexy saw a bobbing light ahead of her.

"Lexy! Whoa!"

Milo.

She threw herself on him.

Tyman windmilled to a halt a few feet away, then tried to sprint past them.

Milo didn't even hesitate. Seeming to swell in size, he pushed Lexy behind him and leapt forward in one movement.

Tyman crashed to the ground with a yell.

Milo knelt over the prone form. "Well, don't just stand there," he snapped. "Get my torch."

Numbly, Lexy bent to pick it up from the path where he had dropped it.

Milo shone it over his victim. "Better make sure I haven't killed him, I suppose."

"And … have you?"

"Nah. Just unconscious. He'll come round in a minute. You're OK, are you?" He shone a light over Lexy.

She nodded.

"So – and forgive me if this is a silly question – but what the sodding hell's going on here?"

"Foxes," came a voice from the darkness. They whirled around.

Ward limped into the halo of light cast by Milo's torch, leaning heavily on a piece of wood, gun at his shoulder. He looked like a victim from the trenches. His face was Dover cliff white. "We were… after foxes. We weren't expecting to see her up here." He jerked his head at Lexy.

"But when you did, you decided to take the opportunity to deal with me." Lexy took a step forward.

Ward hesitated, eyes narrow. He was trying to remember where he'd said those words.

"Outside the pub," Lexy prompted him, her voice rising. "That's what you said, wasn't it?"

Did Ward summon up a ghostly smile?

Lexy felt Milo's restraining hand on her arm.

Tyman gave a faint moan from where he lay on the path.

"I should get your brother home and looked at if I were you," Milo remarked. "He may have concussion. He fell rather heavily just now."

Ward bent stiffly over Tyman, then with a grunt of pain, collapsed on to the path beside him.

"My ankle. Killing me." He lay back with a grimace.

Milo produced a mobile phone.

"You won't get a signal." Lexy was right.

"OK. We're going to get some help for you," Milo told Ward.

"Just get my father. Down… at the farm. Don't call an ambulance or… anything." He meant no police. Lexy wondered what he'd say if he knew he was talking to a detective inspector.

"And don't be long."

"Don't be long?" She gave an incredulous snort.

Milo bent and picked up Ward's gun, using a white handkerchief.

"Hey! Don't touch that." Ward tried to sit upright and yelled out in pain. "What are you doing?"

"This." Milo cracked it open, removed the cartridges, and put them in his pocket. "I'll take it down with me. So it's out of harm's way."

"Who do you think you are? You can't do that."

"Watch me."

"Great." Ward lay back again.

"Ready?" Milo nodded at Lexy. They set off down the path at a jog, the torch lighting their way.

"You've done that before, haven't you?" said Lexy. "That thing with the gun?"

"I may have had some training."

She took a sideways glance at Milo. She couldn't believe she'd hurled herself at him like that.

"Thanks for… back there," she mumbled.

"Glad to be of service."

"It was like something out of Superman."

"I'm not usually like that."

"What were you doing up there?"

"I came to see you. Bit late because I was tied up with work."

"Thought I heard an engine."

"You've got sharp ears. I parked further down the path and walked up, because I didn't want to wake the whole cottage up. I was coming up into the clearing when I saw you creeping across the lawn."

"So you followed me?"

"I wasn't going to start yelling to you. Anyway, I was curious."

"Lucky you were, as it turned out."

"Why was he chasing you?"

"Who, Tyman?" Lexy paused. "You're not going to like this."

"Tell me anyway."

"Milo – I was right all along. They're trying to kill me. At least Ward is. He fired that gun straight at me tonight – deliberately."

"And Tyman?"

"He was trying to stop him, but Ward told him to get out of the way. Tyman shouted at Ward not to shoot, but he did anyway. I couldn't believe it. And when Ward realised he'd missed, he ran straight for me. He was going to have another go, at close range. The only reason he didn't was because he fell and dropped the gun – at which point he had the goddamn nerve to ask me if I was all right."

"Lexy, I know you're stuck on this idea that the Gallimores are after your blood, but are you certain Ward was running in for another shot at you? Did he have the gun raised?"

"Yes!" Lexy jogged on for a few more strides, then slowed. "Well, actually, no. He was holding it down low."

"Has it occurred to you they simply didn't realise you were there?"

It made sense, but Lexy wasn't going to give in to reason yet. "I tell you, Milo – when he first saw me, Ward aimed that gun right at me. He must have known I was there. Tyman was screaming at him not to shoot me. Stop a sec." Lexy paused at the side of the path to get her breath, trying to think straight about what had just occurred. "You know, it would be the perfect way to get rid of me, wouldn't it? A shooting accident. After all, I'd been trespassing on private land – land I'd already been warned off… "

"Give over."

"Listen – the Gallimores definitely had something to do with Elizabeth's death. They know that I know, and now they're trying to arrange a similar accident for me. It's so… bloody obvious. I can't understand why you won't see it."

"It's not for lack of trying. Believe me, I've trawled those files – spent half of last night doing it, actually. I still can't find a motive."

"I'll get you one." She could have at least thanked him.

"Wish you would. Speaking of which, you haven't mentioned what you were doing up the hill tonight."

"I saw one of the Gallimores creeping up there earlier. At least I assume it was one of them. I wanted to know what he was up to. So I followed him."

"Just can't leave it alone, can you?"

They ran along in silence for a while, until Four Winds Cottage came into view, and they slowed. "Want to go in?"

Lexy shook her head. "No, I'll come down to the farm with you."

Milo led the way down the steep track to the farm, the grass, already damp with dew, soaking their feet.

Bruce was up when they got there, pacing the yard. He'd been waiting for his sons to get back. When Milo had given him an edited account of what had happened, leaving out Lexy's accusations against Bruce's first born, the farmer ran for the Land Rover, his florid face wobbling in concern.

"Get in, get in." He started the engine and swung the vehicle around. Lexy and Milo jumped into the back seat.

"So, what were you doing up there?" Bruce shouted above the engine as they bounced up the rutted track.

"Kinky ran off up into the woods earlier," Lexy improvised. The farmer didn't know she'd off-loaded the chihuahua. "Luckily Milo turned up, so he came to help me look."

"Did you find him?"

"Yes. He's safe and sound." In Edward de Glenville's ancestral kitchen.

"Well, that's something. Wouldn't like to think of him…" Bruce's voice trailed away.

He managed to get the vehicle part of the way up through the woods beyond Four Winds Cottage. They piled out and walked the short distance to where Ward and Tyman had been left.

Tyman was conscious again. He'd managed to bind Ward's ankle with a torn-up t-shirt and get him up, supporting his brother along the path, but their progress looked painful. Bruce pushed himself under Ward's other arm.

He looked across at Tyman. "Understand you fell hard, son."

"You could say that." Tyman gingerly felt the back of his head, throwing a resentful glance at Milo.

Bruce helped his sons into the Land Rover. "We don't need to mention this incident to the authorities, do we?"

"I don't know. Do we?" said Milo.

"No one was shot. No real 'arm done."

Milo gripped Lexy's shoulder just as she opened her mouth to protest.

"Agh!"

"What's that, pet?"

"Nothing. Lexy and I will walk down to the cottage from here," said Milo. "It's not far."

"Right you are." The Land Rover lurched off.

"Why'd you stop me?" Lexy shouted.

"Because I want to get my head around what happened first."

"Why don't you believe me?"

"Tell me about the shooting bit from the beginning."

Lexy sighed. "It was dark, and I'd gone off the path. I heard Ward shouting at Tyman to get out of the way. I heard Tyman shouting at Ward not to shoot. Then I heard an explosion right next to me. Practically deafened me."

"So Ward might have been aiming at a fox all the time."

Lexy shrugged. "Then why did Tyman warn him not to shoot?"

"That's one of the two questions we have to ask ourselves."

"And the other?"

"Why did Ward ignore him?"

"There you are!" Steve strode out of the garden shadows when they reached the cottage. "I heard a shot on the hillside. It woke me up, and the girls too. Then we heard the Land Rover – we went downstairs and found you were missing. Didn't know what to do – whether to call the police, or go up there ourselves and try to find you. Are you OK, Lexy?"

He had taken her hands. She was aware of Milo looking on. "Yeah, of course I am."

Rowana ran out of the cottage, looking hysterical. "You'd gone from the sofa. We thought you'd been shot."

Gabrielle stood framed in the doorway in a flimsy nightdress.

"Oi – get a dressing gown on," Steve called.

Lexy withdrew her hands. "I was…" Damn, she couldn't use the Kinky line here. "… out badger-spotting and the Gallimores were out shooting. Bad combination."

"Shooting badgers? That must be illegal – shouldn't the police be told?"

"They were shooting foxes, apparently," said Lexy, eyeing Milo.

"And I am the police," he announced.

Steve's head jerked up. Rowana went white.

"Technically, the only person who's broken the law is Lexy. She was trespassing on private land. But I don't think they're going to prosecute," Milo added.

"I should bleedin' well think not," Lexy muttered.

"So what exactly happened?" Gabrielle asked. They were all in the kitchen, sipping hot tea.

Lexy felt like she'd scream if she had to go over this one more time. "I was just heading up the path to where I knew the um... badger sett was, and there was this sudden commotion, and I heard Ward and Tyman yelling."

She didn't bother repeating exactly what she had heard Ward and Tyman yelling. It wasn't going to do her any good.

"Then I heard a shot, and I threw myself to the ground, thinking I'd been hit. Ward came rushing up, fell over and injured his ankle, then Tyman turned up, I ran off, he came after me, and Milo suddenly appeared and knocked Tyman out."

"Bit like a Carry On film, in fact," Milo remarked.

"Yeah, it was a laugh a minute."

"But Ward *is* all right?" Gabrielle demanded.

"Think so." Lexy drained her tea. "I'm fine as well, thanks."

"I'd better be off." Milo pushed himself up.

Lexy went to the door with him.

"Why'd you come and see me so late, anyway?"

He looked beyond her up the hall.

"It was about your husband again."

"What?"

"He caught up with you earlier, didn't he?"

"How do you... ?"

"Someone reported an incident in the supermarket car park earlier today. Involving a lime green Fiat Panda and a bloke with a wrench."

"Oh... crap."

"Let me see your arm." Milo pushed Lexy's jacket sleeve up before she could stop him. "He do this?"

"Just before he smashed my windscreen."

"Never a dull moment with you, is there?"

"Well, you know – I like to keep busy."

"Where is Kinky, by the way?"

"That's why Gerard was smashing his way into my car. He

decided he wanted him back."

"Seriously?"

"Yup. For some reason it seemed to annoy him when I explained I'd donated his half million quid to a bird sanctuary. He made a sudden decision to take Kinky in lieu."

"I take it he didn't succeed."

"'Course not. But it was a close run thing. I left Kinky with Edward – told him to keep him shut in for a few days over at the manor. The mutt won't like it, but at least he'll be safe. Just in case Gerard's looking for me."

"Probably for the best." Milo hesitated, as if he wanted to say something else.

"Can you look in on Kinky?" Lexy asked. "If you get a chance?"

"What – and run the gauntlet of Edward and Peter?" Milo gave her his crooked smile. "No problem."

Lexy awoke with a jump the next morning. It took a few moments for her to register that she was safe on the sofa in Four Winds Cottage, rather than at the wrong end of a shotgun barrel. Or a long-handled wrench. She really had to get more choosy about who she associated with in future.

It was raining heavily outside. She lay there, listening to the overflow from the gutter splash on to the patio, able to stretch her legs out because Kinky wasn't there, but for that same reason not really enjoying the luxury.

Her mind was still playing out the drama of the previous night. The trip up the hill at midnight, in pursuit of a mysterious figure. The deafening gunshot, whistling past her ear. Did Ward really have a fox in his sights? The more she thought about it, the more she had to admit that Milo might have been right. The questions that really needed answers were exactly as the detective had said – why had Tyman warned Ward not to shoot? And why did Ward ignore him?

The obvious answer was that Tyman must have seen Lexy at

the last second, while Ward was taking aim at an unfortunate fox. But one sometimes had to look beyond the obvious…

There was a knock at the door. Steve came in, holding a mug of tea.

"Thought you might like this."

"Oh – thanks."

He set the mug down on the coffee table in front of her and cast an eye over her. "You look good all rumpled up like that."

"Behave," said Lexy.

He smiled and left.

It was hard not to smile too.

Her next visitor was Rowana.

"Why didn't you tell me Milo was a policeman?"

"He's a secret policeman." Lexy took pity at the girl's aggrieved expression. "Look, Rowana – he's a friend. He's not going to prosecute you under the Witchcraft Act."

"I know that," she muttered. "But I still think you might have told me."

"Sorry." Lexy seemed to be saying that a lot lately.

"It's all right. You can't help it if your boyfriend's a policeman, I suppose."

"He's not actually my… "

Rowana slipped out of the room.

Lexy fell back with a groan.

She listened to the sounds of breakfast being made, but couldn't summon up an appetite right then. She spent some time lying in the bath first. She had bruises on top of bruises, thanks to the events of the last couple of days.

When she went downstairs, the kitchen was empty. She made herself tea and toast, then went back to trying to make sense of the previous night's events. She was going to have to get those crucial questions about the shooting answered. But how?

Lexy made up her mind. She'd go down to the damned farm and ask them. Much as it irked her to confront Butch Cassidy and the Sundance Kid again so soon, perhaps if they were incapacitated by injury, it might be easier to persuade one or other of them into an indiscretion.

Outside, the rain had cleared up but the skies were still grey. She glanced over at the shed as she walked down the garden path. The happy combination of hammering and whistling was again emanating through the half-closed door.

Stopping at the bottom of the hill, she checked her phone for a signal. It was weak, but it still had a pulse. Worth a try.

"Edward?"

"Lexy!" Edward sounded manic.

"Kinky all right? Not giving you any bother is he?"

"No! No! Kinky's… absolutely fine." The signal was breaking up. She could hear voices in the background.

"Lexy?" Crackle. Hiss.

"Yes?"

"Peter here. Kinky's fine. Nothing to worry about."

"I wasn't worried." But she was now.

"Want to talk to him?"

"Eh?" Fizz. Beep. A shout.

"Only kidding. When are you back, by the way?"

"What's he done, Peter?"

"Who?"

"Kinky. What's he done?"

"Nothing. Couldn't be better behaved."

"OK." She looked dubiously at the phone. "Perhaps I'll try and pop in tomorrow."

"Tomorrow? Right. Just give us a…" The line went dead. But not before she'd heard Edward screech "Tomorrow?" in the background.

"Great. That's really put my mind at rest," she muttered.

17

Lexy pulled the bell cord outside the farmhouse, and moments later a large, blurred shape approached the opaque side window.

Bruce looked taken aback to see Lexy.

"Oh… er… 'allo, pet."

"Sorry to bother you. I just wanted to check how Ward was. And er, Tyman, of course." And grill them 'til they squeaked.

Bruce snorted. "Tyman's in bed with a great big lump on the back of his head. Serves him right, bloody young idiot. Ward's in the living room, with his foot in plaster." He frowned at her uncertainly. "You want to see him?"

"Yes, please."

"Go on, then, you know the way."

"Lexy." Ward was lying on the sofa, his right foot in a cast. His eyes glittered in his pale face. "Last person I expected to see."

"So, how are you?" she enquired coolly, perching on an armchair opposite him.

"Managed to break a bone in my ankle. I've been in casualty half the night waiting for someone to set it." His lips twitched. "I suppose you reckon I deserve it."

"Depends, really," said Lexy.

"On what?"

"On what you were really doing up there last night."

Bruce poked his head around the door. "Tea?"

"Oh… er… yes, thanks," said Lexy.

"Not for me." Ward shifted, wincing.

They heard the sound of crockery being rattled.

"I told you what happened," Ward said. "I… "

He was interrupted by a shout from upstairs, followed by an exclamation from the kitchen. Bruce's head appeared again.

"Need to go and see to his lordship. Would you mind doing

the honours with the brew, love?"

Lexy got up and went into the Gallimores' shiny kitchen.

A mug was sitting on the worktop, with a teabag brewing in it. She opened the fridge to look for milk and was confronted by three enormous raw steaks on a platter. Had Edgar the bull met his end? With a shudder, Lexy added two sugars to her tea, squeezed out the teabag and took it through.

"You were saying," she prompted Ward.

"Like I told you. We were out after foxes, and you got in the way. Simple as that."

"Why was it only you with a gun then? And how come I didn't hear any shots until you fired it at me?"

He hesitated. "I was on my own up there, all right? Tyman came to find me, to talk me out of doing it." His voice was low, eyes preoccupied. "My brother's softer than I am where animals are concerned. He showed up just as I was taking my first aim."

"And this is the delicate soul who turns into Mr Hyde when he's on his own with a woman?"

Ward wouldn't meet her eyes.

"So that's why you ignored him when he told you not to shoot?"

"Yes. Neither of us saw you until I'd fired." But he was still looking away.

"The other day Mrs Mangeot told me that you lot would have trouble humanely destroying a hen. Are you sure shooting foxes is your style?"

"Is that what she said? Good old Mangeot. Listen, we've got sheep out on the hill."

"Have you?"

Again, he hesitated. "Yes." He was lying. Why?

"I've never seen any."

"I can assure you we…"

Ward was interrupted again by a shout from outside the door. It was Tyman this time.

"Hey! She's here! I saw her coming down the track from Four Winds!"

"Oi – I told you to calm down." Bruce's voice rang out sharply, followed by muffled conversation.

Ward closed his eyes and leaned back on the sofa.

"What was all that about?" Lexy demanded.

"I think Tyman must be pleased you've come to see us. As well he might be."

She stared at him. "Yeah, all right. I'm going now."

Ward sat up again. "No – hang on a minute…"

Shaking her head, Lexy went through to the hall. Must be the medication.

She heard voices in the kitchen, and without really thinking what she was doing, Lexy slipped into a downstairs cloakroom and pulled the door almost closed. As she watched through the crack, Tyman appeared, looking as spaced out as Ward, a smile spreading across his face. Chivvied by Bruce, he went back upstairs. After a minute, Lexy came out of the cloakroom, walked quietly to the bottom of the stairs, then went up. Time to talk to laughing boy.

She already knew which was Ward's bedroom. Lexy put her head around the room next door to it. Empty, the bed roughly made up. She walked down a small corridor, following the sound of a television, and tapped on the door at the end.

"Yes?" came Tyman's voice.

"Surprise." Lexy walked in.

He was sitting on the bed, wearing what she'd just seen him in, black track suit bottoms and a t-shirt.

"Lexy!" He pointed a remote at the TV, and killed the sound. "What are you… ?"

"Doing here?" Lexy gave him a crocodile smile. "Came to see how you are, Tyman."

"Bit of a bump." He pointed to his head. "Otherwise OK. Better than OK, actually. You?"

"Oh, I'm fine. Just can't quite work out what happened up

there last night." She sat on a chair, after first moving a pile of clothes.

Tyman watched her. "Well," he began, "it was like we said. Ward and I were up there shooting foxes…"

"You're not a fan of the fox, then?"

"Well… no. Not… as such. I mean… "

"Must have been quite a shock when I popped up just as Ward was about to blast Basil Brush into oblivion."

"'Course it was."

"You actually saw me then?"

"Ye…es."

He hadn't seen her.

"And you shouted to Ward not to shoot?"

"Yeah. What is this, Lexy? I'm not really up to the Spanish Inquisition at the moment."

"You looked pretty happy when you were downstairs just now."

Tyman started. "You… er… saw me, did you? I was just stretching my legs. I get really bad cramp."

She nodded.

"Lexy… " Tyman frowned. "Where did you get to yesterday morning? After you ran up the hill? I looked everywhere for you. Thought you'd been abducted by aliens, you disappeared so quickly."

"I got abducted, all right," Lexy muttered.

"Sorry?"

"Just… try asking your brother, Tyman."

"Everything all right?" Bruce appeared in the doorway. "Oh, you're in 'ere now, are you?" He goggled at Lexy.

She stood up. "Just going, actually. Thanks, Tyman. You've been very helpful."

Tyman was still looking mystified.

"My brother? What's he got to do with it?"

18

When Lexy got back to Four Winds, she found that Steve had rolled the absurd-looking little red car from the shed on to the lawn, and was lying with his head under it.

"Accident in Toytown?" she called, crossing the lawn.

He eased his way out.

"Reckon it hasn't been driven since 1990." He showed Lexy the tax disc.

"Perhaps it belonged to Elizabeth's husband," she said, examining it. "He must have died at around that time."

Steve's face darkened. "Robert," he said, with a glance towards the cottage. "Never occurred to me it might have been his."

"Did you know him?"

"We met."

"But you didn't get on, I'm sensing?"

He shook his head. "He lived for the army. I didn't have a lot in common with him."

"Surprised Elizabeth did."

"She didn't. Main problem was that Robert didn't want kids, and he didn't want a divorce, either. He was moving up through the ranks, and a marital split wouldn't have helped his case."

"Can't have been easy for her."

Steve took his time before answering. "No."

"Want anything from the shop?" Lexy asked. "I'm just going down there for a paper." And perhaps she'd get a couple of bottles of wine, too, because Lexy had a vague picture in her head of later on that evening, which involved herself, Steve and a couple of bottles of wine.

"Rowana might. She's cooking tonight."

"I need a few things for this curry I'm doing," Rowana confirmed, when Lexy put her head around the kitchen door.

She reeled off a list of ingredients.

"I'm not sure cardamom pods have reached Nodmore." Lexy fumbled in her jacket pocket for a pen. "Or quinces."

Lexy was thoughtful as she got into her car and set off down the tree-canopied track. On top of the continuing peculiarity of the Gallimores, there was that little nugget from Steve.

Elizabeth, stuck in a loveless, childless marriage, with no hope of a divorce. A small part of her must have been relieved when her husband released her from this predicament by dying in action. It would have been her chance to start again. Lexy wondered why she hadn't.

"What do you think, Kinky?" It wasn't until the words were out of her mouth that Lexy realised her sidekick wasn't sitting in the passenger seat. And remembered why.

After she turned out of the farm gate, she checked in her rear view mirror at frequent intervals. No sign of a black BMW containing a perma-tanned nutter with a long-handled wrench. That was good. But Lexy wondered about the wisdom of venturing out in her rather distinctive car while Gerard was still at large. He might have his spies out.

Just outside Nodmore, she turned into a side road and parked out of sight of the main thoroughfare – although to call the one-track lane that passed through the village a thoroughfare might have given it an over-inflated sense of its own worth.

Lexy walked the few hundred yards to the village centre, pushed open the door to the shop and braced herself.

Behind the counter, Maureen's head jerked up. She was serving someone.

"… well, it meant I sold a few more papers than usual, didn't it, luvver?"

"So, all was not lost." The answering voice was gravelly.

"Exactly. And you know what they say. Today's news is tomorrow's fish and chip wrapper. Soon be forgotten."

"Don't say that, Mo – I'm enjoying the infamy. Raised the price of my paintings by twenty per cent. Perhaps next time I'll deck someone really famous." This was followed by a rich smoker's cough.

It was Archer Trevino. Just the person she wanted to meet. Lexy rushed around the shop, chucking items into her wire basket.

The two of them were still conversing when she got to the counter.

"All right, moi luvver? Still up at Four Winds Cottage, are you?"

Maureen was showing off her gossip acumen. It certainly had an effect on Archer. He turned sharply to Lexy. Up close, his face was battle-worn, his silver hair unkempt. He held a bottle of whisky in each hand.

"This young lady is a friend of the Patersons, them that got Elizabeth's place," Maureen informed him.

He looked her up and down boldly enough, but Lexy was sure she saw a shadow in the eyes Elizabeth had captured so well in her painting.

"Hello," she said. "Saw you in the pub the other night."

"Not surprised. Home from home for me. Now, I must be going, Mo. Ciao."

"Bye, luvver."

He whisked out. Annoyed that he didn't take the conversational bait, Lexy heaved her basket on to the counter. "Don't suppose you've got any cardamom pods?"

"Not in the shop, not enough demand for them, but I've got some in my kitchen out back. 'Ow many d'you want?"

"Are you sure? Half a dozen should do it."

"Keep an eye on things here a tick, then."

You can't beat the countryside, Lexy thought. Where else would someone give you supplies out of their own kitchen, and leave you in charge of the shop while they went to get them?

"'Ere you are – two extra for luck. Curry tonight is it?"

"It's looking that way."

"I like a nice curry. They planning on staying long, the

206

Patersons?"

Here we go. Lexy shook her head. "I think they have to get back to London."

"Selling the cottage, are they? To them Gallimores?"

"Not that I'm aware of."

"There's a surprise! Thought they'd put an offer in?"

"Yeah, they did. But it wasn't nearly enough." Lexy smiled. That would be all round the village by tomorrow.

She left the shop, weighed down by two bags. Halfway back to the car, around a bend that put the shop out of sight, she heard heavy footsteps behind her.

"Here – let me carry those bags."

Lexy stopped, surprised.

It was Archer Trevino, speaking through wreaths of cigarette smoke. He'd obviously off-loaded the whisky. Smelt like he'd had a snifter before doing so.

"Thanks," she said. "I feel like my arms have grown another three inches. Name's Lexy Lomax, by the way."

"Archer Trevino." The hand he offered her was calloused and stained with paint and nicotine.

"New to the village, I hear?" He bent to pick up her shopping.

"Just a temporary guest. My home's back in Clopwolde."

"Ah, Clopwolde – the great metropolis! Good god, woman, what have you got in these bags?"

"We ran out of a few things up at the cottage. Don't worry, my car's just down the road."

"Why didn't you park outside the shop? We're not exactly overrun with yellow lines and parking wardens in Nodmore."

"I enjoy the exercise."

"You don't need it, darling. Mind you – I do. And I have an ulterior motive for being gentlemanly."

"Oh, yes?"

He stopped to wipe his brow. "It concerns the family Paterson up at the cottage."

Lexy hid a smile.

"I wondered how long they plan to stay. And if they plan to sell."

"Are you interested in buying the place, then?" she said, innocently.

"Maybe."

"Or are you just trying to avoid them?"

His eyes narrowed. "Perceptive of you."

"Just happened to notice you leave the pub in a hurry the other night when you recognised them."

"And observant. Well, as it happens I'd rather not run into them, for reasons that go back a long way."

"Back to 1990?"

He exhaled, coughing out smoke as he did so. "Who told you?" His eyes were no longer decadent – they were sharp and concerned.

"All I know is that Steve and Jackie Paterson fell out with Elizabeth that year."

"How long have you been a friend of the Patersons?"

"Not that long."

"Er... Lexy... " He leant towards her, giving her the benefit of his whisky-enhanced breath. "I know it's a bit of an imposition, but any discussion regarding past events with Elizabeth, Steve and Jackie – could you keep it under your hat? This is a small village, and they do love to talk." He went into a spasm of coughing.

"No problem. Look, my car's just down this side road," Lexy said. "I can take the bags from here." She didn't want the bloke expiring on her.

"Sure you're not trying to avoid someone too?"

"I like to keep a low profile."

"What – in that thing?" He'd spotted the Panda.

"Would you want to park it in the middle of the village?"

"See your point."

"Thanks for the help with the bags."

"My pleasure. I... er... suppose it was you Steve was visiting here a few weeks ago?"

Lexy frowned. "When, exactly?"

"I don't know, exactly. Yes, I do. It was the day before my Liz fell over that bloody balcony."

Lexy felt a curious sense of detachment. "Steve Paterson was here then?"

"In Clopwolde, certainly. Saw him driving through the village. I noticed the name on the side of the van first. Paterson's Fine Cakes. Then I realised it was him behind the wheel. Quite a blast from the past." His expression was rueful.

He's an old lush, Lexy's brain urged her. He probably imagined it.

"Then he turned up in the pub the other day," Archer went on. "And I somehow knew it wouldn't be long before…"

Lexy took the weight of the bags. Wild conclusions were starting to race through her mind.

"…anyway, speaking of the Unicorn, you know the night when you were all in there…?"

Lexy nodded distractedly.

"The two girls – I thought at first they were with the Gallimore lads, you know, girlfriends. But then I realised they were…" He hesitated. "Steve's daughters, weren't they?"

Lexy nodded again. "Guess you never met them."

"Jackie had a toddler with her, last time I saw her back in 1990."

"That would have been Gabrielle – Steve's daughter with his first wife. The younger girl, Rowana, probably wouldn't even have been born."

"No. No, of course she wouldn't."

Archer was still standing on the corner of the road after Lexy had turned and driven past.

When she arrived at the gate to Pilgrim's Farm, she pulled in and stopped, her mind churning. Archer's words echoed in her head.

Steve had been in Suffolk, driving through Clopwolde. Twenty minutes away from Nodmore. The day before Elizabeth went over the balcony.

But how long had he stayed?

She sat for a moment, trying to think. OK. He was in the vicinity the day before Elizabeth was killed. That's all she knew. Could have been another reason he was here.

She knew that Steve, Jackie and Elizabeth had secrets. Secrets, she now realised, that were shared with Archer Trevino. Four of them in it. Two now dead. Lexy gripped the steering wheel, her heart in her mouth. Steve couldn't possibly be behind Elizabeth's death, could he? It seemed unthinkable. But what if he'd already known about the will? Been so desperate that he'd decided to capitalise on it early?

She shut her eyes briefly. There was nothing for it. One way or another, she was going to have to find out exactly what time he'd got back from Suffolk. And she wasn't sure if she was going to like the answer.

Funny how Milo had picked up on that point right from the beginning.

Lexy got out of the car to open the gate. How the hell were Rowana and Gabrielle going to deal with it, if it turned out to be true?

She blinked. The farm gate was already open. Furthermore, a large wooden sign had appeared – WELCOME TO PILGRIM'S FARM. Instructions were in place for visitors to follow the signs to the parking area. Someone must have only just erected the sign, because she was certain it hadn't been there when she drove out of the gate three-quarters of an hour ago.

Disorientated, Lexy got back into the car and drove slowly up the tarmac track. It occurred to her that if Steve, god forbid, had been behind Elizabeth's death, the Gallimores were off the hook.

And if that was the case, Lexy thought, staring over at the huddle of farm buildings, why on earth had they been practically falling over themselves to behave so suspiciously, to deceive, hijack and generally lead her a merry dance ever since she'd met them?

She needed someone to bounce ideas off. Lexy pulled over halfway to the cottage, and tried Milo. The signal was faint and he was still unavailable. She sent a text in the end: *Call me asap.* Not much point, she thought, dismally. The chances were that the signal would have gone completely by the time she got to the cottage.

Steve was still under the car on the lawn when she got back. He was tapping hard at something and didn't seem to have heard the Panda's engine. Lexy found herself giving him a wide berth, practically sneaking into the kitchen. She couldn't face him right now.

Rowana was pleased to see her.

"You got the cardamom!"

"I wasn't so lucky with the quinces."

"Doesn't matter." Rowana began unpacking the bags. "Would you like a coffee?"

Oh, yes. Lexy sat down heavily at the table. "Black, please, two sugars."

She watched her set the cups up and pour.

"Are you all right?" Rowana asked.

"Got a couple of things on my mind."

"Anything I can do to help?"

Yes, thought Lexy. You can tell me what your dad was up to in Suffolk six weeks ago, while you were prancing around your magic circle. But to ask the question outright was impossible.

"Thanks," she smiled. "But this is just a temporary glitch I'm suffering."

"Is it money…? I mean, I must owe you some by now."

"No, you're all right. Let's sort it out at the end of the week." Which wasn't far away. Lexy just hoped the event wouldn't be marked by Rowana's dad being carted off to Lowestoft nick for questioning.

"Could you take this to Gabby? She's in the living room." Rowana handed her a cup of coffee.

A portable radio was playing when Lexy went in, and Gabrielle was humming along to it.

"It's the theme tune to the new *Wuthering Heights*," she told Lexy.

"What, the Hollywood remake? Have you seen it?" Lexy tried to pull herself together.

"Yes. Opening night in the West End. Russell took me up there." Gabrielle sighed. "Only time he ever took me to the movies. I cried buckets at the end."

Only time he ever took me to the movies.

Lexy tried not to stare boggle-eyed at her. She had a sudden image of Rowana, sitting opposite her, at her desk in the fisherman's cabin on Clopwolde quay, telling Lexy why she'd had to abruptly end her invocation in the greenhouse.

I heard noises. It was Gabrielle and Russell, back from the cinema.

Lexy was finding it difficult to catch her breath. "That was the night your dad was away, wasn't it?"

Gabrielle thought for a moment. "Yes." She reddened. "How did you know?"

Lexy reckoned that Gabrielle's blushes were to do with the fact that Russell had spent the night in the flat over the shop.

"Rowana mentioned it. She said it was one of the few times your dad had ever been away overnight." It was a bit of a weak stroke, but it got the boat moving.

"Yeah – and he hated the idea of leaving us alone, even at my age. It was embarrassing. Like he didn't trust us." Again she reddened.

"Still, I bet he got back early the next morning to make sure you hadn't been having any wild parties." Lexy was gripping the coffee mug hard enough to break it.

Please say he got back before nine.

"No, actually he didn't get back until lunchtime."

"Oh, crap."

"Sorry?"

Lexy put the coffee cup down abruptly and walked out.

212

She needed to go somewhere quiet to think. She needed Milo, and she needed Kinky. Neither of whom was currently available.

Avoiding Steve, this time by going out of the back gate, she walked down the steep hill. She didn't get a signal until she was practically at Pilgrim's Farm.

There was a text message from Milo.

In court all day. Problems?

She rang him. Voicemail again. It was too complicated to explain. She tapped a text in.

Pls come to 4 Winds when u can. Yes – problems.

There was a woodpile near the farm gate. Lexy sat on it. Slowly, she tried to get her scattered thoughts in order.

Every instinct she had was telling her that that Steve Paterson couldn't murder a woman in cold blood. But the facts, from Gabrielle's unwitting lips, and from Archer Trevino's whisky-soaked ones, told a different story. If Archer was to be believed, Steve had been in Clopwolde the day before Elizabeth died, and if Gabrielle was right, he hadn't returned to London until lunchtime on the day of her death. Elizabeth died around nine o'clock in the morning. It took about three hours to drive from Clopwolde to London.

Meaning – swift push over the balcony, and back in time for lunch.

It was beyond coincidence. Lexy's heels kicked at the logs. Steve must have known about the terms of the will. It would explain his initial reaction to the news, as described by Rowana, and, as the reality of what he'd done sank in, his reluctance to visit Four Winds Cottage.

Any guilt that he suffered must quickly have worn off, though. She plucked a long stem of grass and chewed the end thoughtfully. He certainly hadn't been acting like a man with murder on his conscience. Surely he would be weighed down with remorse?

Could there be any other explanation for Steve being here on the morning of Elizabeth's death? Lexy was sorely tempted just to stride up the hill and ask him straight. But if he had been involved, that could be a dangerous move. If Lexy were to meet with an unfortunate accident, too, DI Milo might never get to the bottom of it.

Lexy got her phone out again and sent the detective another text.

SP may have been here the morning EC got killed.

There, that should clarify matters if it came to the crunch.

Lexy tried calling Edward next. No reply. Same with Peter. Odd.

She pushed herself up and trudged back to the cottage. There wasn't much else she could do.

Rowana had made the promised curry. Lexy sat down with the Patersons and tried to act normally, but it wasn't easy. She was aware of Steve eyeing her quizzically, and with some effort she turned to his younger daughter.

"This is really good – how did you make it?"

"Oh, I fried the spices first, then added the garlic and sliced onion and…"

Lexy wasn't really listening. Her thoughts kept drifting to the Gallimores, for some reason. There was still something nagging at the back of her mind. She was sure it was Tyman… something Tyman had said… She shook herself. Why was she bothering with that? All her attention should be on trying to find out what Steve was doing in Clopwolde the day before Elizabeth died.

"I can write it down for you, if you like," Rowana said.

"What?"

"The recipe."

Everyone looked up at a tap on the door.

It was Milo. Thank god. He looked tired, deep lines under his eyes.

"Hope you're not hungry," said Steve, looking at the empty dishes.

Milo shook his head. "Thanks, I've already eaten."

"Tell you what, I'll wash up," said Lexy. "You three go and relax."

The Patersons trooped through to the living room. "See you later," said Steve to Lexy, as he went.

She gave him a tight smile.

Milo picked up a tea towel and stood next to Lexy.

"I assume you didn't get me here just to do the drying."

Lexy waited until she was sure the other three were out of earshot.

"Didn't you see my text?" she said. "About Steve."

"I got something from you... wasn't sure..."

"I ran into Archer Trevino today," Lexy said quietly. "He said he saw Steve in Clopwolde, six weeks ago. The day before Elizabeth fell."

Milo was instantly alert. "Could he have been mistaken?"

"Don't think so. It was the Paterson's Fine Cakes logo on the van that got his attention. When he looked, it was Steve driving it. 'The day before my Liz fell over that bloody balcony,' to quote him. That's how he remembered it."

"Perhaps Steve drove back that same night."

Lexy shook her head. "That's the big problem. Gabrielle said he didn't get back to London until lunchtime the following day."

Milo swore under his breath. "How did she know?"

"She remembered going to the cinema the night before with her ex, Russell."

"OK. Does Steve know that you know?"

"Not unless Gabrielle brought it up. But I think I was circumspect enough not make her suspicious."

"Even so, we'd better go outside and talk." Milo looked at his watch. "In fact, let's go to the pub."

"How did Archer know Steve?" Milo negotiated the rutted track. The suspension in his car was a lot better than the Panda's. Lexy leaned back, relieved to have someone to talk to at last.

"Through Elizabeth. Steve admitted he knew her."

"Really?"

"Something he'd never told his daughters."

"Why the skulduggery?"

"Some kind of mysterious parting of the ways that had occurred between him, his second wife, Jackie, and Elizabeth."

"Thought it was too good to be true that they didn't know each other."

The Unicorn was as dark and quiet as it had been when Lexy and Milo met there four days ago. They even got the same alcove table.

Lexy glanced over at the bar. Archer wasn't in. Perhaps the Unicorn wasn't as much of a home from home as he made out. Or perhaps that whisky for dinner got the better of him.

"Do you think Steve and Elizabeth were having an affair?" Milo asked. "And Jackie found out?"

"I wondered about that, but I don't think so. From what Steve said, it was more about Jackie doing Elizabeth a big favour, and Elizabeth doing her one in return."

"The mind boggles. But it doesn't sound like the scenario for an acrimonious split. Let's have a look at that photo again – the one of the three of them."

Lexy felt in her inside pocket and took the photo out.

"Did you show this to Steve?"

Lexy nodded.

Milo winced. "What was his reaction?"

She thought. "I think he said something like 'Poor Elizabeth – I didn't realise.'"

"Didn't realise she still held a torch for him?"

"That's a quaint expression, Milo."

"I suppose the real question we should be asking ourselves is – did Steve know what was in Elizabeth's will?"

"And did he act on it in desperation?" she finished for him.

They contemplated one another.

"So, what am I going to do now?" said Milo. "Go to the DCI tomorrow morning and tell him I want to re-open this case in light of new evidence? Pull in Steve Paterson for questioning?"

"I'm just telling you the facts. Up to you what you do with them." Lexy hesitated. "The only thing that doesn't tie in is that Steve doesn't act like a man whose conscience is troubling him."

"Perhaps he hasn't got one."

Lexy screwed up her face. "So we're proposing that Steve came here six weeks ago with murder on his mind. Drove up to Four Winds in his cake van, got Elizabeth out on to the balcony and pushed?"

Milo shrugged. "As we said before, he was broke, and if he knew what was in the will, and felt confident Rowana would share it..."

"It's an incredibly cold-blooded, callous act though, isn't it?" said Lexy. "It doesn't seem to tie in with him as a person at all."

"I've told you before – there is no typical murderer."

"Anyway," she pressed on, "how could he have got Elizabeth into position without a struggle? How could he even have been sure the fall would kill her? I bet plenty of people would survive a fall like that. Maybe with fractures and ruptures, but still alive to tell the tale."

"If it was planned, he was taking a gamble, certainly."

"Perhaps they argued, and he pushed her in a fit of rage?" As soon as she said the words, Lexy immediately thought of Tyman, struggling with his mother on the high wire – allegedly. But who was going to take a clown seriously?

"Never know unless we ask him." Milo scratched his chin. "I think I'll have a quiet chat with him. Nothing heavy. Just tell him I need to clear up a couple of points. Mention that I know he was down here at the relevant time. See which way he jumps."

"Don't do it in the bedroom with the window open, then."

Why was she wisecracking? Must be a nervous reaction, because Lexy didn't find the prospect of Steve being questioned like this remotely funny.

217

Milo finished his drink. "Listen, I'm going to drop you back. I need to sleep. I'm giving evidence first thing tomorrow in Norwich Crown Court. Long drive." He smothered a yawn. "Meanwhile, just try to act normally around the Patersons, and I'll come over tomorrow evening and take Steve for a ride in my car."

"OK." Lexy wasn't sure she could wait that long. She'd have to do a bit of digging on her own.

"Oh – by the way, I stopped off at Edward's on the way over tonight."

"Is Kinky all right?" How could she have forgotten to ask earlier?

"No one was in, actually."

"Did you hear him barking when you rang the bell?"

Milo shook his head.

"Well, I suppose the kitchen is quite a way from the front door." But Lexy was uneasy. She located her phone. "Excuse me a sec."

She pressed Edward's number. It rang a couple of times, then went to voicemail. Same with Peter's. Lexy snapped the phone shut.

"No luck?"

"Nope. I spoke to Edward earlier. He sounded a bit strange, to be honest. I wonder if I should be worried." She ruffled her hair. "But he said Kinky was fine. And Peter said he was fine."

"I'm sure he's fine, then."

"Hmm." Lexy wasn't so confident. If she hadn't had a drink she would have driven straight over to Edward's to find out, even though it was close to eleven. She glanced at Milo. She couldn't ask him to take her there, he was dead on his feet.

Milo's own phone suddenly vibrated on the table, making them both jump. He pulled a face, and put it to his ear. "DI Milo."

Lexy saw his features stiffen. He threw a look at her, then shifted back in his seat, pressing the phone closer to his ear. "I... er... can't talk now, but I'll come straight over – all right?"

He listened, his face concerned. "Hmm. Yes. Just… er… hang on in there. Won't be long, OK?"

Lexy tried not to look as if she was straining her ears to listen. It didn't sound like a work call.

He clicked the phone shut. "Got to go."

"I'm ready." She got up. "If you need to hurry somewhere you could always drop me at the farm gate."

"No, you're all right. I'll take you back."

Milo was silent as they drove, his foot firmly on the accelerator.

"Problem?" Lexy enquired.

"Just a… personal thing. Need to go and see someone."

A personal thing. Lexy tried to imagine who Milo might be rushing through the night to see. Whoever she was, she sounded like someone he would drop everything for. The thought made Lexy strangely dissatisfied.

When she arrived back at the cottage, the kitchen door was still unlocked. Rowana was finishing the washing up.

"Ah – sorry," said Lexy.

"That's all right. I don't blame you for going off with Milo. He's nice. It's all right if you want him to stay over, by the way."

Lexy gave a small snort. "He's just a friend." Anyway, it sounded as if he had a hot date somewhere else that night.

"Dad would only get uptight if it was one of us," continued Rowana. "Over-protective father syndrome."

Lexy dragged her mind from speculation about Milo. "Is that something you've put to the test yourself?"

Rowana blushed. "Not personally. But Gabrielle has a few times."

"Like the night you were in the greenhouse?" It was out of her mouth before she'd had time to think.

Rowana frowned, thought back, and nodded. "Oh, yes. Gabby brought Russell back that night, because she knew Dad wasn't going to be back until the next day." She squinted at Lexy. "How did you know that?"

"Gabby mentioned it."

"Did she?" Rowana finished drying and took her time about hanging the tea towel on its hook. "Well, I'd better get to bed. See you tomorrow, Lexy."

That was a bit formal. Lexy watched her walk stiffly out of the kitchen.

Later, in her sleeping bag, Lexy thought about this exchange. Something had clicked in Rowana's mind when Lexy mentioned Steve's absence on the fateful morning. He must have given Rowana and Gabrielle some kind of account of where he'd been. Could this be the first time Rowana had thought to question it?

Lexy lay back on the pillow, instinctively waiting for Kinky to jump up. It took a few seconds to remember he wasn't there. What was he doing now, she wondered? Sleeping on a cushion in front of the range, with any luck. On an impulse she leaned down to find her phone. Hallelujah, she had a signal. She called Edward, even though it was nearly midnight. Three rings, then voicemail.

"Edward, can you call me? I just wanted to check that Kinky's still all right."

She fell into an anxious sleep, her phone by her hand.

19

At eight o'clock the following morning Lexy drove down to the gate at Pilgrim's Farm, stopped and called Edward.

It rang. He answered. Thank god.

"Ah… Lexy, it's you. Right…"

"Hi, Edward. Did you get my messages? Is Kinky all right?"

"Um… yes. He's here with me now," he panted. "We're out having a little walkies on the beach, aren't we, Kinky? How's London, sweetie?"

"I came back early." Did she hear a suppressed scream? "Have you got him on a lead?"

"What?"

"Kinky. Is he on a lead?"

"'Course he is. Don't you worry about anything. Ah – here's Peter. Must go. Byeee."

"Edward!" But he'd switched his phone off.

Lexy swore softly. What was going on? She didn't like the thought of Edward taking Kinky as far as the beach. He'd better have him on a lead. What if they met another dog? Kinky had a reputation for not allowing other dogs to pass him without taking a piece out of them. And if there was a choice, he always went for the large pedigree breeds.

Lexy winced at the thought. On balance the chihuahua would be safer with her. She'd done nothing but worry herself silly about him ever since she'd left him there. Lexy tried Edward again, and as she did so, her phone bleeped to announce its battery was low and promptly switched itself off.

She ground her teeth. Should have put the stupid thing on charge overnight. Tossing it into her bag, she turned into the lane.

Fifteen minutes later Lexy pulled into the long driveway that led to Edward's manor house. If they weren't back, she'd wait it out.

It started off well enough. The maroon Jaguar was there, and next to it Peter's immaculate black 1946 Alvis. Result. Lexy parked with a flourish, jumped out and gave the bell pull a good yank.

It was a minute or two before the huge, studded door swung open. Edward stood before her in his dressing gown, looking, for him, positively dishevelled. He stared at her aghast.

"Well, hello!" said Lexy. "Am I glad to see you!" She looked beyond him to the open kitchen door, expecting a small, caramel-coloured whirlwind. "Where is he, then?"

"Peter!" Edward shouted.

"I don't mean him."

A door opened upstairs.

"Now what?" Equally tousled, Edward's partner appeared at the top of the sweeping oak staircase. He gave a small shriek as he spotted Lexy.

"What's happened?" Lexy seized Edward's silk dressing-gown sleeve.

"It's all been a bit of a nightmare, lovie."

Peter was running down the stairs, slippers pattering. "I told you to call her!" he yelled at Edward.

"I was going to!"

Lexy found herself shouting, too. "For god's sake – what's happened to Kinky?"

"Right – let's all stay calm. Now – the main thing is, he's all right." Peter ushered Lexy in, prising her fingers from Edward's sleeve and shutting the front door, then led the way to the kitchen.

"At least he was the last time we saw him," Edward clarified, sinking into a chair.

"Tell me he's joking," Lexy said to Peter.

He grimaced. "You know when you left Kinky here?"

"Yes – two days ago." Lexy was feeling very tense.

"Well, Eddie and I needed to go out that evening for a quiet drink, because what with the antiques fair, and worrying about the kittens and so on, our relationship was getting a little strained."

"Even more so than usual," Edward pointed out.

"So we decided to take Kinky with us, in case he got lonely."

"But I specifically asked you to keep him here at all times." Lexy stared, dismayed, at Edward.

"We thought you were just being over-protective, lovie." Edward twisted a tea towel. "I mean, who would have thought …?"

"In the Jolly Herring, of all places…" agreed Peter, scandalised.

Lexy stared from one to the other. "So you took Kinky to Clopwolde, to the Jolly Herring."

"Yes," said Edward. "And he was with us all evening, eating crisps, perfectly happy. Then, just before last orders, we happened to leave him – it can only have been for, what, two minutes?"

Peter nodded confirmation. "I was in the loo, and Eddie was at the bar. And when we got back…"

"Gone! We nearly died, sweetie," said Edward. "Searched the pub from top to bottom, then had all the punters out looking for him up and down the street. Had to offer a reward, of course."

"Hang on, hang on," said Lexy. "Was he tied up when you left him?"

"Yes, his lead was tied to the table leg – it had been all evening." said Peter.

"Since that incident with the cocker spaniel," Edward reminded him. "But he must have pulled it free."

Or perhaps someone had deliberately untied it.

"Let me guess," said Lexy. "Was Gerard Warwick-Holmes in the Jolly Herring that night?"

"Gerard was there, as it happened, yes," said Peter. "He's staying there, actually."

"I suppose he was out looking, too, after Kinky disappeared?"

"Yes. In fact, it was the most helpful he'd been all week."

"I bet it was, the bastard," she said quietly.

Edward and Peter exchanged bemused looks. "The thing is, sweetie, we haven't been able to find Kinky anywhere," said Edward, pushing himself up, and pacing up and down the kitchen. "It's been the most traumatic episode in my entire life, and that's saying something. We've had the whole village on red alert. When you called us, we totally panicked."

"No, you panicked," snapped Peter.

"You were the one who told her he was all right."

"Only because you already had, you great f…"

"Shut up," said Lexy.

"Then we agonised about whether to call you back," Edward continued, his voice shaking.

"But we kept hoping he'd turn up," said Peter.

"And we stupidly left it longer and longer, and you kept trying to contact us, and basically we haven't been able to sleep a wink since it happened. We were up all last night, driving around Clopwolde with packets of Doggy Chomps. Just about to try to grab an hour now, before going out knocking on doors. God, darling, we've been to all the dogs' homes and rescue centres for miles around…" Edward slumped at the table, his eyes glistening. "We should have told you right away, lovie, but we know how much he means to you, and we just wanted to get him back in one piece without…"

"We even called your policeman," interrupted Peter.

"You called Milo?"

Edward frowned. "Fat lot of good that did us. He came round here, we explained what had happened, he asked a couple of questions, then off he went, like he had a poker stuck up his…"

"Edward!" Peter took over. "One has to say he didn't make any helpful suggestions, and when we asked if we should report Kinky as stolen through the official police channels, he said don't bother."

"Don't bother?" Lexy repeated.

"Well, he was in a tearing hurry," said Edward. "Clearly our little trauma was beneath him."

"Perhaps he had other things on his mind," said Lexy, darkly. "Anyway, forget him. Listen, is Gerard still in Clopwolde?"

"He's due to leave this morning, and good riddance. But what's he got to do with all this?" Peter was bemused.

"Everything." Lexy checked her watch. "Gerard is my husband."

"What!"

"I know. Hard to believe, isn't it? Imagine how I feel. Right – get dressed. We're going out."

"Yes, but… how?" Edward began, his round brown eyes widening. "Why did you never…? When did you…?"

"I'll tell you on the way."

"No – now." Edward propelled Lexy upstairs and she hovered in the doorway as the two men hopped around the bedroom, pulling on trousers, shirts and socks.

"Fourteen years? You've been married to Gerard Warwick-Holmes for…?" Peter shoved his foot into a tasteful leather brogue. "Does that mean you were that blonde…"

"Bimbo. Yes."

"Can't wear brown with black, lovie," Edward muttered.

"… in *Heirlooms in the Attic*?" Peter began to pull the shoe off again.

"Yes."

"The one who used to bend over a lot in tight jeans?"

"Yes. And boys – this is an emergency. Brown with black is exempt for the day. Come on."

Lexy led the way downstairs at a run.

"Where are we going?"

"The Jolly Herring. You'll have to drive, Edward."

She couldn't risk Gerard recognising her car. Not now it had a new windscreen.

On the way, Lexy gave the two men a potted history of her marriage to the washed-up antiques show presenter. She didn't tell them about the half million she'd nicked from his safe, but she mentioned that when he last saw her, Gerard had laid claim to the chihuahua.

"He was very keen to get his hands on Kinky," Lexy said. "Which is why I thought I'd put him in a safe house."

"And instead," said Edward, "I took the poor little mutt right into the lion's den. I'm distraught, darling."

"It's my own fault. I should have told you all this before."

"So you reckon Gerard's got Kinky hidden in his room at the JH?" Peter intervened.

"I'm certain he has. He must have swiped him when you two weren't there, and sneaked him up the stairs."

"Yes – now I come to think about it, we were sitting right at the back of the bar, by the door that leads up to the bedrooms," snorted Edward. "The bloody nerve of the man."

"And that... arse... actually came up to me at one point and asked about Kinky," Peter said. "Asked if he was ours. I said he belonged to a friend."

"That would have been enough for him." Lexy slipped her seatbelt off as they approached Clopwolde high street. "Drive round the back of the pub, and drop me off. You two are going to have to chat up the landlord and find out what room Gerard's in."

Edward swept the Jag into a space next to the pub kitchen, and Lexy slipped out and crouched between a row of wheelie bins, praying that her two friends wouldn't screw this up.

After five minutes, Edward put his head around the corner of the pub wall.

"What's the news?" Lexy whispered.

"He's in the Pilchard Room, right at the top. Peter's distracting old Fanny Adams..." Edward was referring to the pub landlord, Francis, "... so we can nip up the back stairs."

Edward led the way up three flights of carpeted stairs. The Pilchard Room was at the back of the creaky old Victorian pub. They crept up to the door. It had a Do Not Disturb sign hanging from the handle.

"He might be asleep. Try knocking," Lexy whispered. "I'll hide around the corner."

"What shall I say?"

"Whatever, Edward. Anything. Say you've come to wish him goodbye and thank him for all his hard work at the antiques fair."

Edward harrumphed.

"All you need to do is get in there and get a glimpse of Kinky. I'll do the rest."

When Lexy was in position, Edward rapped on the door. He waited a minute then rapped again.

He shook his head at Lexy. "No muffled barks. No rustle of quilt."

She hurried to join him. "Right." Lexy felt in her inside pocket.

"What're you doing? Ordering room service?"

"They didn't call them access cards for nothing." Lexy swiped the rectangle of plastic hard down between the door and frame, and on the second attempt, the lock sprang back and the door swung open.

The room was empty. It had been left in a hell of a mess – bedclothes in a twisted bundle, damp towels on the floor, half-drunk whisky bottle on the table.

But the most disturbing thing was the blood. Blood spattered across the sheets, the towels and the carpet.

Edward clutched her.

"It's OK. Kinky probably bit him."

Lexy tried to keep calm. She checked the bin. Among the used tissues and discarded newspapers were five empty dog food pouches. The cheap kind. A bowl of water had been left in the corner of the room.

"He was here all along – right under our noses." Edward balled his fists. "If I'd even guessed…"

Peter put his head around the door.

"He's left," he called in a stage whisper.

"We know," said Lexy.

"Is that…"

"Yes – blood."

Peter swayed. Lexy and Edward helped him back down the corridor. "Gerard actually called Fanny just now," Peter said, when he could talk again. "While I was standing there. From what I could gather, he said he'd had to leave in the early hours of this morning, so he paid his room bill over the phone."

Lexy swallowed. Gerard had been gone hours.

"Going to need to go up to London, then, aren't we?" said Edward, briskly. "Still got your key to Gerard's house, Lexy?"

Lexy shook her head. "I wasn't ever intending to go back."

"Well, I'm sure we can find a way to get hold of Kinky. Gerard's got to let him out in the back garden sometime, hasn't he? Don't worry, sweetie, we'll get him back, exactly the same way that slimy, red-faced gargoyle nicked him from us." Edward dangled his car keys in front of Lexy's face, and she and Peter followed him through the pub.

There was a chance Edward was right, but Lexy wasn't banking on it. She wasn't sure what Gerard intended to do with the chihuahua, but she knew it wouldn't involve giving him a loving home in South Kensington. All her husband had really wanted to do was to part Lexy from the dog – which he had successfully done. What he did with Kinky from now on was anyone's guess, although one thing was for sure. If Gerard was true to form, he'd offload him as soon as possible. And he'd already had several hours' start.

Lonny, Lexy's neighbour, was standing at the bar with his cronies as they passed through. He waved cheerily to her. "That you, luvver? Didn't recognise you with your clothes on."

The group of fishermen hooted.

"Just – let's not go there," said Lexy, at Peter's enquiring glance.

"Ah – you should've seen 'im." Lonny returned to his original subject. "Two lovely black eyes. Jumped in that thirty grand Chelsea tractor of 'is, and drove out of the village like Old Shuck himself was after 'im."

His friends roared with appreciative laughter.

Lexy had only just caught Lonny's words as she followed Edward and Peter through the door. She stopped and went over to the bar.

"You talking about Gerard Warwick-Holmes?"

He put an arm around her. "Yes, my darlin', I am. Four o'clock this morning, when I was heading for the beach with my rods, past the back of this 'ere pub, he came rushing out the door with two shiners and a bloody nose. Looked like someone had given him a right pasting."

"Did he have anyone... or anything... with him?"

Lonny shook his head. "Nah. Apart from that poncy designer suitcase."

Perhaps Kinky was already in the car. "Right. Thanks."

"What for, darlin'. I haven't given you anything yet. Could do, though, if you like?"

More hoots.

So Gerard had been in a fight. Wouldn't be the first time. Lexy just hoped that Kinky hadn't been caught up in it, too.

Edward was gunning the Jaguar outside the pub, Peter sitting next to him, pulling at his seatbelt.

They arrived at the South Kensington villa two and a half hours later.

Edward parked at a discreet distance, ignoring the yellow lines and 'residents only' signs. Gerard's ostentatious car wasn't parked in the drive.

"Is there a garage?" Peter asked.

Lexy shook her head. She couldn't trust herself to speak. All the way there, against her common sense, she had got up her hopes that Gerard would be at home with Kinky, and somehow between the three of them, she, Edward and Peter would be able to recover the chihuahua. Gerard's car not being in the drive was the first blow.

"Perhaps he dropped Kinky off earlier and went on somewhere, Edward mused.

229

Yeah, the hospital, if what Lonny said was right.

Edward pushed open the car door. "I'm going to have a listen through the letterbox."

"Yes," said Lexy, eagerly. "If Kinky's there he's bound to bark. Just be quick in case Gerard turns up – we need the element of surprise."

She hoped that none of neighbours was watching as Edward sidled up the drive in a pair of shades and an old trilby he'd found in the boot of the Jaguar.

"He couldn't look more like a housebreaker if he tried," Peter muttered. "Why doesn't he just stride up there... oh, sod it..."

A traffic warden had appeared. Peter slid into the driving seat and he and Lexy drove off, leaving Edward to it. The only parking space was two streets away.

Edward called Peter's mobile, minutes later. "Not a sound from inside. I'll be waiting on the other side of the... hang on..." His voice fell to a hoarse whisper. "The chihuahua has landed."

"Yes!" Peter started the engine. Lexy felt her heart surge.

But when they pulled up beside Edward, who was lurking behind one of the lime trees that lined the road, he shrugged his shoulders apologetically, pointing to a woman holding a lead. "Different chihuahua. Sorry."

"They're practically compulsory around here." Lexy gritted her teeth to stop the tears of disappointment that threatened to well. She looked over at the villa. "Sorry, guys, I need to know if he's in there."

And before either Edward or Peter could stop her, she had marched over to her old home, walked down the side passage and scaled the locked wooden gate that led to the back garden.

"Kinky," she called, jumping down. "You there, boy?"

He wasn't. Not outside, at any rate. She stared through the conservatory window, shading her eyes against the sun. God, the place was a mess – Gerard had always been a stranger to housework. Clearly hadn't found anyone yet to take on the job for him. Lexy felt vindictively glad.

She checked all the downstairs windows at the back, calling and tapping on the glass. But there was no familiar returning bark. She knew it had been a long shot.

Lexy, Edward and Peter spent the rest of the day slumped in the car, watching the villa. At least, Lexy did. Edward and Peter both fell asleep. She couldn't blame them, although she wished Peter didn't mumble so much in his sleep. Especially as all he mumbled about was antiques.

Edward awoke with a start late in the afternoon. He blinked round at Lexy. "Anything?"

She shook her head. "Might as well give up. We could be here all night at this rate."

"I'm so sorry, sweetie. Tell you what, we'll come straight back here tomorrow morning and …"

"I think Gerard's already found another home for Kinky, Edward."

Hopefully it wasn't the bottom of the Thames.

Lexy was very quiet on the drive back home.

When she returned to Four Winds Cottage, nursing a heavy heart, it was gone ten, and the Patersons were out – they'd left a note to say that they'd gone to the Unicorn and Lexy was welcome to join them.

She didn't think she'd be great company that evening.

She fished her phone out of her bag, and went back out to the car to find the charger.

The faint sound made her look up. Someone was coming. She could hear the crunch of shoe on gravel. Lexy ducked down by the car.

After a minute a dark figure walked into the clearing, then disappeared into shadows at a corner of the wall surrounding the cottage. Lexy next saw him looking in at the kitchen window.

He went around the side of the cottage.

Was it Tyman? Bruce? Couldn't be Ward because of his ankle. Whoever it was, he was checking whether anyone was in.

231

The figure reappeared at the other side of the cottage, then walked off down the rutted track.

Lexy wondered whether it was someone from the village, casing the joint. If whoever it was had bothered trying the kitchen door handle, they'd have been able to get in and have away whatever they wanted.

Lexy felt too exhausted to trail the interloper, but she went back to the cottage and systematically locked all the doors and windows. Just after she had gone to bed, she heard muffled voices as the Patersons returned. They had a key, luckily. Lexy listened to the creaking of the stairs as they went to bed.

She lay back in the darkness, trying to push away images of what Gerard might have done to her dog. Unsuccessfully. In the end, she put the light back on and turned on the portable radio Gabrielle had been listening to earlier. She tuned it to something classical and lay back.

After a long while, Lexy had a plan. In the morning she would go back up to London on her own and talk to Gerard, if he was there. Find him, if he wasn't. Plead with him if necessary. And if that didn't work, she'd threaten to expose him over the stolen painting. Somehow or other, she'd get the chihuahua back. If he was still…

Lexy lay back, letting Mozart soothe her mind, trying to think about something other than Kinky.

She allowed her thoughts to drift to the Gallimores. Even with the recent revelations about Steve, Lexy still held on to a slim strand of belief that they had something to do with Elizabeth's death. But on what basis?

Count the ways, Lexy.

Their behaviour from the word go. Their seemingly irrational attitude towards her presence at Four Winds Cottage, and the news of Rowana's inheritance. The way Bruce had lost no time at all in making an offer for the place, and in encouraging his sons to sweet-talk Gabrielle and Rowana with the same end in mind.

They wanted the cottage – but why?

Bruce had cajoled Lexy to leave the place, and when that didn't work, he made some kind of pact with his elder son to get her out by more drastic means: a pact that excluded Tyman.

Was Tyman the key to all of this?

Lexy conjured up Tyman's good-natured face. She tried to think why the trip she had made with him up the hill on September Eve had been such a big problem to Ward. So much so that he felt the need to ambush her like something out of… Tarzan. It just didn't make sense. On balance, there seemed to be more evidence pointing to Ward Gallimore being the one with problems.

And the ambush was nothing next to the gun incident.

Get out of the way, Tyman!

No! Don't shoot!

Then that ear-shattering explosion that Lexy would remember for the rest of her life.

It wasn't Lexy who Tyman saw at the last minute, when he warned Ward not to shoot. He hadn't seen her – that much was obvious from what he'd stammered out when she'd questioned him about it. So it had been the fox he was trying to save. Why not just admit that in the first place?

She shook her head, confounded.

There were other odd things, not least the way Tyman flinched every time Elizabeth's fall was mentioned. And the fact that the Gallimores were constantly watching the cottage through binoculars. And that other falling incident concerning Tyman's mother and a circus high wire.

Add to that the oft-referred-to sheep on the hill, the sheep that Lexy had never actually seen. And the incident with the bull.

"The bull that also never was," Lexy said to herself.

On top of all of that was the frankly bizarre behaviour of Tyman and Ward when she went to the farm the previous day. What was all that about?

Why had Tyman started yelling?

Because he'd seen her coming down the path from the cottage. Big deal.

Bruce had shut him up pretty quickly, but what had Ward said when she'd queried it?

I think Tyman must be pleased you've come to see us.

Lexy hadn't realised that she'd come to mean that much to Gallimore minor.

An earlier incident suddenly came to Lexy's mind. When she'd been hiding under Ward's bed, on the night they'd been invited to the Gallimores for dinner.

Tyman had been trying to find her.

Well, she's not in here, Ward had said, unwittingly. *Perhaps she decided to give you the slip?*

Yes, well, we wouldn't want that, would we?

That was it. That was the thing that had been lurking at the back of her mind.

Why hadn't they wanted her loose on the farm? What hadn't they wanted her to see? Something incriminating? Something that might link them back to Elizabeth? She must…

Lexy felt her eyes closing.

The next thing she knew was a tap on the door. She pushed herself up, blinking. The table light was still on, as was the radio. She glanced at the clock. It was five-thirty in the morning.

"Who is it?" Lexy stood up, alarmed.

There was another quiet tap. It was someone at the patio door.

Lexy went over cautiously. The curtain was half pulled across. Cupping her hands she put her face against the glass to stare out into the iron grey dawn. No one there. Was she expecting the dark figure who cased the joint earlier? Surely he wouldn't knock before entering.

Plucking up courage, Lexy unlocked and opened the door. "Who is it?" she called, quietly.

No one. Had she imagined it? But there wasn't even a breeze

to blame for making the leaves of the rhododendron tap against the glass.

Lexy was just closing the doors when she heard a sound.

One she recognised. Scampering feet.

A second later Kinky appeared. He leapt up at her with a joyful bark.

Lexy was almost too stunned to greet him.

She stared beyond him, went out on to the patio. There was no sign of anyone.

"Tell me it wasn't you tapping," she said to the excited chihuahua. She checked him over. He seemed the same as ever. No new scars. No additional limps. Had he somehow escaped from Gerard during that fracas, and made his way back here? He'd be pretty footsore if he had, and he clearly wasn't. And, anyway, surely he'd go home, to the cabin, if he was loose in Clopwolde?

"Main thing is, you're back, mate," said Lexy, the realisation finally hitting her. She closed her eyes, sinking on to the sofa. "You're back."

20

Lexy awoke to a familiar discomfort. She was squashed up on one end of the sofa, and Kinky was spread out at the other end.

It hadn't been a dream. The dog opened one eye, then jumped up and shook himself, demanding breakfast.

Lexy heard the sound of murmured voices, and pushed open the living room door to listen. Sounded as if Steve, Rowana and Gabrielle were talking together.

She quickly dressed, and pushed open the kitchen door.

The Patersons were indeed sitting at the table, heads bent together, talking intensely.

"Hello," Lexy said.

They all jumped.

"He's back," said Rowana, as Kinky trotted past them to the larder.

"Yup – like a bad penny," Lexy smiled. She opened a packet of dog food for Kinky.

"We're having a council of war," said Steve.

"Oh, sorry. I didn't mean to butt in."

For a moment Lexy wondered if things had come to a head. Perhaps, thanks to her broaching the subject with each of them, Rowana and Gabrielle had discussed the morning of Elizabeth's death, and the fact that their father had been absent during that crucial time, and now they were questioning him themselves.

But Steve looked far too pleased with himself to be on the wrong end of an inquisition.

"Actually, we could do with your advice."

"Really?"

"Really." Rowana pushed out a chair for her. A drift of papers, covered in scribbles, figures, bullet points and question marks lay across the table.

Gabrielle poured a cup of tea and put it in front of Lexy. The girl was becoming positively human.

"So…?" Lexy looked around at them, her face going a little rigid as she met Steve's eyes. Whatever they were cooking up here, he wasn't out of deep water yet.

"We've discovered something about ourselves since we've been here," he began.

"Don't tell me – you're all aliens from the planet Zarg."

"Nah – we knew that already. What we've actually discovered is that none of us wants to start up the cake business again."

"We've had our fill of cakes," Gabrielle reiterated.

"In a manner of speaking," Rowana added.

"So we're going to have a go at something we really want to do for a change – seeing as we've been given this opportunity," said Steve.

But were you given it, or did you engineer it? Lexy couldn't return his smile.

She got up to let Kinky into the garden.

"The thing is, I'm not going to sell the cottage," Rowana announced. "We're staying here. I already love Four Winds Cottage far too much to part with it. So do Gabrielle and Dad."

"But how will you…?" Lexy began.

"Well, there's a little boutique over in Aldeburgh that's advertising for a full-time assistant." Gabrielle had anticipated her question. "I called them this morning and they've asked me to come over for an interview."

"And I'm going to start restoring vintage motors," said Steve.

"Big surprise there," added Rowana.

"Won't make any money from it, but what the hell. I'll try to get some work in a local garage to make ends meet."

Lexy said a silent prayer that Steve wouldn't be studying car manuals in a prison cell instead. She turned to Rowana, eyebrows raised.

Steve and Gabrielle were grinning like a couple of Cheshire

cats that just got a large dollop of double cream on top of their cream.

Rowana blushed. "I've been accepted into art college in London. Just told Dad and Gabby."

"Wow!" Lexy made like she didn't already know.

"I'm going back there in a couple of weeks, to find digs," the girl continued. "But I'm coming back here at weekends."

"I couldn't be prouder of both my daughters," said Steve.

"Leave it out, Dad," said Gabrielle.

"So – what was that advice you wanted?" Lexy asked. "If you were going to ask me whether you should take the plunge and follow your dreams, I'd say you've already answered that question."

The Patersons smiled sheepishly.

"Even though Elizabeth's dead," Lexy went on, "it seems like her influence lives on." She was watching Steve carefully. "Without that old car in her garage, you might have taken Rowana up on her offer to sell the cottage and gone back to London to start another confectionery business."

"True." He returned her look with steady good humour.

"And Rowana might have decided to sacrifice her place at art college, so she could help you."

Rowana nodded.

"Not that I'd have let her," Steve said.

"And I might still be wishing I'd married Russell," said Gabrielle. "And I'm glad to say I'm now completely over him." But did her sapphire eyes look a little wistful?

"What about Ward?" Rowana said, quickly. "After all, we are going to be neighbours with them now."

"Not my type," returned Gabrielle. "And that book he lent me was about a completely different Tom Jones. I think the sod was laughing at me."

Lexy and Rowana exchanged looks.

"I'd better get ready to go to Aldeburgh." Gabrielle pushed her chair back. "It's OK if I borrow the van, isn't it, Dad?"

"Yes, of course. Good luck, darling." He hugged his elder daughter.

Lexy watched them, struck by the similarity between the two, in looks at least.

"I'll be in the studio," said Rowana. "I'm going to sort out Elizabeth's paints. Best of luck, Gabby." She, too, embraced her sister. But they were chalk and cheese. Just as Steve had said.

Steve and Lexy were left alone in the kitchen.

"I'm glad you're going to be staying here," she said. "Hope things work out."

"It's going to be a struggle." Steve drained his tea. "But I think we'll get by."

"It's a nice place to get by in."

"It'll be even better when I get that window fixed. But right now, I feel like stretching my legs. Fancy a walk up that legendary hill?"

"I do," said Lexy. Time to get some answers.

"Give me ten minutes, then." Steve stood up. "I'd better make sure Gabby gets off all right."

"I'll meet you by the back gate," said Lexy. "Just need to make a phone call." Might as well put Edward and Peter out of their misery.

She left by the kitchen door and headed down the track, checking her phone at intervals until she got a signal.

"Lexy!" Edward had the manic voice again. "We'll come and pick you up now. Where are you, exactly? Peter and I have talked about this Gerard business, and we think we might have to resort to violence. I know someone who…"

"Edward… Edward… it's OK."

"… might be able to get us a…"

"Edward. Kinky's back," Lexy shouted.

"What?"

"He's back with me. Arrived at half five this morning. On his own."

Lexy had been wondering whether Edward and Peter had

been involved in Kinky's mysterious reappearance, but it seemed unlikely, judging by the loud sobbing coming down the phone.

"Thank god – finally we can sleep!" she heard Peter wail.

"Yes – you two do just that, and I'll… catch up with you later. Er… Edward… would you really have held Gerard at gunpoint for me?"

"I have been quite overwrought about all this, sweetie."

"Bloody lucky you came back when you did, Kinky," Lexy muttered, as they went back up the hill. "Otherwise I'd have had a gay version of Bonnie and Clyde on my hands."

Gabrielle was just leaving in the van. Steve waved from the door.

Lexy frowned, her hand slipping into her inside jacket pocket. But this time she didn't take out the photograph of Steve, Gabrielle and Rowana.

She took out the one of Elizabeth Cassall, the one she should have looked at properly in the first place.

After all, it had been staring her in the face all the time.

21

"So, when were you going to tell her?"

"What?"

"I said, when were you going to tell her?" Lexy had to shout to make herself heard.

She and Steve had walked to the summit of the hill.

It was a fresh, breezy morning, with low white clouds scudding across the sky, but it wasn't the wind that was giving them hearing problems.

It was the sheep.

Lexy couldn't understand how she'd missed them on her previous trips up the hill – the summit was seething with brown and white ovines all bleating hoarsely at one another.

Luckily she had a lead for Kinky, or rather a piece of string she kept in her bag for emergencies, seeing as the chihuahua's usual lead had disappeared during the incident at the Jolly Herring. The dog was uncharacteristically uninterested in the sheep though, and stuck close to Lexy, a worried frown seeming to furrow his brow.

"Rowana. When were you going to tell her who her real mother was?"

Steve caught her arm, his face grey. "Who told you…?"

"Let's go over there." Lexy pointed to a free patch of ground close to the cliff edge.

The sheep parted like a woollen version of the Red Sea to let them through.

They could finally hear each other.

The sea undulated below, white-cuffed waves reaching greedily to the soft sand at the foot of the cliff.

"Elizabeth told me." Lexy took out the photo.

Steve took it from her, and this time he looked at it for a

long time.

Lexy inspected the ground, kicked a couple of dried sheep droppings over the cliff and sat down facing the sea. Steve dropped down beside her. Kinky paced around behind them.

"Jackie couldn't conceive," Steve said, without preamble. "We tried for two years. Really tried. I'm talking practically every night."

"That's a lot of detail," said Lexy.

"I was... knackered. Literally..."

"So is that."

"... and Jackie was distraught. Doctors, fertility clinics, old wives' tales, we did the lot. She got suicidal in the end, even though we had Gabrielle, and... I thought... everything to live for."

The breeze tugged at the photo in his hand.

"Then, one day, when I was just about at the end of my tether, Jackie got a phone call from an old friend of hers." He inclined his head. "Elizabeth Cassall. Said she was in some kind of trouble, and Jackie went straight off to visit her on the next train out of London, leaving me with Gabrielle to look after and a shop to run."

He paused, a muscle twitching in his cheek.

"When Jackie came back a week later, there was a change in her. Suddenly life was good again. She was almost manically happy. Every couple of weeks she'd go to Suffolk, and she'd come back happier each time."

Lexy frowned. The explanation wasn't going quite how she expected.

"Then after a couple of months had passed, she announced she was going to stay with Liz for six weeks. By which point I started to wonder what the hell was going on."

So was Lexy.

Steve stared hard at the photograph again. "I couldn't have even imagined the truth. It was the time of the Gulf War. 1990. Elizabeth's husband Robert had been over there in the thick of it. And while he'd been out on manoeuvres, Elizabeth had a very ill-advised one night stand with …"

Here we go. So he was going to own up to having an affair, after all. Lexy had suspected it for a while, but it was still disappointing to find that…

"… Archer Trevino."

"What?" Lexy felt a wave of shock pass over her. "But… ?"

"I know." Steve closed his eyes briefly. "Two months later she realised she was pregnant. She also knew that when Robert got back from the Gulf he would realise the child couldn't possibly be his. She wasn't even going to think about telling Archer – he was a drunken, womanizing… libertine." He shook his head. "But she didn't want to take a life. So she called her old friend Jackie, desperate to work out what to do. And, unbeknown to me, Jackie had this great idea."

He gave her a grim look.

"My god," whispered Lexy.

"Yes. Somehow they managed to keep it quiet between them. It didn't show on Elizabeth until the final months. At which point, she shut herself up here at the cottage, and Jackie looked after her. Helped her give birth, then they called a doctor in Clopwolde just afterwards and said Jackie had unexpectedly gone into labour."

"*Jackie*… not Elizabeth," Lexy whispered, incredulous.

"Yup. And she came back home to me with a newborn daughter."

Lexy shook her head in disbelief.

Elizabeth Cassall. Rowana Cassall. Or perhaps, Lexy reminded herself, Rowana Trevino. Daughter of the painter who lived in the thatched cottage in Nodmore and drank whisky. Perhaps he'd stop now he had someone other than himself to consider.

"Must have been something of a surprise."

"Tell me about it." Steve picked up a stone and flung it at the sea far below.

Kinky's ears pricked up. Lexy tightened her hold on the piece of string to which he was still attached. "It explains that big mutual favour between Elizabeth and Jackie," she said, half to herself.

"Yes. Elizabeth gets to keep face, and Jackie gets what she was prepared to do anything for. A baby." His mouth jerked. "At first Jackie tried to convince me Rowana was ours. I almost believed her, god knows, I wanted to. She was a beautiful baby – and Jackie was in seventh heaven. But I knew I had to make her and Elizabeth put it right between them. Tell the truth to everyone involved. I came down here – spoke to Elizabeth. I thought perhaps Jackie and I could try to legally adopt Rowana. But Elizabeth told me to go and never to contact her again. And the irony of all this was that Robert never came back from the Gulf anyway. I didn't find that out till years later.

"Then Jackie got ill. It was so… quick." He shot a look at Lexy. "I couldn't put her through any more pain than she was already in. So I promised I'd look after Rowana as my own. It was my last promise to her."

They were silent for a while.

"Did you tell Elizabeth that Jackie had… passed away?" Lexy said.

He shook his head.

"Whose names are on the birth certificate?"

"Mine and Jackie's."

"It must have given you a hell of a shake up when you heard about this inheritance out of the blue."

Steve nodded. "I'd been living in denial for nearly seventeen years. As far as I was concerned, Rowana was my daughter and that was the end of it." His fingers pulled at the short grass surrounding them. "Elizabeth and I never did have any contact. But there was a part of me that lived in fear of something happening one day. Old sins cast long shadows, and all that.

"In a way, the worst of it was hearing that Elizabeth had died. I opened that letter from the solicitor two months ago and I looked over at Rowana and it finally struck home that she'd had a mother who'd lived and died just two counties away from us, and she'd never known a single thing about her."

Lexy felt herself reach out and squeeze Steve's hand.

He shot her a grateful look. "Like I said, I'd no idea that Elizabeth had left her estate to Jackie, let alone Rowana. Couldn't get my head around it at first. Even made me angry that Elizabeth had put us in this position. And through it all, I had to keep up this pretence that I was surprised, you know, this 'how amazing that an old friend of Jackie's has left Rowana this huge inheritance' routine."

He frowned. "One of the oddest things was the way Rowana reacted to it all. I mean, you would have thought she'd be just the tiniest bit pleased that she'd inherited all this money from someone she'd been told was a friend of her mother, someone she'd never met, so would never mourn. And at a time when we were so desperate for money."

"You'd have thought so."

"But right from the start she treated it like a poisoned chalice. She didn't even seem to want to come here and see the place, which made two of us, frankly – but at least I had good reason. I was very worried that Rowana was going to find something here, a letter or… diary… or… god knows what… that would reveal the truth about her parentage. I didn't even want her seeing snaps of Elizabeth."

"I can understand that." They both glanced down at the photo Steve still held in his other hand.

He sighed. "Gabrielle was the one who chivvied us into coming straight down here, even though we didn't have a key, and the paperwork wasn't signed off. Naturally, she couldn't understand why Rowana and I were dragging our feet. We had a look around the outside, and I discovered the back door key under a pot, when they were round the other side of the cottage."

Lexy's lips twitched. Rowana had found the front door key under one pot, and Steve had found the back door key under another one. Elizabeth didn't believe in sophisticated security measures.

"I didn't want Gabby knowing," Steve continued, "because she'd be straight in there, so I pocketed it, and that first night, when they were asleep, I nipped back to the cottage and gathered up all the letters and photos I could find, in every drawer and cupboard."

So that explained the strange absence of paperwork in the place. "Lucky the Gallimores didn't spot you," said Lexy.

"Would have taken a bit of explaining, wouldn't it? But as luck would have it, I got the whole lot back to my room in the B&B at Clopwolde, unseen, and I sat up for the rest of the night sifting out everything I thought might give a clue to Rowana's background."

"Find anything?"

"Not really. Elizabeth had been pretty careful. There were a couple of photos of her, looking just like Rowana, which I got rid of. But I think the most incriminating thing of all was that one I missed – the one of Rowana, Gabby and me."

They looked at one another.

"Wonder how Elizabeth came by it?" said Lexy. "Guess she must have gone up to London and taken it in a mad moment."

"A moment of regret, more like." Steve stared hard at the grey-green sea below.

Lexy still had hold of his hand. They sat like that a while. She wondered whether to tell him about the inscription in *The Language of Flowers*. No – perhaps she'd leave him to find it himself one day.

The language of flowers. Lexy smiled.

"Unusual name, Rowana," she remarked.

"Yes. It was the only thing Elizabeth requested."

Lexy thought she knew why. It was so that Elizabeth could remember her daughter whenever she looked out at the tree she'd planted sixteen years ago in the garden of Four Winds Cottage.

The mountain ash, otherwise known as the rowan.

"So when were you going to tell her?" Lexy asked, again.

Steve shook his head. "I wasn't. And now she's off to art college in London in a couple of weeks. I want her to go with an untroubled mind. Whatever it was that was bothering her when all this business started seems to be over, and she's happier than she's been for a long time. Elizabeth, god bless her, is dead now. Why upset the apple cart?"

"Archer Trevino?" suggested Lexy.

"He doesn't know."

Lexy hesitated. Archer's ravaged features swam before her eyes. Did he know? Or perhaps guess? What was it he'd said as they parted?

'... speaking of the Unicorn, you know that night you were all in there... the two girls... Steve's daughters, weren't they?'

When Archer looked across the pub that night and recognised Steve, did he also see Rowana and make the connection? Did he recognise Elizabeth in her? Or even himself?

"He very nearly did, though," Steve continued.

"Really?"

"A couple of weeks before we learned about this inheritance I came down here intending to see him."

Lexy sat stock still.

"I was going to beg money from him," said Steve. "Because he was rich, and I'd spent the last sixteen years bringing up his daughter. Stupid idea, and dangerous. I would never have gone through with it. I think I just needed to get away for a while. I got as far as Clopwolde, booked myself into a fussy little B&B for the night, sat in my room and drank a bottle of Scotch. Woke up fully clothed on my bed the following morning with the landlady standing over me."

"Er... about what time was it?" Lexy asked. "When she was standing over you?" She realised she was squeezing Steve's hand with some force now.

He looked down at his crushed fingers. "Nine? Quarter to?

I hadn't shown for my pre-booked breakfast. Major sin at the Wharf View B&B. Apparently the cleaning lady had let herself into my room when I was meant to be at the breakfast table, thought I was dead, and started having palpitations." He paused. "Er... my fingers are starting to go black, by the way. Not that I don't like you holding my hand."

Lexy loosened her grip. She realised that she'd started laughing.

"What is it?" Steve regarded her quizzically. "What's so funny?"

"Just nice to have my instincts confirmed."

"What – that I'm a drunken slob?"

"No. That you're a good man."

"I try my best." Steve started laughing too, and before Lexy knew it, he had leaned over and kissed her. And she kissed him back.

"I'm sorry." He took hold of her other hand. "Couldn't help myself."

"Me, too. Weak moment."

They eyed one another.

"Better get back."

"Yes."

He stood, stretched, pulled her up and held her close to him, suddenly serious. "I'm going to have to tell Rowana, aren't I?"

"Up to you." Lexy let her head rest on his shoulder. Just for a moment. Kinky stared up at her askance.

"I guess I owe her the truth," Steve went on. "But it's going to be messy."

He was still holding that last photo of Elizabeth, the one that looked so painfully like Rowana. The wind made it flutter.

He and Lexy watched it.

"I could just let go of this."

"And let her find out some other way? You'll always be looking over your shoulder."

"Lexy – I… er… suppose there's no chance of you staying on at the cottage, is there? I mean, with me?"

Stay at Four Winds Cottage? Lexy imagined herself living

there, with Freshing Hill on her doorstep every day. A romantic new relationship, a ready-made family, domestic bliss…

She felt herself shaking her head.

"I know, I know," said Steve. "Too soon to ask. Anyway, you're a free spirit. And I'm a forty-five year old bloke with a lot of explaining to do."

He'd got that about right.

They made their way back through the sheep. Steve held the photograph of Elizabeth in his hand, until they reached the gate of the cottage, then he slipped it into his pocket.

"I'm returning to the underside of my small red car to think," he said. "Just in case anyone wants me. And I enjoyed that kiss, by the way."

22

Lexy let herself into the kitchen and pulled out a chair.

"God, Kinky, what a tangled web," she murmured, watching the dog circle the kitchen floor, sniffing suspiciously.

At least one good thing had come from this. Steve was out of the frame as far as Elizabeth's death was concerned. She would still check his alibi though, go and talk to the fearsome landlady and her cleaner at Wharf View B&B. They'd be sure to remember the disgraceful drunk.

But Lexy knew that it would be a formality.

"And you know what this all means," she said to the inattentive dog. "The Gallimores are back on centre stage again."

She felt almost too tired to contemplate it.

In fact, it was tempting to draw a line under the whole Elizabeth affair, pack up her stuff and head back to the cabin a day early, now that Gerard was gone. Lexy couldn't quite trust herself to get through another night on the sofa after that kiss, and she didn't want to complicate matters with Steve any further. It would be tough to leave, though...

But leave she must, Lexy told herself, for all the reasons Steve had said. But before she went she would have to square things with Rowana, and convince the girl that her magic in the greenhouse wasn't in any way responsible for Elizabeth's death.

No time like the present. She went to the studio, but Rowana wasn't there. She wasn't in the garden, either. Lexy went upstairs and called outside the room she was sharing with Gabrielle. No answer. She opened the door to Elizabeth's room, and went over to the window, gazing down the hill towards Pilgrim's Farm. Was that Rowana walking up the tarmac track? Lexy fetched the binoculars, but the figure was too far away to identify.

Perhaps she'd drive down there.

Lexy collected Kinky, who was now outside the kitchen door, sniffing around under the hydrangea bush where he'd last had his teeth in that delicious bone.

She ushered him into the Panda, stuck her key in the ignition and turned it. The car coughed raucously, spat and died.

Lexy sat there with her eyes shut counting to one hundred. She'd got to eighty-eight when a tap on her window made her jump. She wound it down.

"Problem?" Steve enquired.

Lexy found herself blushing like a teenager. "Arsing thing won't start – again," she said gruffly.

"Well, it can't be the spark plugs." He lifted the lime green bonnet and propped it.

Lexy got out. "Listen – you don't have to…"

"It's OK." Steve bent over the engine. "Although I have to say it's not looking good in here."

"I knew it hadn't got long to live." Lexy sighed. She'd miss the Panda – they'd had an action-packed three months together. And she'd just bought the ungrateful bastard a new windscreen.

"Oh, she'll go again," said Steve. "I just need to get a couple of parts. There's a scrap yard just outside Lowestoft…"

"Hey – don't go to any trouble." Especially after she'd just given him the brush off.

"It's no trouble. I welcome any excuse to go to a scrap yard. Just don't tell the girls. Last time I went for some replacement door handles for the van, I came back towing a Hillman Imp."

Lexy swallowed. Why did he have to be so endearing?

She squinted down the hill. "Think I can see Rowana down there – I might go and meet her."

She set off, the chihuahua at her heel, aware that Steve was watching after her. "What do you, reckon, Kinky?" she murmured. "Am I being too hasty turning him down? After all, it would be brilliant living here all the time."

Kinky gave her the briefest of pained glances. He was sniffing at the path like a minute bloodhound.

"Oh, yeah – I forgot how you felt about the place," Lexy went on. "You've never really taken to it here, have you?" She looked at the scenery all around. "Can't imagine why."

Kinky gave a series of sharp barks.

Lexy ignored him. The thought of living at Four Winds was so intoxicating. But was it that, rather than the thought of living with Steve? Would she be even contemplating it if he lived in a council flat in Ipswich? Anyway, she'd only met the bloke a few days ago. And she didn't really know him – not beyond a brief kiss. Lexy felt herself redden again. No – she couldn't just stay and hope things worked out. What if they didn't? And how would Gabrielle and Rowana react when they discovered Steve and her in the throes of an affair? Didn't bear thinking about – especially as Rowana was her client.

But what if Steve was her soulmate – that once in a lifetime person she'd never come across again? Was she going to regret this forever? Lexy was so absorbed in this dilemma that she walked all the way to Pilgrim's Farm without being aware of it. It was only when Kinky gave another disconcerted bark that Lexy focused on her surroundings.

Mrs Mangeot was in the yard, loading bags into the back of a small car.

"Why, 'allo, dear," she said. "Come to see the boys? Been in the wars they 'ave. Both of 'em fell up in the woods the other night."

She obviously didn't know that Lexy was already aware of this.

"They were out badger watching. Badger watching! Must have scared off every badger for miles around, the clumsy buggers. I could tell them a thing or two about it, and it doesn't involve crashing around in size nine boots and tripping over tree stumps, either."

Lexy had to stop herself from snorting out loud. The Gallimores had told their housekeeper that they'd been out badger watching, rather than killing foxes. No wonder she thought they were such angels.

"Anyway, I'd best get on." Mrs Mangeot squeezed herself into her car. "I was meant to be meeting my daughter at the farm entrance but the poor girl's walked all the way up here now."

Lexy looked up to see a figure trudging towards them, the same one she'd seen earlier. Not Rowana, then.

Mrs Mangeot pulled off with a wave.

Lexy looked over at the front door.

What was it at Pilgrim's Farm that the Gallimores wanted to hide from her?

The door was ajar. Lexy pushed it open.

"Anybody home?" she called.

Silence.

Lexy went to the living room, expecting to find Ward still laid up on the sofa. But all she found was a neatly folded quilt with two pillows stacked on it. There were two tracks visible in the carpet leading to the kitchen. Ward must have found a way of getting up and about.

Lexy compressed her lips, and pushed open the kitchen door.

Three cups with dregs of coffee stood on the draining board.

There was a door at the far end of the kitchen that opened out on to what looked like a scullery. She went across and pushed it wide. The small room contained a washing machine and a pile of damp washing in a basket. And a door leading outside.

"You'd better stay here," Lexy said to the chihuahua, pushing him back into the kitchen and shutting the door. She didn't want him having a close encounter with the world's rarest chicken, or whatever it was the Gallimores kept here.

She went through the scullery and found herself in a covered passage with a corrugated roof. Kinky had started barking – sharp, warning barks.

Steeling herself, Lexy followed the passage past a row of woodsheds with cobwebbed windows. It ended at an old-fashioned tiled path that curved away past a bank of faded pink hydrangeas. She paused. A printed sign with red lettering informed her that she was entering a quarantine area. Authorised Personnel Only.

The double track that had made an indentation across the living room carpet was visible in front of her as two damp tyre tracks. Shrugging, Lexy made her way along the path, feeling the warmth of the morning sun on the back of her neck, Kinky's barks fading into the distance. It wound on, until she felt marooned in hydrangeas and silence.

Then she turned a corner, and found herself looking at a high brick wall. It had a sturdy wooden gate in it, with a heavy steel bolt, drawn open. A padlock with the key in it hung on a rusty nail beside the bolt.

Lexy slowly pushed the gate open.

23

She found herself in an untidy garden. Clumps of pampas grass were dotted around a muddy pond. A large fallen tree pointed broken branches to the sky.

It wasn't what she expected a quarantine yard to look like, particularly given the neat and tidy appearance of the rest of Pilgrim's Farm.

Wrinkling her nose, Lexy skirted a battered-looking privet bush.

Ah – there were the cages, at the far end of the garden. She made her way towards them.

Halfway across, two things struck her.

One, it wasn't so much cages, as one large cage.

And, two, it was open.

Lexy stopped dead. Later she would say she felt it before she heard it. Felt a warm gust just behind her. Then that low rasp.

She turned and froze.

"Don't move," said a voice.

Seemed like a sensible suggestion.

Tyman appeared, walking slowly towards her.

Ward was coming across the enclosure too, propelling himself in a wheelchair that made parallel tracks across the grass.

"So – you've finally discovered our secret," he said. "Now, we really will have to kill you."

"Shut up, Ward." Tyman slipped past Lexy. "Come on, darling." He put a hand on the mottled brown shoulder and began to walk slowly back to the cage, Ward bumping along beside them.

Lexy stood aside to let them pass, then followed, transfixed by the thick, black-tufted tail that twitched languidly from side to side.

Finally, it all made sense.

This was why the Gallimore family had been so dismayed to

find someone staying in Fours Winds Cottage – why they tried to get her to leave. Why they were watching the place with binoculars all day.

This explained the escaped bull that no one actually saw. The sheep that were meant to be on the hill, but were crammed in a paddock on the farm until now. The bag with the dark red stain, and the tear in Tyman's jeans. The fact that Pilgrim's Farm had been closed to visitors.

This explained why Ward had ambushed her on the hill like something out of Tarzan, and shepherded her back down to the cottage.

This explained why Kinky has taken such a fearful dislike to Four Winds Cottage.

Poor Kinky – always trying to warn her, right from the beginning. How could she have been so blind?

Again, Lexy heard Ward's voice outside the pub, speaking in lowered tones to his father. *We'll just have to deal with her the hard way. It's the only option.*

Then Tyman shouting outside the door when she was at the farm the day before. *She's here! I saw her coming down the track… !*

"In you go." Tyman locked the cage.

"It's OK," he said, turning to Lexy with a smile. "She's mostly harmless."

"*Mostly?*" Lexy stared hard at him.

Tyman's smile faded and he glanced resignedly over at Ward. "Might as well come clean, I guess."

He sat on a bench outside the cage, gesturing Lexy to do the same. Ward angled the wheelchair next to them.

"Where do we start?" he said.

"Let me guess," said Lexy. "This – what's her name?"

"Lola."

"Lola here caused the accident with Elizabeth."

Tyman dropped his head. "She got out two months ago. Dad – well, all of us – had got a bit lax with security." He put a hand through the bars of the cage to scratch a scarred ear. "Trouble is,

Lola's been a pet since we rescued her years ago."

"Rescued her?"

Ward grimaced. "We'd been touring Eastern Europe with the circus, and when we were in Romania, some kids tipped us the wink that a man in their village had a lioness for sale. I mean, we never used performing animals ourselves, but I guess the kids associated the circus with lions. Anyway, it sounded like there was something fishy going on, so we ended up going with them, and we discovered this ignorant sadist starving Lola, and torturing her. See, she's still blind in one eye."

Lexy frowned at the scarred face.

"God knows how he'd got hold of her in the first place." Tyman's voice was tight. "From what we could gather it was from a local zoo that had gone bankrupt, and was just selling the animals, or giving them away. Anyway, I… er… broke into his place that night and took her."

"Nearly getting himself killed in the process," added Ward.

"By the owner, rather than by Lola," Tyman confirmed. "He had the sort of gun that puts ours to shame. Anyway, to cut a long story short, we took her with us, back to our base in France." He gave Lexy a defiant look.

"Risky," she commented. Who was she kidding? She'd have done the same.

"Then, when Dad bought Pilgrim's Farm last year," Ward continued, "we smuggled her over the channel on a boat."

Now, that *was* dodgy. Lexy had to stop herself looking admiring.

"She's always been fairly placid, for a lion," said Tyman. "And she's getting pretty old and arthritic now. She's normally out in her paddock during the day, and the gate in the wall is always shut and padlocked. No one knows she's here. She's well away from the farm, and she never makes a noise – there's something wrong with her throat. The loudest she can manage is a sort of low cough."

"So I heard," said Lexy. Just now in the paddock, right

behind her. And several nights ago, outside the cottage. The sound she couldn't place because it was out of context. But then a lion is somewhat out of context on a hill in Suffolk.

"Anyway," Tyman continued, "the day she got out there was a misunderstanding. Her cage was unlocked, but she was still in it. Dad came down looking for me, thought the cage was locked and left the gate in the wall open. While he was round the back of the paddock, Lola pushed her way out of her cage and wandered out the gate."

"I happened to be out in the garden de-fleaing Django," said Ward. "He suddenly did the dog equivalent of going pale, and I turned round, and saw Lola strolling up the path. My biggest immediate fear was that Mrs Mangeot would see her. Much as she loves animals, there are limits. I tried to corner Lola and chase her back down the path, but she was in no mood for games. She dodged round me, jumped over the garden wall, and legged it straight off up the hill."

Tyman gave a grim laugh. "Dad didn't even realise what had happened. He was still in the paddock. Ward got hold of me, and the three of us tracked and chased her for... what?" He glanced at Ward for affirmation. "Twenty hours... ?"

Ward nodded.

"... but she'd gone completely to ground. Left us with a hell of a dilemma."

"I'll say."

"We didn't want to contact the police. A scandal like keeping an illegal lion could have ruined our business, to say nothing of the fact that they'd want to take her away from us, maybe even have her put down. So we just kept patrolling the area, night and day, to try and track her down and catch her."

"We had to keep a very close eye on Elizabeth," Ward said, "to make sure she didn't accidentally come across Lola. We were constantly watching the place through binoculars. Then one morning Elizabeth came marching down to the farm. Someone had stolen a whole salmon that had been defrosting on her kitchen table. I think she thought it was one of us.

"Well, it was pretty obvious that Lola was starting to get hungry and she'd managed to get into the cottage," Tyman went on. "Elizabeth tended to leave the patio doors open from the time she got up until she went to bed. So that night, Ward and I went up to Four Winds with some bait and lay in wait for her out the back. We were pretty sure Lola would come to us if we had some raw steak, and we'd spiked it with horse tranquilliser – just enough to make sure she was completely calm to get back to the farm."

"Just when we'd given it up as a bad job," Ward continued, "about eight in the morning, I went back down to the farm to check she hadn't sneaked back in our absence."

"I decided to stick around the cottage for a few more minutes, just in case," said Tyman. "And lo and behold, she turned up on the track. As soon as she saw me she went skittish and raced back up the hill. I couldn't get a signal on my bloody phone, of course, to call Ward back, so I spent the best part of an hour circling behind her and slowly herding her down myself, praying that Elizabeth wouldn't come out."

"Everything was fine until we got to the back of the cottage. Then suddenly Lola was over the wall, straight across the lawn and through the patio doors."

Lexy drew in a deep breath. There was a kind of ghastly inevitability about it all.

"Scared the hell out of me," said Tyman. "I ran in after her and got to the hall, just as she was coming out of the kitchen. She couldn't get past me back out the patio doors, so the bugger ran upstairs. I followed her, meaning to try to shut her in one of the bedrooms. Stupid idea, but I wasn't thinking straight by then." He shot Lexy an anguished look. "The radio was on in the bathroom. I thought Elizabeth was safe in there. Then when Lola went straight into Elizabeth's bedroom and I heard a scream, I was… well… paralysed."

"Think I can guess the rest," said Lexy.

Elizabeth, minding her own business in her bedroom, hearing a noise, looking up, and seeing a full grown lioness walking towards her. Not many people would be able to cope with that. It was bad enough finding one standing behind you in a paddock. Lexy could certainly understand why Elizabeth started screaming.

"She started backing up, right?" said Lexy. "Stumbled out through the windows, on to the balcony and went straight over."

Rather like the scenario Lexy had first dreamed up, when she'd found the trail of goose grass burrs on the carpet. Except Lexy's imagined culprit was a man who deliberately wanted Elizabeth dead, rather than an elderly lioness hoping for another salmon.

"The screaming suddenly stopped," said Tyman, swallowing. "I thought Elizabeth had just fainted. I managed to get my legs to take me to the bedroom, and I looked in. But she wasn't in there."

He shook his head. "Just the open window, and Lola looking at me as if to say *whoops*."

He coloured. "I lost it, and started shouting and yelling at Lola, and she leapt right past me, knocking me flat, gashing my jeans on the way, straight down the stairs and out of the cottage. She was scared out of her wits.

"I dashed round to the front. There was nothing I could do. Elizabeth had broken her neck. Died instantly. I ran back down to the farm in a panic. Ward got the gist of it and dragged me out of the kitchen before Mrs Mangeot got an inkling."

"We called an ambulance," cut in Ward, "and they got a doctor out to certify the cause of death. Even though there was a police investigation no one suspected it was anything other than an accident." He gave Lexy a sober look. "It *was* an accident."

"After that we were more desperate than ever to catch Lola," Tyman said. "But she just kept evading us. She was lying up somewhere during the day, and coming out at dusk, which was her normal feeding time at the farm, then prowling around until dawn. All we could do was patrol the hillside with spiked meat. One or other of us was usually out there all night. We had to go back to the vet twice for horse tranquilliser. He must have thought we were getting high on it or something."

"That's what you were carrying in the bag the other day, wasn't it?" said Lexy. "Spiked meat." Probably explained those huge steaks in the fridge, too. "And that's why there were no sheep on the hill."

"They were all crammed into one of our lower fields until yesterday morning," said Ward.

"Can you imagine how we felt when you suddenly turned up in the middle of it all?" said Tyman. "It was like a nightmare."

"Cheers," said Lexy. "But I can see where you're coming from. Couldn't at the time though. I thought you were all mental."

"Lola hadn't been down to Four Winds since the accident, but a complication like you was we all needed," said Ward. "Together with a bite-sized dog. Dad was practically apoplectic after meeting you that morning. We knew we had to get you out of there.

"When we got over the shock of seeing you in the pub that night with the Patersons, Dad took the opportunity to try to get them to sell him the cottage. He would have bought it too, just to get rid of you all quickly. He made up the story about the break-ins, hoping it would put you off going back that night. But it didn't work, and he started to go into panic mode." Ward glanced at his brother. "I said I'd go and shoot Lola, but we didn't tell Tyman, because we knew he'd try and stop me. I mean, Lola's Tyman's lion, really. He was the one who risked his life rescuing her, and I think she knows it."

Lexy looked at the huge cat, quietly panting as Tyman rubbed her ear. Lola knew it.

"When I overheard you talking to your dad about dealing with Lola," said Lexy, "I thought you were talking about me. I thought you were going to do away with me – because I knew too much."

Ward and Tyman exchanged wry looks. "You must have thought

we were the Suffolk Mafia." Tyman gave her a weak smile.

"The awful thing was," Lexy went on, "I couldn't make anyone believe me. I thought I was losing my mind. And when Ward came dashing into the cottage the next day…"

"You thought that's when I was going to kill you," Ward said. "No wonder you looked so petrified. I'd just seen Lola near the cottage, so I had to find a reason to keep you all from wandering out there. The only thing I could think of at the time was to tell you that Edgar was loose. As if he'd hurt a fly."

"He's OK, is he, Edgar?" Lexy asked quickly.

"Yeah. He was lying in the sun when I checked him earlier."

Rather than on a plate in the fridge. Good.

"So, given that all this was going on," Lexy said to Tyman, "why did you invite me up the hill at dawn?"

He smiled into her eyes. "Just seemed like a good idea at the time."

"Yeah, really intelligent, Tyman," Ward snorted.

"What did happen to you that morning, anyway?" Tyman asked Lexy.

"I followed you, idiot," Ward cut in. "When I saw what you were doing I escorted Lexy back to the cottage."

Escorted?

"Thanks a lot. Didn't you hear me shouting?"

"Frankly, I didn't care."

"She wouldn't have been in any danger," Tyman said, quietly.

"Is that why you were toting a gun?" Lexy enquired.

"Just wanted to be on the safe side."

"I assume none of it was true, then?" Lexy turned to Ward, hiding a grin. "What you told me about..." She angled her head at Tyman.

Ward coloured. "Only thing I could think of at short notice."

"What's this?" said Tyman.

"I'll let you explain," Lexy told Ward.

"Explain what?" said Tyman.

"Later," Ward growled.

"But when we were up on the hillside the second time," Lexy said to Ward, serious again. "The night of the shooting. It was Lola you were shooting at, wasn't it – not me?"

"Of course. How could we have known you were there? You appeared at the last moment. Lola was right behind you."

"She has a habit of doing that," said Lexy.

They contemplated the lioness in silence for a moment.

"When I came down to the farm, that morning after the shooting… " Lexy began, slowly.

"Lola must have been about five minutes behind you," Ward went on.

"So when Tyman was shouting that he'd seen her coming down the hill," Lexy said.

"I was talking about Lola," Tyman finished. "She'd finally had enough of roughing it. Came back of her own accord."

"No wonder you lot were light-headed with relief. And there was me thinking you were all just mad as a box of frogs."

Tyman put a hand on her arm. "The question is – are you going to tell anyone about her?"

Lexy found herself looking into Lola's gold-flecked eye.

"I don't think you should have let things go on the way they did," she began, slowly, "although god knows I can understand your reasons. But I'm going to leave it to you to decide about going to the police."

"I suppose you think we should?" said Ward.

"It's not up to me. But if you decide to, can you go and break the news to Rowana first?"

"Why?"

"Elizabeth Cassall was her mother."

"Christ." Another silence descended.

"I'd better go and get my dog. He's shut up in your kitchen. Fortunately." Lexy imagined Kinky hanging off Lola's long, tasselled tail.

She made her way back to the gate, leaving the Gallimore brothers to wrestle with their consciences.

Kinky had barked himself hoarse in the Gallimores' kitchen. Lexy raided their biscuit tin and gave him four custard creams, along with a full apology.

They arrived back at Four Winds Cottage at the same moment as Gabrielle. The girl leapt from the van and ran across the lawn to where Steve was still working.

"I've got a month's trial at Fandango, starting next week," she shrieked. "I might be even able to sell some of my clothes in the shop, because the manageress really liked what I was wearing, and she couldn't believe it when I told her I'd made it."

"I knew you'd do it, sweetheart." Lexy watched Steve kiss his daughter.

A white estate car pulled up next to the van. Lexy felt her features tighten.

"How did it go? You got it, didn't you, Gabby?" Rowana, obviously back from wherever she'd been, ran out from the kitchen door, paint stains on her hands. Like... Archer Trevino. Funny, that.

"Isn't she brilliant, Dad?"

Steve looked over at Rowana, shading his eyes. He hesitated for a split second.

"Not now!" Lexy screamed under her breath.

"Yes, my love, she's amazing. You both are."

Far away in the distance a mechanical grumble broke the still, hot air.

Milo walked up the path to stand next to Lexy. She glanced coolly at him.

Kinky, however, ran up to the policeman, tail waving. Milo bent to pat him. Odd. Kinky and Milo didn't object to one another, but so far they'd never been enthusiastic.

Milo straightened. "What's new?"

Lexy almost broke out laughing. He wouldn't believe it if she told him. She was having trouble herself.

"Edward managed to lose Kinky, but he came back again," she

said. "That's about it."

"Lose him?"

"Long story."

"Would this be a good time for me to have that chat to Steve?" Milo said, quietly.

Lexy hesitated. "Probably won't need to now."

"Oh?"

"Yeah. I went up the hill with him this morning, and…"

"You seem to go up that hill quite a lot."

In the background, the grumble increased. Kinky's ears pricked up. Lexy saw Steve's eyes flicker.

"It's because it's forbidden. I can't resist it."

"Is that right?"

"Anyway, I found out a lot. Tell you later." She indicated the Patersons. "How was court?" she murmured.

"Complicated." Milo's ice-grey eyes were focused on Lexy. She didn't notice because she was looking at Steve.

"You win the case?"

"Yup."

"Good."

"So he's fixing your car, is he?"

"Who, Steve? Yes. He's a dab hand with sprockets."

"I can imagine."

The mechanical growl had now turned to a roar. It seemed to thicken the very air.

"Lotus 7," Steve said, absently.

Gabrielle put her head to one side with a small frown.

With a final, throaty growl, a low, green and yellow sports car burst into sight and slithered to a halt outside the cottage.

A round pink face gazed out at them and broke into a wide smile.

"Gabrielle! At last!"

The pink-faced being clambered out of the car, pushed his way through the gate and bounded along the path, oblivious to everything except Gabrielle, who was regarding him with a mixture of delight and despair.

"Do you think that might be Russell?" Milo enquired.

"Gosh, I dunno." Lexy shot him an exasperated look. "Of course it's ruddy Russell."

"Do you still want to… ?" Russell blurted.

"Yes! But what about the blonde woman?" Gabrielle shrieked.

Russell's circular face regarded her with mystification.

"I saw you with her on the night before we left the shop. Leaving your house together."

He frowned, then beamed.

"You never did meet Mummy, did you? She's a bit eccentric, to be perfectly honest." He lowered his voice. "Lots of work done. You know, on the face. I take after my father, of course," he added.

"Oh, Russell," Gabrielle murmured, huskily.

"Oh, Gabrielle." He clasped her to his chest.

"Oh, god," remarked Milo. He inclined his head towards the gate. "Fancy another walk up this illicit hill?"

24

"Lot of sheep." Milo looked around him in surprise.

"Yup. The Gallimores have suddenly started putting them back up here. As of this morning."

Lexy had Kinky back on the makeshift lead again, and the dog led the way, listening to the loud bleating with a lot more interest than he had shown earlier.

"This morning when you were up here with Steve."

"Yes. Now listen to this. He's got an alibi for the time Elizabeth fell."

"Really?" Milo's grey eyes narrowed.

"Might as well sit down. Over here, by the cliff edge, where it's quieter. It's a long story. Starts back in 1990."

Lexy told him Steve's saga.

"God help that girl when he finally tells her who her real parents are," he said, when Lexy had finished.

And that's not the worst of it, Lexy mused, thinking of Lola.

"He is going to tell her, I assume?"

"Think he's realised he's going to have to face up to it," Lexy said. "In fact, there was a horrible moment earlier in the garden when I thought he was going to blurt it out there and then."

"So how did you get him to tell you all this?"

"I guessed that Elizabeth was Rowana's mother – from that photograph of her in the studio."

Milo gave a short laugh. "Should have noticed it myself. They are remarkably similar."

"And once that was out in the open, he told me the rest. I can't get over the Archer Trevino bit. I mean, how would you feel if someone suddenly told you he was your father?"

"I don't even want to go there."

"Might not be so great for Rowana," Lexy pondered, "but you

never know, the old bastard could be quite pleased to find he's got a kid like her."

"Especially a kid who paints." Milo leaned back, shutting his eyes against the sun.

"That's quite a cut you've got over your eyebrow," said Lexy. He had a bruise on his cheek, and grazed knuckles, too. "Been beating up suspects again?"

"Police brutality," Milo murmured. "The reason I joined the force."

Lexy stared at him for a further minute, then exclaimed softly, "It was you, wasn't it?"

"Me who what?"

"Knocked seven bells out of my husband."

"I don't know what you're talking about."

"In the Jolly Herring. And it was you who brought Kinky back this morning."

Milo was silent.

"Why didn't you stick around?" Lexy demanded.

"It was five-thirty, I was in a hurry and I didn't have time for explanations." Milo looked shifty. "As it was, I'd had him with me all of yesterday because I didn't have a chance to get him back to you. Had to take him to Norwich Crown Court and back."

"Bloody hell, Milo – why didn't you tell me you'd got him? I was going out of my mind. And as for Edward and Peter…"

The detective gave her a sideways look. "For one thing, your phone wasn't switched on. And for another, I didn't want you knowing it was me who laid into Gerard. Doesn't exactly look good, does it?"

"Looks good from where I'm sitting." Lexy considered him. "But how did you know Gerard had Kinky in the first place?"

"Edward called me when you and I were in the pub the other night – told me Kinky had gone missing."

Lexy bit her lip. So much for Milo's hot date.

"I went round there and got the rest of the story," Milo

continued. "And put two and two together, just like you must have done. I knew Gerard was staying at the Herring. I told Edward not to report it, and I went over to the pub to persuade Gerard to hand Kinky over. Nicely. But he was such a…"

"I know," said Lexy.

"He was drunk, too. He swung at me, and I… kind of lost it. Not my usual style, but there it is. He won't have any lasting damage, and frankly, he had it coming."

Lexy regarded him in admiration. "You got my dog back and you ran my husband out of town. That's pretty impressive, Milo. I'm…"

"Think nothing of it," the detective interrupted. "What's up with these sheep, by the way?"

The beasts were milling anxiously around the summit, filling the air with aggravated baaing.

Lexy stood up, causing further consternation among them. One headed in their direction just as Milo was rising. It barged into the back of his legs, and would have knocked him clean over the cliff if Lexy hadn't grabbed his arm.

He clutched at her jacket. "They've turned into Fair Isle killing machines."

Lexy's eyes widened. Something had jumped up from the steps, straight into the middle of the flock.

"It's the black dog!"

"Eh?"

"The black dog," she yelled. "Y'know – Old Shuck. In among the sheep!"

With a sudden snarl, Kinky jerked the string lead clean out of her hand. He pelted towards the flock.

"Stop!" Lexy raced after the chihuahua.

Milo stared after them.

A piercing whistle resounded across the cliff top. All the sheep looked up as one. Kinky dived into their midst just as Bruce and Tyman Gallimore appeared over the ridge of the hill. Tyman wasn't wearing the bandage any more, but he looked pale.

Didn't stop him shouting at the top of his lungs, though.

"Oi – what the hell are you doing?"

Lexy supposed it didn't look good – her up the outlawed hill yet again, this time running like a berserker at his precious lambkins. She hoped they'd missed the sight of Kinky disappearing into the flock.

They certainly wouldn't miss the frenzied growling and snapping. Kinky must have caught up with Old Shuck at last.

"Is that your dog in our flock?" Bruce shouted.

"No," she yelled back, crossing her fingers. "This one's a bit bigger." And blacker.

"What are you…?" Milo had caught up with her.

"Stay with me on this," she hissed.

The Gallimores pounded over to join them.

"Whose is it, then?" Tyman squinted at the flock.

Bruce was pulling a shotgun from a holder on his back.

Lexy hesitated. The barking had stopped. She found herself clutching Milo's arm.

"You said it was a big black one," said Milo. "Old Sugar, or something."

"Old Shuck? The ghost dog? Didn't sound like a ghost to me." Bruce shouldered his gun.

Lexy frantically scanned the brown and white sea of wool. "Look – he's in there. Towards the back – facing the cliff edge. Black and shaggy, big shoulders."

She tried to see whether the beast was gripping anything small and caramel-coloured in its jaws.

"Bugger me – that's Satan," said Bruce.

Lexy and Milo stole a glance at him.

"Well, I wouldn't go that far…" Lexy began.

Tyman swore. "And there's us thinking he'd been… consumed."

"Yet 'ere he is, alive and kicking." Bruce began to move towards the flock.

"I'll keep them talking, you go and start the car," said Milo to Lexy.

"It's all right. Satan's a…" Tyman began to move in the opposite direction from Bruce.

"… long-'aired Greek." Bruce finished.

"Now I'm really worried." Milo was still trying to see the creature.

Lexy closed her eyes. "Satan's a rare breed, isn't he?"

"Aye, that's what we've been trying to tell you. Easy does it. Hang on… he's pushing those sheep towards the cliff edge."

Everyone stopped dead.

Satan was clearly visible now. A big, burly male goat, with a shaggy coat and horns that curled tightly back against his head.

"Yes," said Milo, squinting. "From a distance, in the mist, it could almost be mistaken for…"

"Thank you," Lexy muttered.

The goat was advancing towards a small group of sheep that had split from the main flock.

"We'll lose them, Dad." Tyman, his face white, bent low and started running towards them.

But someone beat him to it. Kinky. He struggled out from under one of the cliff top sheep and ran directly at the black goat. It bunched its legs. Was it going to toss the chihuahua clean over the cliff? No – it pirouetted, and raced off, Kinky at its shaggy heels.

They were heading straight for Bruce.

The farmer lunged forward and grabbed the goat in capable arms, pushing it to the ground.

Kinky trotted back towards Lexy, snorting and shaking his head. He had wool trailing from his collar.

"So you thought he was the legendary Black Dog, did you?" Tyman, panting from the run, was grinning all over his face now.

"I've seen your ruddy Satan here, there and everywhere," admitted Lexy. "Thought I was losing my marbles."

Tyman drew closer to her. "You haven't…?" He jerked his head at Milo, who had moved out of earshot to congratulate Kinky.

"Told him about Lola? No."

"After the… Elizabeth incident, when things got desperate, Dad tied Satan up here as bait for Lola."

"Bit drastic," said Lexy.

"I know. He wasn't thinking straight. He didn't tell me until afterwards – he knew I'd have stopped him. Didn't work, anyway – good old Satan must have got loose. Er… Lexy…"

"Yes?"

"If… if… we decided to go to the police…"

Tyman had always been the one with the pricking conscience.

"… would it be best to talk to Milo first? He is a policeman, isn't he?"

Lexy saw Milo quietly pull a hank of black wool from the chihuahua's mouth. Kinky obviously hadn't been able to resist a quick nip.

"Yes," she said. Milo would be sure to thank her for that. "But leave it a while. The Patersons are going to have some other complications to deal with first."

Tyman nodded, hurrying after Bruce.

Lexy, Milo and Kinky followed the flock down the hill, quietly peeling off when they reached the cottage.

Rowana and Gabrielle were sitting together on the kitchen doorstep, golden head against black. "I mean, I'm still going to do this job," Lexy heard Gabrielle say. "I want a career in fashion. I've already told Russell that."

Lexy let Kinky loose, and he ran straight over to the hydrangea bush.

Steve was standing by the Panda, talking to Russell. He smiled over at Lexy, pointing to the car and giving her the thumbs-up.

Milo leant on the gate. "Purely out of interest," he said, "is there something going on between you and Steve Paterson?"

Lexy perched herself on the garden wall beside him. "My golden rule, Milo. Never get involved with a client's father."

"I'll bear that in mind. That your only rule?"

"No. I've got others – just can't think of them at the moment."

They relaxed in friendly silence for a moment.

"So what are you going to do now?" said Milo. "Now that Steve isn't a suspect? Hey – you're not going to start looking at the Gallimores again, are you?"

"Nah. I think I was on the wrong track with them. Like you said, I've been making a mountain out of a molehill."

Milo raised his eyebrows. "Wonders will never cease."

"So, I think I'm going to call it a day and head on back to Clopwolde, seeing as Gerard appears no longer to be there."

"Yes, and I'd prefer it if you didn't mention that incident to anyone." Milo inspected his grazed knuckles. "What are you going to do about Rowana and the magic… thing, by the way?"

Lexy shrugged. It was a good question. She'd done what she'd set out to do, and discovered what happened to Elizabeth Cassall. Found out that it was more to do with a lioness than a goddess.

But she wasn't going to tell Rowana. It was up to the Gallimores to do that.

"I'm going to tell her that as far as I can establish, Elizabeth fell by accident."

The truth, in other words.

MEET LEXY AND KINKY IN
DEAD WOMAN'S SHOES
KAYE C HILL'S CRACKLING DEBUT NOVEL

All she wanted was to get away – and suddenly it's raining cats, dogs and bodies…

Lexy Lomax has run away from her obnoxious husband, taking with her a cool half million of his ill-gotten gains and a homicidal chihuahua called Kinky. Holed up in a decrepit log cabin on the Suffolk coast, Lexy finds herself mistaken for the previous owner of the cabin, a private investigator, now deceased. Before she knows it she's embroiled in a cocktail of marital infidelity (possibly), missing cats (probably) and poison pen letters (definitely).

Oh, yes – and a murder or two…

Praise for *Dead Woman's Shoes*:

Into the prevailing noir of contemporary crime fiction Kaye C Hill brings a welcome splash of colour and humour.
– Simon Brett

I just love Lexy – and Kinky. I hope I'm going to meet [them] again.
– Jean Currie, The New Writer

Crisp prose and a plot laced with animal tomfoolery will keep readers… eager for a sequel.
– Publishers Weekly (USA)

ISBN: 978-0-9551589-9-5   £7.99

You can also meet Lexy Lomax again in
CRIMINAL TENDENCIES
**a diverse and wholly engrossing collection
of short stories from some of the best of the
UK's crime writers.**

**£1 from every copy sold of this
first-rate collection will go to support the
NATIONAL HEREDITARY
BREAST CANCER HELPLINE**

She lay on her face, as if asleep. I turned her over and saw the deep wound on her brow…
– Reginald Hill, *John Brown's Body*

Her mouth was dry and she was shaking badly. Terror was gripping her; the same terror she previously experienced only in her dreams…
– Peter James, *12 Bolinbroke Avenue*

His lips were thin and pale. "She must be following us. She's some sort of stalker."
– Sophie Hannah, *The Octopus Nest*

When he thought he was alone, he squatted down and opened the briefcase. I was interested to see that it contained an automatic pistol and piles and piles of banknotes.
– Andrew Taylor, *Waiting for Mr Right*

Published by Crème de la Crime
ISBN: 978-09557078-5-8   £7.99

MORE GRIPPING TITLES IN 2009
FROM CRÈME DE LA CRIME

SECRET LAMENT
Roz Southey

Italian actors…
French spies…
At least the thugs are English…
Charles Patterson is not happy. It's the hottest June for years; he's stuck in musical rehearsals with a family of Italians; some local ruffians are after his blood; and someone is trying to break into the house of Esther Jerdoun, the woman he loves.

When a murder is discovered he fears Esther may be next. It's time to ask some tough questions.

Who is the strange man masquerading under a patently false name? Are there really spies abroad in Newcastle? Why is a psalm-teacher keeping vigil over a house in the town?

And can Patterson find the murderer before he strikes again?

Praise for Roz Southey's previous Charles Patterson mysteries:

… an elegantly-written and atmospheric mystery which continues to surprise and satisfy to the very last page.
– R S Downie, author of the Ruso historical mystery series

Southey has a real feel for the eighteenth century…
– Booklist (USA)

ISBN: 978-0-9557078-6-5   **£7.99**

DEAD LIKE HER   Linda Regan

Sex, drugs – and Marilyn Monroe…
A potentially lethal combination.

It seems like a straightforward case for newly promoted DCI Paul
Banham and DI Alison Grainger: the murdered women all bore an
uncanny resemblance to Marilyn Monroe and worked for a lookalike
agency.

But the enquiry soon unearths connections with a covert investigation
into drug-running and people-trafficking. A new member of the team,
uniquely qualified but inexperienced, is placed in a dangerous situation
– made more difficult when love rears its complicated head!

Can Banham and Grainger save her from the villains – and from
herself?

Praise for Linda Regan's previous Banham/Grainger mysteries:

*Regan exhibits enviable control over her characters in this skilful
and fascinating whodunit.*
– Colin Dexter OBE

I loved it. Don't miss it.
– Richard Briers CBE

Regan is a writer well worth keeping an eye on.
– Martin Edwards, author of the acclaimed Harry Devlin mysteries

… one of the best up-and coming writers
– Peter Guttridge, the Observer

ISBN: 978-0-9557078-8-9   **£7.99**

BLOOD MONEY   Maureen Carter

When family loyalties are at stake can a woman can be as hard as a man?

Detective Sergeant Bev Morriss is in a very dark place.

Personal tragedy has pushed her close to self-destruct mode; both colleagues and friends have started to give her a wide berth.

But Bev is still a cop, and there are villains to battle as well as demons. Enter the Sandman, a vicious serial burglar who wears a clown mask and plays mind-games with his victims.

When the violence spirals into abduction, blackmail and murder, the bad guys soon discover Bev is in no mood to play...

Praise for Maureen Carter's earlier Bev Morriss titles:

If there was any justice in this world, she'd be as famous as Ian Rankin!
– Sharon Wheeler, Reviewing the Evidence

British hardboiled crime fiction at its best...
– George Easter, Deadly Pleasures

I liked [it] so much that I have ordered the first 3 books in this series.
– Maddy Van Hertbruggen, I Love a Mystery Newsletter

ISBN: 978-0-9557078-7-2   **£7.99**

LOVE NOT POISON   Mary Andrea Clarke

A husband dead in a fire – but was it an accident?

A wife hysterical – but is it with grief?

The Crimson Cavalier is in search of the truth…

In the 1780s young ladies are expected to apply themselves to the social round and the business of finding a husband – but Miss Georgiana Grey is no ordinary young lady.

The death of ill-natured Lord Wickerston in a fire leads her to ask questions, to the chagrin of her strait-laced brother Edward, and the alarm of her friend Mr Max Lakesby.

Who would want Lord Wickerston dead? Does Edward know more than he is willing to say?

And how is the notorious highwayman known as the Crimson Cavalier involved?

Praise for Mary Andrea Clarke's first Crimson Cavalier adventure:

… *sparkling period crime fiction with a lively touch*

– Andrew Taylor, award-winning author of The American Boy

… *a delightful and entertaining novel with an engrossing plot.*

– Historical Novels Review

Clarke captures the flavor of the period…

– Publishers Weekly (USA)

… *fans of Georgette Heyer… will snap this title up. Another winning tale from Crème de la Crime.*

– US Library Journal

ISBN: 978-0-9560566-0-3   **£7.99**